What read

"Readers who like steamy sex and trilogies will enjoy Henrietta's Redemption, the second book in The Partners Series. I loved it and I can't wait to read Monique's story, the final book in the series, and neither will you."

Ann Cantrell
Author

"I hate to think of this series ending. In this second book of The Partners Series, Janet Lococo takes you on a roller coaster ride through the lives of two of southern Louisiana's beautiful people. Henrietta, a kick butt lawyer, and recently divorced Bradley Graham. The gap between them grows larger as circumstances reveal themselves.

Mrs. Lococo has the talent to weave a story you don't want to put down. You fall in love with the characters and cheer for their happy-ever-after."

Charlotte Parker (CJ Parker)
Author

HENRIETTA'S

REDEMPTION

by

Janet Foret Lococo

JANLO Services Publishing
PO Box 6
Lockport, Louisiana 70374

HENRIETTA'S REDEMPTION

Published by JANLO Services Publishing
P.O. Box 6
Lockport, Louisiana 70374-0006

www.janetflococo.net
Email: janlopub@me.com

Cover Image: www.creativeparamita.com/

ISBN 10: 0-9856077-3-4
ISBN 13: 978-0-9856077-3-9

~ *Dedication* ~

To Dominique Cecilia Lococo,
my wonderful granddaughter, proudly serving our
country in the United States Navy.

To my children: Gaynell, Ted and Pauline.

To my readers who never seem to tire of my stories.
I could not continue to do this without your loving
support.

And to Castranzio Theodore Lococo,
my husband of 55 years, who has finally learned not
to disturb me when I'm writing.

~ *Acknowledgements*~

A completed book is never the work of the author alone. Several people helped me get this story from my head to paper and to publish this steamy romance novel, some unknowingly.

Fellow SOLA members served as my critique partners. They are listed alphabetically:

Ann B. Cantrell, fellow self–published author, supported me and read and edited the final manuscript and the back cover blurb. Her books include: *Legacy of Time*, *Legacy of Revenge*, *Legacy of Conflict*, *How Many Frogs Must I Kiss*, and *Calico Queen*. Thank you.

C.J. Parker, author of *Fugue Macabre: Ghost Dance*, *Fugue Macabre: Bone Dance,* and *Misty Dreams*, has encouraged me since I began writing my very first novel and taught me so much about the craft. She read my completed manuscript before layout in spite of working on her own epic story. I would not consider publishing a novel without her honest assessment of my work. Thank you.

So, with all that help, you'd think this book would be "perfect." I'm sure it's not, and any errors you spot are mine alone.

Prologue

Eager to leave Cut Off, Louisiana, Henrietta Blanchard earns a full scholarship to Nicholls State University with a perfect high school grade point average and high expectations.

She meets Gloria Babin and Monique Boudreaux when they begin pre-law undergraduate school in 1979 and are assigned to the same dormitory suite. The three soon form a sisterhood.

Following graduation from Nicholls State University, they move on to Harvard Law School. Following graduation and bar exams in 1987, they establish their own law firm in Houston, Texas. Their focus is representing women in post–divorce property settlements. Their firm makes it into the big time when they are successful in obtaining a thirty million dollar settlement for the ex-wife of a billionaire banker.

This is Henrietta's story.

Janet Foret Lococo

Chapter 1

Two days before Christmas of 2010, Henrietta drove her rental car into her mother's driveway until the front bumper almost touched the garage door. She relaxed as soon as she noticed her mother was not home from work yet. That would give her a chance to chill before *the inquisition* began. Spending the holiday season in her hometown had not been her idea, but her mother had insisted. And since her law partners both left Houston for the holidays, she would've been alone. So here she was, in the small town she couldn't wait to leave.

The decision to return to Cut Off, Louisiana, had not been an easy one. She'd always hated the small town atmosphere and the way people gossiped about everything for as long as she could remember. They forgot and forgave nothing–even things that had occurred many years earlier.

She imagined wrinkled faces frowning as one old bitty after another whispered about unfortunate occurrences in the lives of others. Once they knew she was in town, Henrietta figured she'd be the subject of their tongue-wagging, even though more than thirty years had passed since the darkest day of her life.

And now, she was stuck here until January 2, 2011. She sighed at the thought of spending ten lackluster days with little to do. There were very few restaurants to enjoy—and none of the five-star quality she frequented in Houston, Texas. Somehow, she'd manage to survive. She was, after all, a real survivor. That thought alone eased her insecurity.

She pulled her luggage from the trunk, took the key from its hiding place, and let herself in through the back door. Memories—both good and terrible—slammed through her mind as she stepped into her mother's kitchen. Her clammy hands slid off the luggage handle, and her bag fell to the floor with a thump. She wiped her hands on the sides of her pants and drew her lips into a tight line as she vowed not to allow her visit home to upset her as it always had in the past. That was easier said than done even though the closet had been removed.

Henrietta's gaze slid around the kitchen. Everything looked new. *Mama must be doing well with her job.* She grabbed a Coke from the refrigerator, popped the top, and took a big swallow. *Um. Icy cold.* God, she was so thirsty, and this hit the spot.

An image of Gloria Babin, one of her law partners, suddenly popped into her mind. Pregnant by Jesse Martin, she was in New York City over the Christmas holidays because she feared returning home to Thibodaux, Louisiana and running into the man of her dreams.

Henrietta couldn't fathom loving someone the way Gloria adored Jesse. And for what? A baby in her belly her religious conscience wouldn't allow her to rid herself of? No. She'd never be like that. She was positive there was no man alive who could make her feel that way. She'd just completed reading a book by a Louisiana author with a demon lord character. This demon was handsome, capable of both black and white magic, could fuck all night long and lead his lover to orgasm after orgasm. That was more her style. No love. Just sex.

A male friend had once told her he treated women like postage stamps. He'd admitted, "I lick 'em, stick 'em, and send 'em on their way." Henrietta had gotten a kick out of his statement. That's exactly what she did.

She knew Gloria and Monique, her other law partner, worried about her promiscuous lifestyle. But it was Gloria who always warned her of the danger of sexually transmitted diseases. Henrietta was no dummy. Beginning with her very first sexual experience in tenth grade, she'd never had sex without a condom. Not only to prevent disease, either. There was no way she'd ever take a chance on getting pregnant.

She took a big gulp of her soda. Although she'd screwed many men, Henrietta had never loved anyone or had an orgasm other than with her dildo. Go figure.

She dragged her luggage into her old room and set it on her bed. A fresh coat of off-white paint covered the walls, and the curtains and bedding looked new. She moved into the living/dining room. Again, everything looked brand new. Her mother's house had gotten a complete makeover since her last visit.

When she heard the back door slam and her mother's squeal of excitement, she stepped out into the hall, into her mother's waiting arms.

"Retta, Retta, Retta," she purred and tightened her hold around Henrietta's waist. "I'm so glad you're spending the holidays with me. This year, for the first time in a long time, all my children will be together for Christmas." She pulled her into an even tighter hug. "My baby," she whispered, "is so beautiful and all grown up." She pushed Henrietta away, let her eyes roam from the tip of her head to her toes and beamed. "You look like a model." Then she hugged her again. "All of you will come with me and Grammy to midnight Mass. We'll sit together."

Although Henrietta could hardly remember the last time she'd been to church, she kept that information to herself, didn't argue, and began to unpack and quickly changed the subject. "So how are my brothers?"

"They're doing great." She hugged Henrietta again. "Your brothers are healthy and happy, and their charter fishing business has grown to three fishing boats. And like your dad did with them, their boys are learning about the business early. They're making a lot of money. As a matter of fact, the complete renovation of this house is my Christmas present from your brothers.

"You've been gone so long. I know it pains you to be down here, but we've all missed you terribly." She drilled Henrietta's gaze with her own. "I'm sure your nephews and nieces will not like going to midnight Mass any more than you will, but that's just tough."

Henrietta couldn't help but laugh at her mother's comment. Undaunted, her mother continued, "We'll probably need two pews for our family. Our Christmas meal will be in the evening so your brothers can have lunch with their in-laws." She planted a kiss on Henrietta's cheek. "It's mighty generous of you to get the entire thing catered. I can't believe I won't have to cook a thing." She nodded her head forward and back and broke into a huge smile. "That's a first for me. Nothing to do but relax and enjoy."

"You deserve it, Mom. You've always had to work hard after Daddy died. He was so young." She lifted the curtain and looked out of the window. "I'm glad they didn't tear down the wharf."

"I'd never allow that. I remember how you loved sitting out there seemingly mesmerized by the water as the current ambled down the bayou and carried the few water lilies south of the Intracoastal Canal toward the Gulf."

"It's always been my favorite place to daydream…"

Chapter 2

Henrietta took her mother to a local seafood restaurant for supper, as the evening meal was called along the banks of Bayou Lafourche. Seafood cooked the Cajun way was the only thing she missed now that she lived in Houston. In her opinion, nobody cooked seafood better than the people of South Louisiana. She missed nothing else.

She passed on the boiled seafood listed on the menu since her brothers might host a seafood boil while she was home. She licked her lips as she thought of the big blue crabs they usually caught and hand-selected the fullest ones to boil. After studying the food choices, she decided to try the shrimp pistolette. Hot and stuffed with a creamy sauce full of seasonings and rough-cut shrimp, it was delicious and messy.

Her mother laughed and commented, "Retta, you've lost your touch with eating sloppy but delicious food in South Louisiana. You've two large spots on your expensive-looking silk blouse." She laughed again.

Henrietta looked down. Sure enough, two spots of sauce

now decorated her costly top. Turning her gaze to her mother, she laughed, too. "Give me a couple of days and I'll be back up to snuff." She bit into the crispy pistolette; this time, she kept her face over her plate."

Her mother grinned. "See, you're getting better at it already."

After their meal, they drove up and down streets so Henrietta could see the Christmas decorations. Some were awesome. Some were very tacky–a mishmash of everything Christmas. *Some things don't change.*

"Is there a man in your life?" her mother inquired.

The beginnings of a small fire of anger burned at Henrietta's butt. She should've seen that coming. Her mother wanted her settled down and married. *No way.* "No, Mom. I have a lot of male friends, but nothing serious. You should know by now that I still do not like men in general. I don't think I could ever give my heart to one man. I can't trust them. Nevertheless, I'm not the house with shutters and a white picket fence type. I like where I am in life." She nodded her head once and hoped her mother would see it as an exclamation point.

"It's just that I hate to think of you being all alone in your old age. Once I'm gone…"

"You've been alone for thirty-plus years, and you've handled it. What makes you think that I'd be any different?"

"I had children to ease my loneliness. You don't."

Henrietta's pulse quickened with uneasiness at her mother's words. She swallowed and kept her eyes on the road. "Don't worry about me. End of story, Mom."

Although it was only ten o'clock when they returned to her mother's house, Henrietta was overwhelmed with exhaustion. She hugged her mom and smacked kisses to both her cheeks. "I'm whipped. Would you mind if I showered and went to bed?"

"Not at all. And feel free to sleep in since we have no pre-Christmas dinner cooking to do."

Henrietta pecked another kiss to her mother's cheek before heading for the bathroom. The hot water slammed onto her skin and soothed her muscles. She could almost feel each one relax under the steady stream as she lathered her body and shampooed her hair. After drying herself with a thick towel, she slipped into her pajamas, dried her hair, and slid beneath the cool sheets of her old bed. Before she knew it, she was fast asleep.

Chapter 3

Sleep brought vivid dreams. *She was in the tenth grade, and Johnny Brown approached her as she reached in her locker for her notebook and textbook for her biology class. "Hey, Retta. Hold up. I want to ask you something."*

She'd looked up into dark chocolate-brown eyes. "What do you need help with, John?"

He appeared to be gun-shy as he cleared his throat. "I don't need any help." He looked down at the floor before eyeing her again. "I was hoping you'd want to come to prom with me."

She frowned. Was he teasing her? She pressed her lips into a fine line before asking, "Is this some sort of a joke?"

"It's no joke. I'd like you to be my prom date."

His dark brown gaze searched hers as he waited for her answer. "I'm not sure my mother would allow it. I don't date."

He dragged his foot forward and backward repeatedly. His big brown eyes looked anxious. "Why don't you ask her? That is if you'd like to go. I could call you tonight."

"No. Don't call. I'll let you know tomorrow. Regardless of

11

the outcome, thanks for asking."

Henrietta smiled as he turned and walked away. Of course her mother would say yes, hoping she'd changed her mind about guys in general; but she hadn't, and she wouldn't. Except for her father, she lumped all men into the same category– users of women.

She wondered about it, though. John's tall, so that I could wear high heels. He's handsome and muscular... a star on the football team. We'd probably look good together. He's a senior. She had no romantic feelings whatsoever about this guy and wondered why he had asked her. She decided that if she went to prom with Johnny, she'd screw him to see what it was like since her friends said it was wonderful.

The scene in her dream changed to where she and Johnny were in the backseat of his father's big Lincoln Town Car parked on an unplowed strip of land in a sugarcane field. Her dress was on the front seat, and her underwear was on the floor of the car. Johnny was still completely dressed, but she quickly removed his shirt and his belt. His eyes got big when she pushed him down on the seat before straddling him.

"What are you doing?" His voice sounded raspy, and his breaths came close together.

"I want to see what having sex is all about. Come on. Take off your drawers."

When his underwear was off, she saw his dick standing almost straight up. It looked kind of like a tree in a sea of dark brown curly grass. It looked pretty big. She threw all caution aside and wrapped her hand around it to satisfy her curiosity about how it would feel. Velvet wrapped around a steel rod.

His voice shook, and his body trembled. "Have you done this before?"

A light film of sweat was visible on his muscled neck and chest. The smell of his cologne, GatorBait by Ralph Lauren– the same her brother wore–strengthened in the closed car. "No, but I've decided it's time I try it. Please tell me this is not your first time, too."

His reply was shaky. *"It's not, but I don't have a condom and I'll be damned if I'll chance getting you pregnant. At the very least, I know that much."*

She opened her purse, drew out a foil packet, tore it open, and rolled it on him. His eyes widened even more. *"Are you sure you've haven't done this before?"*

"I'm sure."

"I've never had a virgin, but I know it'll hurt the first time."

"I know. I'm far from stupid." She pinched her lips together. She'd lost her virginity long before, but he'd never know. She fisted her hands on her hips. *"Look. Do you want to fuck or not?"*

"Of course I do. I don't know any straight guy alive who'd refuse an offer of sex."

He slid his finger between her labia. *"I'll caress you with my fingers to get you wet so I'll slide more easily inside of you."* He found her nub and rubbed it.

That felt as good as when she did it herself. She positioned her opening at the tip of his shaft and eased it in a little at a time. Johnny moaned, *"Oh, sweet Jesus. More, Retta. More."*

She took him in and groaned, surprised that it hurt when he pushed himself inside and sank fully into her. He whispered, *"That's the worst part."*

He filled her, and Henrietta moaned and groaned to make him think she was enjoying this. She'd read enough romance novels to know what was expected. *"Now. Now. Now,"* she breathed as he stiffened and came into the rubber." A surge of power engulfed her when he shuddered and cried out her name. A victorious feeling enveloped her like one of Grammy's old quilts. To think she was capable of doing this to a guy.

He kissed her and told her how good it was and what a surprise she'd been. He had not expected sex. They were both sweaty with the car windows up, trying to keep the mosquitoes away.

13

"How will you explain the blood that'll be in your panties?"

"I brought tissues and a pad to wear home."

He shook his head and seemed puzzled. "You seem to have thought of everything." Then he helped her get dressed before putting on his clothes. He took her face in his hands and planted a sweet kiss on her lips. "I had a wonderful time, Retta. Thank you for sharing your virginity with me."

She woke with a start; glad it was only a dream. What in the world triggered that? She'd not dated John again although he'd asked her many times.

That prom date had been the beginning of her promiscuity. Why did she even do it since she derived no satisfaction from the sex act? Because she loved knowing that a man was at her mercy until she brought on his orgasm. Wielding power over a man made her feel like a winner. Perhaps it was a form of revenge for what Uncle Carl had done.

Sometimes she felt ashamed of her behavior, but she couldn't seem to stop it. No longer sleepy, she slipped into her robe and slippers, grabbed her iPad, and quietly moved outside. The weather was balmy–usual for Christmas in Cut Off–since the coldest weather usually didn't arrive until January. She sat on the wharf in the early dawn and took in a deep breath of the earthy smell mixed with the dank aroma of the water. This was the smell of home. A *pirogue* slid noiselessly over the water. The man paddling it down the bayou waved, and Henrietta returned his greeting with a wave of her own. She wondered if the man had hewn-out the long narrow canoe from a solid tree trunk as she watched a small green water snake slither toward the bayou bank.

Henrietta doggedly pondered her dream. Why had the loss of her virginity been its focus? Perhaps she should study herself, beginning with her astrological signs, and hopefully learn the reasons for her sexual behavior.

She searched online on her iPad. Born on the cusps of Leo and Virgo–she read she was honest, creative with words, logical, organized–to a fault according to her partners–ambitious, and dramatic. Henrietta was usually optimistic. As she read further, she agreed she was stubborn, blunt, quarrelsome, and a perfectionist. Umm... Was she really cold and stuck on her ego? She didn't think so. *Maybe with men.* According to the research article, these people need to fulfill their needs without losing their abilities to give to others. She wasn't sure about that applying to her. She was a good worker, however, and agreed she was tenacious and persuasive.

Just for the hell of it, she studied her compatibility chart. Not that it mattered. There was no way she would ever marry.

She read that her Leo arrogance was toned down by modest Virgo energies for people born on the Leo/Virgo cusp. It would be helpful to fall in love with a gentle sign that might otherwise be intimidated by Leo, giving them a greater degree of comfort in social situations.

"What a load of crap," she muttered. "People don't walk around with their astrological sign stamped on their forehead."

She switched to her email account just as her mother came outside bearing a steaming cup of her favorite *café au lait*. She took a sip of the hot, sweet coffee and moaned.

"So good," she said looking up. "Thanks, Mom."

Janet Foret Lococo

Chapter 4

Henrietta dabbed Oscar de la Renta's 'Esprit d'Oscar' perfume behind her ears and on each wrist. She dressed in her Christmas-red designer dress of silk for midnight Mass at Sacred Heart Church–better known as Cote Blanche Catholic Church. She wrapped her silk scarf with its red, green, and gold circles and black and white rectangles around her neck. It looked very sharp with her dress. She wanted to look like she owned the world and everything in it. A shiver of pride rode up her spine. She knew the old biddies that did nothing else but gossip would appraise her from head to toe. Let them look… she had nothing to hide.

The sound of the choir singing Christmas carols drifted outside each time the huge entry doors opened to let in members of the congregation. Henrietta remained at her mother's side as they entered the building. Two huge Christmas trees with hundreds of red miniature lights stood on each side of the altar laden with a large number of poinsettias. The tall, golden candelabras gleamed. A beautiful tenor voice sounded above the rest of the singers as the choir sang *Angels We Have Heard*

On High.

Because she wanted her family members seated together, her mother selected two pews midway on the left side of the center aisle and instructed Henrietta to sit behind her and "save" places for the rest of the family. Grammy sat with her daughter. When the hour of midnight got close, both pews were filled with Blanchards of every size and shape.

It had been years since Henrietta had attended Mass. She drummed her fingertips on the wooden seat and admired the stained glass windows while waiting for the beginning of the service. As the church filled, she figured children would become restless and noisy during the sure-to-be-lengthy ceremony. She recalled how she and her brothers had misbehaved in church when they were young and couldn't help smiling. Her mother had not thought their antics cute, and she and her brothers had not relished the well-earned punishments she'd handed out. She smiled at the sight of a young mother seated three pews ahead of them digging into her purse and pulling out a container of dry cereal when her one-year-old started fussing before Mass even began. Times had indeed changed.

Finally, all the bells in the tower tolled, and the choir began singing *Oh Come, Oh Come, Emmanuel*. Again, the lovely tenor voice rang out the melody above the other voices. The sound touched her soul, and her eyes filled with tears from the sheer beauty of his voice.

The altar server carrying the swinging container of burning incense entered first. She hated the smell. It reminded her of her dad's funeral. The altar server holding the Processional Cross, followed by several servers carrying tall, lighted candles, marched in behind the cross-bearer. All of them wore black cassocks topped with lace-edged surplices.

Finally, the pastor-celebrant entered carrying a figure of the Christ Child for placement in the stationary cradle inside the Nativity Scene set at the foot the altar. His chasuble of shiny gold cloth glittered in the bright church lighting,

Then the Solemn High Mass began. When it came time to receive Holy Communion, Henrietta stood in line with all the others in spite of the fact that she had not gone to confession. She recited a silent *Act of Contrition* on her way to receive the Body of Christ. She rationalized her behavior by thinking, "After all, none of us are truly worthy of the Lord."

During communion, the lovely tenor voice sang the *Hallelujah Chorus* from *Handel's Messiah*, raising goosebumps on her arms. The loud and soft parts, the phrasing, the delightful and joyous sound of the singer's voice brought tears to her eyes. To be able to sing like that is truly a gift from God.

After Mass, everyone rushed out. Henrietta tried to keep up with her family. When she thought she heard her name called, her forward motion ceased, and the man behind her plowed into her. He grabbed her around her waist–she assumed to keep her from falling–but he lost his balance and fell flat on his back. She landed right on top of him, between his legs.

"Shit!" She muttered. "You should watch where you're going." When he laughed out loud, she realized he'd heard her curse.

"Such language... and practically on the steps of the church," he jested, still laughing. "Tsk, tsk, tsk." Again, he bellowed with mirth. "I'm Bradley Graham, by the way. I'm sorry to have knocked you over, although it was your fault for stopping so suddenly."

He smelled absolutely delicious–a mixture of scents–spicy, citrusy, musky, perhaps with a hint of vanilla. She sniffed while her face on his chest rested on nothing but hard muscle, and his slow heartbeat sounded in her ear.

"Henrietta Blanchard," she muttered as she tried to rise off him. When she couldn't move because his arms still circled her waist, she furrowed her brow and ordered, "Unhand me."

His silvery gaze studied hers for a moment before he removed his arms from her waist and rolled her off him before quickly jumping to his feet. He gave her his hand to pull her up, and she took it.

"Not very friendly are you?" He frowned before lifting his brows. "Perhaps I should have just let you fall on your ass," he snarled. "Maybe then you'd have been more polite and more appreciative."

As they stood glaring at each other, her mother came up. "Hi, Bradley. I see you've met my daughter."

His mouth dropped open for more than a moment. "Your daughter, Mary Ann?"

"Yes, my daughter.

"She's not at all like you." He wagged his head and started to leave, but turned and smiled at her mother. "Merry Christmas."

Henrietta watched her mother rise on her tiptoes, whisper something in his ear, and kiss his cheek. "Merry Christmas to you, too," she replied and shot him a cunning smile.

He laughed loudly before he turned and strode away.

Driving home, Henrietta asked her mother, "You know that big scoundrel who knocked me down outside of church?"

Her mother smiled. "He's big alright, but not a scoundrel. He's always polite and a real gentleman. We work for the same company, and I think he's ruggedly handsome."

Henrietta pursed her lips and narrowed her eyes at her mother. "Don't even go there, Mom. I'm not in the least bit interested."

"I won't. I only want to say that you could have, at the very least, been nicer when he tried to apologize. I taught you better than that."

"Leave it be, Mom. Just leave it be."

* * *

On their drive home, thoughts of her partner, Gloria, in New York City crossed Henrietta's mind. She hoped she was enjoying the Christmas holiday. She wondered what her other partner, Monique, was doing tonight. She had not been too keen about going home to her tiny hometown on Bayou Lafourche.

"There's absolutely nothing to do in Raceland, Louisiana," she'd complained at the office. "But my mother will hound me to death if I don't go there for Christmas." Henrietta knew that feeling very well. She hadn't wanted to come to Cut Off either.

She'd call them both in the morning.

Chapter 5

To his surprise, Bradley's anger flared white-hot the closer he got to his parked car. His face burned, and his heart slammed against his ribs. He opened and closed his fists. He wanted to hit something. Hard.

It was not generally easy for someone to raise his ire like the woman in the red dress had managed to do. He was ordinarily laid back... usually let things slide... never one to fight over insignificant things. If something was important enough to fight over, however, he made it his business to win.

He pressed the button on his key fob to unlock his car and slid into the driver's seat. He jabbed his index finger at the starter button, and the four hundred horses under the hood of his Porsche awakened and roared, but he didn't drive off. Instead, he sat in the church parking lot to allow his fury to dissipate.

Who did the red-dress-woman think she was to order, "Unhand me?" He scowled. Jesus Christ. What a sourpuss. How could dear sweet Mary Ann have raised this vixen?

He took in a deep breath and let it out slowly before

reviewing what had just occurred. Real bossy. That's what she was, with authentic pain in the ass potential. He shifted in his seat. Nevertheless, she was a lovely vixen... with a nice set of tits that had felt good smashed against his chest when they fell... with long, long legs that would feel good wrapped around his waist... with gorgeous, long, pale blonde hair... and eyes like summer skies.

When his penis hardened, his lip curled, and he wrinkled his nose in disgust. What was wrong with him? *She's a queen bitch, and you have the nerve to want to fuck her?* He rubbed his eyes. He couldn't remember how long it had been since he'd gotten laid, but there was no way he'd become involved with Miss Henrietta Blanchard. She was bad news! He wouldn't fuck her, even if she begged him to. With those thoughts in mind, he peeled out of the church parking lot.

Bradley was determined to remain single following his disastrous failed marriage. He'd been such a fool as a husband that he found it downright embarrassing. He'd almost lost his mind when he learned Saundra had been fucking his best friend during most of their three-year marriage, and he'd never guessed it. Thankful there were no children, he had rid himself of them both. He considered her trash, and he could never forgive his friend. Not in a thousand years.

Bradley enjoyed sex. Long, slow, hot sex that left his partner well satisfied. But that's all he was interested in–fucking with no expectations and no promises. He would NEVER trust any woman with his heart again. No relationships. No drama. Just great sex.

He chuckled when he recalled the words his doctor friend had advised after his divorce from Saundra: "You need to get laid, my friend. Lack-of-nookie is not good for your prostate."

"Not in the mood, Bill. Nookie is part of a woman, and most women want marriage."

His friend had smirked and offered, "We guys constantly chase it until someone manages to tie us down to a one-on-

one relationship. We get taken into their dreams of marriage, babies, a house, and a picket fence. That's the real price of permanent snatch. Now I'm happily married and want to stay that way, but I was happy single, too.

"You mark my words. One of these days, some woman will manage to steal your heart and won't let go. When that happens, you'll be a goner."

His thoughts returned to the church steps after midnight Mass. Henrietta had smelled deliciously wonderful in his arms after they fell. Although it had only been for a moment, he'd recognized Oscar de la Renta's classic scent when it wafted to his nose. *Stop it. Push her out of your mind.*

But his thoughts continued. Why in the world would Mary Ann have whispered an invite to Christmas dinner into his ear? Was she matchmaking? Well, she was barking up the wrong tree. Although he didn't relish spending Christmas alone, Bradley was determined not to show up at the family get-together. But he couldn't help imagining the look on Henrietta's face if he did arrive on her turf. It might be worth going just to piss her off.

Have you lost your mind? You can't be thinking of going. No. He wouldn't go. He'd sleep in for a change tomorrow. Instead of dinner with the Blanchards, he'd eat a light meal he'd prepare himself, finish the Alex Cross novel he'd started that week, have a few drinks, and go to bed.

He could have gone home to Boston, but there was no longer any reason to go there. His parents had been killed in an automobile accident five years ago, and he had no siblings. Since their death, Bradley always experienced nostalgia at Christmas time, sometimes wishing he had brothers and sisters. His mother had always made a big deal about Christmas and New Year. He recalled the way he'd complained while he unscrambled the strings of lights for the fresh-cut blue spruce tree. Everything had to be just so. He still had her priceless collection of tree ornaments stashed in a box in his closet.

He finally drove home. In danger of getting morose, he poured eighteen-year-old Jameson Reserve Irish whiskey into his glass and sipped. He closed his eyes and an image of Henrietta Blanchard in her sexy red dress danced in his head. He tried to rid his mind of her memory, but instead found himself wondering what she'd look like naked... in his bed... Don't even go there. *Too late.* He'd already gone there, and his hard dick throbbed with desire. He emptied his glass and set it on the side table before heading for the shower. No. No. No. He would not think of her. She was definitely off limits.

After a session with Mrs. Thumb and her four daughters in his shower, he slipped into bed without the benefit of pajamas, hoping for dreamless sleep. His hopes were smashed, however, as he removed her sexy red dress and made love to Henrietta Blanchard over and over again in his dreams.

* * *

Henrietta donned her pajamas and slid between the sheets of her bed. Because she was tired, she expected to fall asleep quickly, but her mind remained wide awake. She tossed and turned until she finally allowed herself to think about what was keeping her awake. Bradley Graham. He was tall and ruggedly handsome with absolutely gorgeous silvery-grey eyes, and long, curly eyelashes women would love to have. His thick, almost straight brows gave him an air of nonchalance.

His straight nose was thick, and she was sure his full lips would feel soft. This was no pretty boy. He was a strikingly powerful man. Strong. Confident. Sexy. His dark, almost black hair was long on top, and he wore sideburns.

When she finally slept, Bradley Graham filled her dreams.

Chapter 6

After a restless night, Henrietta greeted Christmas day sitting on the bayou-side wharf, watching the water creep toward the Gulf of Mexico and allowing thoughts to tumble randomly around her mind. The first thing she recalled was her partner Gloria and the way she loved Jesse Martin more than life itself. A pang of jealousy hit home when she remembered the adoring look in her eyes when she spoke of Jesse. She had never looked at any man like that and was sure she never would. *What's with these uncomfortable thoughts? You don't even like men. You believe they are all users of women.*

Monique, her other law partner, had pointed out that she didn't allow herself a chance to look at any man adoringly. And she was right. But her feelings had been hurt upon hearing the words from someone as close to her as a sister. She'd developed tightness in her throat as her shoulders drooped. She pushed away those unsavory thoughts.

Unbidden recollections of the good times she'd enjoyed staying at their state-of-the-art beach house in Grand Isle,

Louisiana, the barrier island where Barataria Bay meets the Gulf of Mexico barged in next. The sandy beach was not a pristine white like the ones in Florida and Alabama. Instead it was darker and sometimes looked dirty–reminded her a little of some California beaches. She loved the smells coming off the salt water and watching the seagulls hunting for food in the late afternoons.

Images of cavorting in the Gulf brought with them feelings of nostalgia. A fierce desire to return to the island gripped her. Henrietta enjoyed the laid back way of life of the natives who call it home. No designer clothes were needed. The thought of the perfect Grand Isle song: Kenny Chesney's *No Shoes, No Shirt, No Problems* lingered as she tried to remember the lyrics. She would talk to J.J. about spending a few days at the beach house their company kept for entertaining customers. She would like to leave tomorrow, stay through Friday, and return home on New Year's Eve. She feared her mother would balk at her decision, but so be it. It wouldn't be the first time.

The smell of French toast wafted from the kitchen, interrupting her reverie. She left her spot on the wharf and headed for the kitchen table and her favorite breakfast food prepared by her mother. The coffee and chicory had been brewed, and a small coffee pot held hot boiled milk to make *café au lait.*

While they ate together, she told her mother about wanting to go to Grand Isle for a few days. Henrietta was surprised by her mother's acceptance of her decision. "I'm pretty sure your brothers are not entertaining customers during this holiday season. The camp should be available."

The caterers arrived at four-thirty and took over Mary Ann's kitchen. Because her brothers were beer drinkers, a case of Budweiser had been iced down since morning. Henrietta had purchased Chardonnay and Merlot for non-beer drinkers.

Henrietta's brothers, their wives, and children arrived at six. Within moments, the house was filled with the noise of adult conversation and children at play. They all munched on tiny assorted sandwiches and hot and cold hors d'oeuvres.

"Wow, Retta, you provided quite a feast for us. This is a nice change from turkey and ham," J.J. remarked. "And you remembered we prefer beer to fancy drinks." He shot her a smile. "Guess we'll just have to give you one of those big A-pluses you always wanted at school."

"Thanks! It's nice for us to be together and enjoy good food and drink without someone having to slave in the kitchen. I rarely cook these days, but I still love to eat."

"You're lucky you can eat all you want without gaining weight," one of her sisters-in-law praised. "I envy you. I have to watch what I eat every darn day."

Once everyone had just about finished eating, the doorbell rang. Johnny Boy answered the door and said, "Well look what the cat dragged in. Hey, bro. Come on in and join us. Mama wasn't sure you'd come."

Henrietta's other two brothers and her mother quickly rose to greet their guest–none other than Mr. Bradley Graham carrying two bottles of wine. Henrietta's face burned. *Who the fuck did he think he was to barge in on their Christmas dinner?* It surely appeared as though her brothers and the son-of-a-bitch were friends. She remained seated and nodded in his direction. He nodded back.

Her mother took his arm saying, "I'm glad you could join us, Bradley. Being with friends at Christmas is much better than being alone." Then she dragged him into the kitchen where the food was spread out on the large table.

After overloading a plate, he joined them in the living room carrying a glass of Chardonnay. Mary Ann brought him a bowl of hot gumbo. Once he'd eaten, he helped her brothers set up two card tables and folding chairs.

Jeremy said, "I didn't hear Mom introduce you when you came in. So how do you know my sister?"

Bradley smiled and eyed Henrietta. "We ran into each

other after midnight Mass."

Jeremy laughed. "So you're the person who knocked her on her ass?"

Everybody laughed except Henrietta. "Ah, come on Sis," teased Johnny Boy with a huge smile on his face. "You were never a wus when you were young. Don't you remember getting into trouble with Ma when you got skinned arms and knees trying to keep up with us? What Bradley said was funny."

"I suppose you're right," she agreed as she moved toward Bradley, surprised by the thunderbolt of desire spearing her belly and spreading to her nether region. *Don't even think of going there.* Her gaze turned up to his face. "I'm sorry I was a wus, Bradley. I'm glad you're here. Merry Christmas." Then she knocked him on his ass with a shove from her crossed forearms."

Everybody laughed, including Bradley. He rose after studying her from her toes to her face. Then he bowed. "Tit for tat. I like that." He swayed his head from side to side before pinning her with his silvery-grey eyes. "You're my kind of woman, Henrietta."

"I'm not anybody's kind of woman, Bradley Graham, and don't you forget it." Then she shot him a broad smile. "Since the entertainment is over, who's interested in a friendly game of Bourré?"

Everyone moved to the card tables and somehow managed to fit around them. Bradley sat between J.J. and her mom, across from her. Jeremy got the high card and dealt the first game. Although Henrietta normally excelled at the card game she'd learned while attending Nicholls State University to study pre-law, she did not excel tonight. Her mind was not on the cards she held, but on the handsome hunk seated across from her. *What is wrong with you, woman! Pay attention to the cards being played. Those eyes of his are mesmerizing. Almost transparent.* She fiddled with her pearls like she always did when she was in an uncomfortable situation.

Bradley left at ten o'clock, and after everything was put away, everyone else left and Henrietta had the key to the Grand Isle beach house.

Janet Foret Lococo

Chapter 7

Bradley smiled as he drove his car home. He still didn't know why he'd decided at the last minute to attend dinner at the Blanchards. *Oh, come on dude. You know you went so you could get another look at the red-dress-woman... to really meet her... maybe even ask her out.* He now knew that would never happen.

He wondered why her behavior was so cold and unfriendly. He recalled feeling that same way after his split with Saundra. It had taken quite some time and the help of a psychologist before he'd realized he was indeed a worthwhile person. I should have listened to my mother. *She'd never liked Saundra.*

He pushed those thoughts aside as he drove into his garage and closed the door before exiting his car. What would he do with all this time off? He wasn't due to return to work until January 3rd and didn't want to sit at home feeling lonely. Maybe he should take a trip. He'd think about it.

After he had showered, he donned what he called his Hugh Hefner silk pajamas, wishing he were at the Playboy Mansion where he could enjoy some totally hot sex, free of any attachments.

Bradley poured himself some Jameson, grabbed the Alex Cross novel, sprawled into his lounger, and raised the footrest. The whiskey burned as it slid down his throat. It was a good burn–a familiar burn.

He tried reading, but soon realized he was reading the same words over and over again, unable to move forward with his thoughts continuously returning to Henrietta Blanchard. He closed the book. He suspected someone somewhere had hurt her and that she no longer trusted men.

He closed his eyes and recalled the image of her after Mass on Christmas Eve. She had looked gorgeous then and tonight. Seated across from her during the card games, he'd gotten a chance to look her over and had found nothing negative except her attitude. She'd become a little friendlier after she had succeeded in knocking him on his ass. He recalled the way she'd laughed out loud when he'd hit the floor.

Her red pants fit her long, slender legs like a second skin. Her full mouth begged to be kissed. Long, golden-brown eyelashes and splendid eyebrows framed her sky-blue eyes. He'd wanted to run his fingers through the long, almost white, blonde hair cascading down her back. He longed to see her naked… to touch her… to kiss every inch of her… to fuck her until they both couldn't breathe.

He would have to go somewhere. Staying in Cut Off would make it too easy for him to pursue her. And he'd be damned before he'd allow himself to be put down by another woman. His boss had left him with the key to the company beach house in Grand Isle. They kept a full-time cook and maid. The island would be deserted. He'd escape there tomorrow.

* * *

Henrietta sipped on Port wine while her mother watched the late news on television. Tonight had been fun. It had been nice to be with her bratty brothers and their wives and children. Were those children ever quiet? It didn't appear to be so.

She was surprised at the immense feeling of sadness that suddenly covered her. She would never have children. So what? Hadn't she made peace with this a long time ago? She had a lot of other things, and children would cramp her lifestyle. She finished the wine. Then she kissed her mother goodnight and stepped into her old room.

Henrietta dressed for bed and slid between the sheets. She'd pack a few things before leaving for Grand Isle in the morning. She wouldn't need anything fancy. Jeans, shorts, and tops would do, but she'd take along a pair of dress pants and a sexy blouse just in case she got bored and decided to frequent one of the bars.

She was asleep almost as soon as her head hit her pillow.

The sun was beginning to set as she strolled barefoot on the beach. It was unusually warm for a winter day in January and so far, the mosquitoes were kept at bay by the insect repellent she'd sprayed on before leaving the beach house.

Henrietta sat on the sand and watched the sky turn from the brilliant light of day into night. This was her favorite time of day. As the sun began to dip down toward the waters of the Gulf, the sky first turned a fiery orange. She watched as a group of Louisiana brown pelicans flew overhead on their way to their roost at Queen Bess Island. Though clumsy on land, they were graceful in flight with their wings spread out wide, and heads held back on their shoulders. Their bills rested on their folded necks.

The orange color of the sky slowly changed from reddish orange into pink before changing to dark blue, and finally to purple/mauve before darkness set in and the first star became visible. The sound of the water lapping onto the shore was peaceful, and she closed her eyes and listened.

The sound of an unfamiliar man's voice startled her. She had not heard his footsteps.

"Want to join me in a walk?" he asked. "I'll tell you all about the stars in the sky," he continued.

She looked up into the silvery-grey eyes of Bradley Graham, and without any thought of consequences or repercussions, she nodded and rose. He took her hand and planted an open-mouth kiss at her wrist before entwining his fingers with hers. She shivered.

"Cold?" He asked.

His voice sounded low and husky. Sexy. "No," she whispered as her nipples hardened into tiny peaks.

He pointed out the stars and planets while they walked for a long while. She wondered how he knew so much about the night sky. When they turned to head back, he wrapped his arms around her waist and pulled her into his body. His chest was hard and muscled. He smelled delicious—a light blend of cologne and man. She could see his pulse beating in the notch of his neck and feel his hardened cock against her belly.

She turned up her head and met his lips. When he dragged his tongue across her lips, she opened her mouth and let him in. She'd never been kissed like that before. This kiss went on and on as his tongue caressed hers. She longed for his mouth on her breasts and the rest of her body. Her genitals pulsed and became wet for him. She had never wanted a man like this.

She awakened when he pushed her away.

Chapter 8

Henrietta had a very special breakfast on the day after Christmas–her mother's made-from-scratch mouth-watering biscuits and *café au lait*. Nobody made better biscuits than Mary Ann Blanchard. As she spread on the butter and slurped her coffee, Henrietta was surprised her mom did not balk at her spending time in Grand Isle now or the night before. Go figure.

She recalled her dream while packing a small bag with necessities. What on earth had made her dream of Bradley Graham? Upon retrospection, she realized she didn't have a clue. She shrugged her shoulders and chalked it up to his unexpected appearance at their Christmas celebration. She was pretty sure her mother hoped to get them together. *No way, Mom. No way. You can stop trying.*

Her mother had put together leftovers from the night before into a picnic basket. She was pretty sure the bar at the beach house was well stocked and that she would find wines she liked there.

By noon, she was on her way, tuned in to her favorite

radio station playing country music, and sang along with Alan Jackson, Brad Paisley, and the like. She stopped at Frank's Supermarket in Golden Meadow to buy a toll ticket and stuck it on the dashboard. This would be her first time driving over the new Leeville toll bridge, and she looked forward to it.

The bridge was fantastic. At some points, it appeared to be rising out of the water. *Of course, dufus! There's water all around.* A mighty edifice it was. She fisted her right hand, pumped it twice over the steering wheel, and said, "Go Louisiana. Great progress. About time!" She pushed all thoughts about Louisiana politics out of her mind.

Henrietta arrived at the beach house located smack dab in the middle of the small island town and pulled into the parking space beneath the building. She got out for a languid full-body stretch, closed her eyes, and deeply inhaled the salty air before grabbing her bag and the picnic basket. She climbed the steps leading to the door and slid the key into the lock.

Everything was neat and clean. Her brothers paid someone to clean up after guests, and J.J. had told her the woman, Mrs. Cheramie, had been alerted to come by daily when he gave her the key.

When she placed her goodies in the refrigerator, she noticed it was well stocked with soft drinks, beer, and Chardonnay. She discovered a treasure trove of wine, Cabernet Sauvignon, Merlot (labels she knew well), and mixers for drinks beneath the counter. She recalled taking J.J. to a Houston liquor store to stock the beach house with good wines for entertaining guests.

Henrietta moseyed onto the screened porch and allowed her gaze to wander to the other buildings. For the life of her, she couldn't understand why the owners called these nice buildings camps and not beach houses. She supposed that was because the older generation had called the simple buildings of the past fishing camps. Those camps had evolved into fancy beach houses, second homes with every convenience. She noted the building next door, owned by the company where her mother worked, was unoccupied. Good. She was not in the mood for neighbors.

Feeling restless after the lengthy drive from Cut Off, she found a straw hat and plopped it onto her head. She needed exercise, and a long walk would be just the thing. She changed into her beach shoes and headed up the beach. She recalled her dream of the night before but shoved it aside. For some unknown reason, she felt sad.

As she walked with thoughts swirling about her brain, Henrietta was unable to understand her melancholy. So what if she was a little jealous of the way Gloria wanted Jesse. Wasn't it normal to want something your friend had? She shrugged her shoulders feeling certain that she'd soon get over it. *Nothing is perfect. There's always at least a little something that could be improved upon.* If they got together, where would they live? That might prove to be a major problem. At any rate, it was impossible to envision herself living with a man for any amount of time, much less the *until death* thing. *Not for me.*

After an hour, she turned and headed back toward the beach house. Although tired from the long walk, the big, ostentatious motorcycle parked beneath the neighbor's house grabbed her attention. The front and rear fenders were blood red, as were some decorative markings on black parts. The seat was black leather and big, silver pipes—she thought they might be mufflers—were visible. It made a powerful statement. She noted the Harley-Davidson logo. Unable to imagine any of the shipbuilding company owners riding this kind of machine, she wondered to whom it belonged. Henrietta had never liked motorcycles. She considered them way too dangerous to ever consider as a means of transportation. There was no way she'd ever ride one.

Once inside, she mixed a couple of lemon drop martinis in the shaker. After pouring one into a stemmed glass, she placed the shaker into the refrigerator. She stuffed her iPhone earbuds into her ears so she could listen to her favorite songs and sat on the back steps, sipping on her drink, and watching the surf endlessly meet the shore. She'd sit there and await the arrival of sunset.

All too soon, her glass was empty, so she left her spot on the steps to mix up another batch while she started on the one in the refrigerator. *I'll make more than two this time.* Her mother's disapproving face came to mind, but she ignored the warning. She wasn't going anywhere, so she'd sip on as many of her favorite martinis as she liked until her mood improved, or she crapped out. Whichever happened first. So what if she got a buzz. She reached for her glass, but she'd emptied it while preparing the next batch. *Time for another.* She filled her glass before placing the shaker in a bucket and adding ice before moving back to the steps.

Henrietta listened to Alan Jackson croon *Remember When.* Yeah, the words written spoke of a life-long relationship. Although beautiful, that was not for her. The words and the idea were so emotional about two virgins making love for the first time…*we made love and then we cried.* She listened until the end and brushed away the tears from her eyes. She pressed the forward button to something livelier and less depressing. She didn't know any men like the one in the song, and she was not at all like the woman. She didn't make love. She had sex.

After a couple more lemon drops, she rose and danced with her eyes closed to Nora Jones' *Don't Know Why.* When she imagined strong arms around her waist, her dreamed-up partner took over the lead. Her eyelids went up, and her mouth dropped open when she gazed into big silvery-grey eyes rimmed with long and gorgeous black lashes.

"That was nice," he whispered.

Her face flushed, embarrassed at being found more than slightly inebriated. Her mind was not working as quickly or as clearly as she liked, and she wanted him gone. She snarled, "Do you make a habit of being where you're not wanted?" Her speech was slurred, and without warning, she felt a little dizzy as she turned toward the steps. She lost her balance and fell into his arms.

"Come on," he urged. "I'll help you up the steps, so you don't fall on your ass again. It seems as though that happens to you a lot."

Anger engulfed her entire being. Her skin burned. She mumbled as he led her up to the door. "I suppose I'll hear about this episode from my brothers until I breathe my last."

"Not unless you tell them." Then he softly dragged his lips along her cheek to her ear. "Your secrets are safe with me."

Her skin warmed with desire now, and she became aware of every single pore. The hairs at her nape made her tingle. An arrow of lust speared her belly, and her pulse raced. *Where did this blinding need come from?* She didn't care as she turned her face so that her lips met his in a heated kiss. Oh, sweet Jesus! What a kiss. She hoped she had not uttered the words out loud. His tongue found hers and waltzed inside her mouth, driving her wild with excitement. He pulled her body in close, her breasts smashed against his rock hard chest, and she felt his growing erection. She wanted him with an ache she'd never known before. She didn't want that kiss ever to end.

He moved her carefully up the steps, and once inside the back door, he asked if she would be okay. She nodded.

Then he moved away from her and said, "I'm not sure how much you drank, but judging from your slurred speech and unsteady condition, I can guarantee you'll have a whale of a headache in the morning. Take care. Goodnight, Henrietta." He left her standing alone in the kitchen and made his way down the steps.

Her cheeks burned with shame and tears spilled onto them. She had brazenly kissed Bradley Graham... had wanted him with every cell of her being. He had to have known that. She sniffed and wiped away her tears with her fingertips. Then the bastard had pushed her away and left.

She didn't dare step into the shower for fear of falling with her unsteady legs. After tearing off her clothes, she slipped into bed. Her last thoughts before drifting off into sleep were that Bradley Graham had walked away from her tonight, just exactly the way he'd done in her dream.

Chapter 9

He had kissed Henrietta Blanchard. Wow! And what a kiss it had turned out to be. Still able to feel her soft lips on his, his fingertips brushed lightly across his mouth. Her body had burned for him. He smacked his cheeks with his hands to chastise himself. He wagged his head. He should never have kissed her. Not in a million years, but he already wanted to do it again. It had all been her fault. She had started it when she captured his lips with her mouth. He'd only improved it. Her moan as their tongues danced drove him on. *So she'd been drunk. So what? Didn't drunks always tell the truth, even if it was self-deprecating?*

Her body had felt like a furnace against his when she pressed herself against him, and his traitorous body had hardened for her. He knew she'd felt his erection. He told himself his lust stemmed from not getting laid in a long while but knew he was only kidding himself. He'd wanted her with a fierceness that frightened him. Sweat oozed from his pores and his heart slammed against his ribs.

He'd always been a predator, so it was natural for him to

be shocked at her taking the lead. Would she remember that kiss in the morning? He doubted it. A small smile turned up the corners of his mouth. If she did remember, she'd surely be pissed.

Bradley had been badly burned once, and there was no way he'd chance that ever happening again. He wasn't at all sure he could stand another deep hurt. No. It had taken him two years to get back his soul. *Why am I thinking of this now?*

At first, he'd been desperate to know why his wife had been fucking his best friend. What had Nate had to offer that he didn't? A bigger dick? No. He recalled seeing it in the men's room, and it was rather small. He fixated on why. Couldn't stop thinking about it. He regretted never cheating on her. At the very least, he could have thrown that in her face.

He'd somehow managed to live through the denial stage but had refused to bargain with the bitch when she offered to try again. He'd not gotten past the anger stage of grief even though his therapist had told him he'd never be happy again until he accepted the breakup. It wasn't about the breakup. It was all about fucking his best friend in their bed. That's when he'd stopped going to his sessions.

He'd stormed at his therapist, "Fuck it. I'm done with them both. I refuse to spend the rest of my life dwelling on Saundra and Nate. I'm moving on." But his inner voice had rejoined, "I'll never trust my heart to anyone again."

He could take care of himself. He could wash and iron clothes as well as any woman and could cook better than most. He'd hired a housekeeper soon after accepting his position at the offshore/shipbuilding company. Free of household chores, he had more time for his beloved photography hobby. He could do exactly what he wanted, when he wanted, and where he chose. The only thing he didn't have was the company of a life partner, and he'd been doing quite well without one.

He walked to his room in the beach house and stripped naked. Then he set the water temperature and stepped into the luxurious shower. His muscles relaxed as the hot water pelted his body, and he relieved his sexual urge with his hand and spilled his seed down the drain. He inhaled the clean citrusy smell of the liquid soap. He would have to remain strong not to give in to Henrietta Blanchard.

After drying with a big, thirsty bath towel, he slipped into bed. Tomorrow, he'd ride out to the dense woods that were home to giant oaks and hackberry trees and take photos of area birds–like flycatchers, thrushes, grosbeaks, and warblers. Fuck Henrietta Blanchard!

* * *

On Tuesday, Henrietta awakened surprised at her nakedness. Her mouth and throat were parched, and the top of her head felt like it might explode from the throbbing pain. She didn't remember undressing, but her clothes were strewn all over the floor. How many lemon drops had she consumed? She couldn't recall. She'd taken a long walk on the beach, mixed a batch of lemon drop martinis, and sat on the steps of the beach house.

Then the recollection hit her full force. Bradley Graham's face. His easy smile... his silver-grey eyes... his hard chest... his arms about her waist... dancing in the sand... "Oh, sweet Jesus," she moaned remembering his kiss. "I made a complete fool of myself. I'm not sure I can ever look him in the eye again. Shit! Shit! Shit!"

She looked at the clock. She'd slept until ten o'clock but still woke with a headache. *No alcohol at all today, kiddo.* The sun shined brightly when she looked through the window on her way to the shower. The glare hurt her eyes. She swallowed two aspirin with a full glass of water before stepping under the stream of hot water.

She dressed in denim shorts and a stretch blouse before slipping her feet into her beach shoes and plopping the large straw hat on her head. Large and very dark sunglasses would make it more comfortable to gaze upon the glistening water while she fished from the end of the long wharf.

The big black bike was gone. *Good!* She hoped he'd returned to Cut Off.

After two hours, she still had not caught a fish. Perhaps Noon was not a good time for fishing. She'd look it up on the internet back at the beach house. She left the wharf and let herself inside. The neighbor's vehicle was still not there. *Amen! Thank you, God.*

Online, she learned that fishing was not something she wanted to do. She'd decided to go to a local fresh seafood market to purchase fresh flounder for her dinner. She planned to grill it, hoping not to burn it. With that thought, she decided to buy two instead of one. She wagged her head. "Admit it, girl. You're not a good cook."

Cooking had never been really important to Henrietta. Although she liked eating, she hated cooking. It was a good thing that she'd done well educationally. As a successful lawyer, she could afford to eat out every day of the week if she wanted to.

Just as she was ready to light the charcoal, she heard the guttural, yet thunderous retort of the Harley. It crackled in sync with her heartbeat, only louder. She closed her eyes. He's back. When she thought he'd gone inside the house, she heard his steps close in on her. A weird excitement spread through her body, making her feel like she might jump right out of her skin.

"Hey!" He called. "Need some help firing up that grill?"

Henrietta couldn't bear to look up at his face. Instead, she held her gaze at his feet. Her heart raced, and her skin warmed. "I think I'll be okay," she responded.

He stopped right in front of her. "I don't. First of all, you've using way too much coal for one item. What are you planning to cook?"

She felt tongue-tied but managed to answer, "Fresh flounder I bought. I tried fishing from the end of the wharf around noon, but the fish were not biting."

He put both his hands in his pants pocket. "Wrong time of day for fishing. The best times are early in the morning and the evening when the tides are changing."

With a flash of anger, she queried, "So are you a fucking authority on fishing AND grilling?"

He cleared his throat. She figured it was to allow him time to come up with a response. "No, not an authority, but I would guess I know more about those things than you do. Why don't you let me start your fire? You only need a few coals for one flounder."

"I bought two." She pinched her lips and scrunched her eyes at him before admitting, "I have a tendency to burn stuff, so I thought it best to be prepared."

His laugh was delightful. "So, have you ever grilled flounder?"

"No." Her face warmed in a blush of embarrassment. "I told you I'm not a very good cook. I don't like to cook at all and hardly ever do."

He chuckled. "Then I've come to your rescue. I'm a good cook and have grilled flounder on more than one occasion. Since you have two, if you'll invite me to dinner, I'll gladly cook the fish."

He had her at a real disadvantage from which she could not gracefully escape. She would have to agree to his cooking the fish. "Okay. I'll make a salad and provide the wine. I'm sure that if I root through the freezer, I'll find a frozen garlic bread to slip under the broiler."

After lighting the fire, Bradley entered the kitchen to season the fish. He certainly looked like he knew his way around seasonings. Henrietta sneaked a peek at his fine ass.

Chapter 10

While Bradley tended to the coals, Henrietta set the table and opened an icy bottle of Decoy Chardonnay. For some unexplainable reason, she was glad Mrs. Cheramie had come to provide maid service while she fished. Correction–tried to fish.

Now this hunk who knew how to cook had returned to her kitchen. A full body flush brought on by his nearness, made it difficult for her to prepare the salad. He patted and rubbed the fish with olive oil and seasonings. He finally finished and took the fish, along with a glass of Chardonnay, to the grill he'd set at the far end of the screened porch.

The aroma of the cooking fish had Henrietta's stomach growling. She realized she'd not eaten anything since waking at ten o'clock. "You can place the bread under the broiler now," he called out. "And watch it every minute as garlic bread is subject to burn quite easily."

"I don't burn everything!" She blew out a breath, determined to watch the bread like a hawk watched a chicken coop. When it was done, she turned off the heat, slid the tray onto the lower pull out shelf, and closed the oven door. When she'd completed seasoning and tossing the salad and served it onto salad plates, Bradley came into the kitchen with fish grilled to perfection. He poured her wine before sitting.

They ate mostly in silence. Once the meal was completed, she said, "Yum, the fish was delicious. Thanks."

He smiled. "The salad is great, and you get a gold star for not burning the bread." He lifted his glass as though in a toast.

Her eyes squinted for a second or two. Before she could say anything, however, he said, "I'm not an ogre, Henrietta. I'm just a plain and simple man. I see no reason why we can't be friends."

Plain, he was not. No, that was not a good description. Handsome. Hot. Those descriptions would be better. She would have bet her last dollar he was not simple either.

"I suppose we could give it a try." Her lips pursed. "Everybody in my family likes you, so I'll give it a try. But I need to tell you that friends do not kiss the way you kissed me last night. So don't do it again."

He chuckled. "I'm surprised you remembered it since you were pretty well blitzed."

"It's the only thing I recall." Oh shit. Did she have to admit that?

"Then I don't suppose you remember you kissed me first."

"I did no such thing, and you know it!"

"Okay, let's not fight. Come on. I'll help you with the dishes, and then we could go for a walk on the beach if you'd like. I promise I won't try to kiss you again."

She didn't know if a walk was a good idea. Walks in the moonlight had a certain mystique and romance about them for most people, and she didn't want to turn him on. Of course, she would not be affected by the allure of the moment. She didn't do romance. She didn't make love. She screwed, then came home to her dildo.

They headed for the beach after cleaning the kitchen. The

waxing moon appeared to be a little larger than last night. The stars twinkled, and Bradley pointed out Venus, the Big Dipper, the Little Dipper, and the North Star. When she stumbled over a stump while looking up, he took her arm and placed it in his.

"The sky is so beautiful," she said. "There is too much light pollution in Houston to see all of this."

"I know. That's one of the advantages of staying in this area. Do you miss living here at all?"

"No." She shook her head. "Houston offers many more things to do. And there are no five-star restaurants or nice clubs around here."

"No bumper-to-bumper traffic either. Low crime," he added. "Why don't you tell me what you're willing to share about yourself?"

"While I was in high school, I couldn't wait to leave Cut Off. I wasn't sure what I wanted other than becoming an attorney. I studied pre-law at Nicholls State University and was assigned to share a suite with pre-law students Gloria Babin and Monique Boudreaux. We became close. They are like sisters to me. We studied together and played together.

"We applied to Harvard Law School after our NSU graduation and were accepted." When he lifted his brows, she added, "Yes, Harvard Law. Is it so hard to believe that women would be accepted there? Especially South Louisiana women?"

"No. I believe in the equality of the sexes. But do go on."

"We rented a three-bedroom apartment and biked to school. We loved the Cambridge-Boston area." She sighed. "There was so much to enjoy. There was no way we'd ever consider living in Lafourche Parish after that. We settled on Houston, so we'd be fairly close to home in the event of family emergencies."

He rolled his eyes at her and laughed. "Did you know that I grew up in Boston?"

Henrietta's mouth dropped open. "No kidding? A Harvard

Law graduate?"

"No. I'm a Yale Law School graduate, as were my father, grandfather, and great-grandfather. There was never any question regarding WHERE I would study law."

"A Yalie. Imagine that. What about siblings?"

"Zippo. I'm an only child. And don't you dare roll those big blues at me. You at least had playmates." They turned around and headed back toward their respective beach houses.

"I was *the baby* and the *only female*. How does *over-protected* sound to you, Bradley Graham?"

"My mother was like that with me. She wanted to keep me safe, so I was always in the company of an adult. I suppose we're both lucky to have turned out the way we did."

Henrietta swallowed the lump that formed in her throat. *Nothing bad. Yeah.* She swallowed again. "Yes," she answered.

"You've never married?"

"No. And I never will."

"Never say never," he warned. "You just haven't met your Prince Charming yet. When you do, you'll change your mind." He raked his fingers through his hair. "I was married once. It lasted all of three years."

"Do I detect a note of anger?"

"More like a whole song. Maybe even an aria from *La Traviata* during Violetta's death scene."

They reached the Blanchard beach house. "Would you like a glass of wine, Bradley?"

"Why don't we go next door? I've got some cold Chardonnay for you. I prefer to sip on eighteen-year-old Jameson Irish whiskey before I turn in." When she frowned, he added, "Have you ever tried really good Irish whiskey?"

"No. I'm not a whiskey fan. I'll have a taste, but then I'll have the wine instead."

He led her to the door, opened it, and turned on the light before guiding her inside. She perched on the sofa and took in the upscale typical beach style surroundings. He popped the cork on a bottle of Chardonnay and poured her a glass.

She sipped. "I've had this wine before, but I can't recall the winery. It's good and cold."

"Alpha Omega," he said.

"Ooh. That's my partner Gloria's favorite. Jesse introduced her to that wine." She sighed. "I believe they love each other. Gloria is pregnant with his child, but he doesn't know it."

He shrugged and handed her a glass of water. "To clean your palate so you won't confuse the taste. He handed her a crystal glass with less than an inch of Jameson inside it. He smiled as he commented, "I'm introducing you to Jameson. Unlike Jesse, I'm not looking for love."

She eyed him and pinched her lips before disclosing, "I already told you I was not at all interested in marriage." She twirled a lock of her hair between her thumb and index finger. "And I'm not sure that I even like you yet. You're absolutely safe from me." She took a sip of the Jameson and rolled it about her mouth.

"Well, how do you like it?" He crossed his right foot over his left knee.

"It's not bad." Her gaze locked onto his. "I prefer wine, however." She handed him the glass with the Jameson, picked up the wine stem, and brought it to her lips.

"So you were raised in Boston?" She asked after taking a sip of her wine.

"Yes. We lived in an ancient brownstone in the Beacon Hill area. My great-grandfather first owned the building. My grandfather inherited it when his father died. He was an only child; his mother died soon after giving birth. My father was an only child, too. There were two more births, but both boys were stillborn."

"I was born in 1970, and although they tried, my mother never conceived again." He shrugged. "It looks like my family is one of only children."

"Compared to being raised in Cut Off, it must have been

nice growing up with all those lovely parks."

"It was, but don't overlook all the great experiences you had growing up along the bayou. Your brothers taught me how to fish, waterski, and hunt once I began my work with the shipbuilding/offshore company."

Henrietta looked at her watch and finished her glass of wine. She'd learned enough for one night and didn't want him to think she was looking for a relationship. "Tonight's been nice, Bradley. Thanks for cooking the fish. I'm going back and getting into bed. Goodnight."

Chapter 11

Henrietta let herself in. She hated to admit it, but she'd enjoyed Bradley's company. He'd made no romantic moves toward her tonight. A woman could do a lot worse. *He's handsome... um... a good cook... um... self-sufficient... um... smart... um... good company.* His clear grey eyes with their tiny darker specks could bedazzle any female. *Even me.* A shudder ran up and down her spine. *No. I was not bedazzled.*

She hadn't asked, but she wondered what had caused Bradley's failed marriage. Maybe he had cheated on his wife. She couldn't help recalling how her law firm's representation of Jesse Martin's ex-wife in their property settlement might ruin Gloria's chance at any happiness with him. He'd paid through the nose to get full custody of his son, and still didn't know it was their law firm that had represented his wife. It was way past time for Gloria to tell him.

Henrietta couldn't put her finger on the reason she thought cheating might have been the cause of Bradley's divorce. Gloria had been married to the bastard, Andrew. He'd admitted to cheating two weeks after their wedding and told her he'd never be satisfied with only one woman when she had learned it five years later. She brushed her teeth and slipped into her nightshirt before sliding into bed. *It doesn't matter. It's not my business anyway.*

She tried to sleep but found it impossible. After tossing and turning for a couple of hours, she put on her beach shoes, grabbed her iPhone and earbuds and sat at the water's edge. Zac Brown crooned *Colder Weather* in her ears. "You're a lover... I'm a runner." That's what she was. A runner. Not a lover. She didn't know why she disliked the guy in the song?

The sound of the surf lapping onto the shore was soothing. The gulf breeze kept her hair out of her face. Her shoulders drooped, and her eyes grew watery. "Why am I so sad?" she whispered.

Henrietta shook her shoulders and swayed to Dierks Bentley singing *Am I the Only One Who Wants to Have Fun Tonight.* She rose, closed her eyes, and danced to Tim McGraw's *Annie I Owe You a Dance.*

A deep voice asked, "I see that you couldn't sleep either. May I join you in that dance?"

Her eyes popped open. Bradley's silvery gaze was only inches away from her face. Her heart raced, her mouth lost all its moisture, and her lips dropped open. Why did he make her feel so totally unglued? *Have to think fast for a smart retort.* Her hands dropped to her hips. "You can't even hear the music. Be real."

"Yes, I can." He pulled her close, removed her earbuds, and dropped them to her neck. Then he turned up the volume on her iPhone. "Don't be stubborn. You know you want to. Don't argue. Just dance."

Unsure of why, Henrietta did his bidding. Bradley pulled her into his warm body that smelled devastatingly sensuous. He danced extremely well, even in the sand. His breath tickled her neck as he hummed the tune. He pulled her even closer.

Her breasts smashed into his chest, and his erection pressed into her belly. Warmth pooled between her thighs.

He didn't miss a step when the song changed to Alan Jackson's *A Woman's Love*, and he knew all the words. His singing voice was nice. Face it. Is there anything that isn't nice about Bradley Graham? "No," she thought she whispered silently.

"No, what?" he whispered into her ear.

"Never mind."

"Harrumph. I will mind. And that's not all," he said right before his mouth captured hers. He dragged his tongue across her lips over and over again until her mouth opened to receive him. Ever so slowly, he slid it inside her mouth and explored every nook and cranny. Boneless, she melted into him. When he pulled his tongue out just as slowly, she felt an immediate loss of what she craved. In and out he went, and she responded. Their tongues mated in a sultry dance. He sucked hard on her tongue with each foray of hers into his mouth. Her panties moistened until she felt the wetness of desire slide down her thighs. She gave in to her feelings and devoured his tongue.

No one had ever kissed her like that. No one had ever made her feel this tumultuous desire. *You do not make love. You screw men into submission.* No good. It wasn't working to dampen her desire or response to his kisses. It was as though he owned her. That frightening thought gave her the strength to push him away.

"No, Bradley," she blurted. She was as breathless as he was. His silvery gaze pinned hers for a minute.

"The lady said no," he said as he backed away leaving space between them. "I'm not sure why, but just so you'll know, I never force my attentions on anyone." He took another step backward, leaving even more space between them. His silvery eyes turned to steel. He didn't blink. She lost all desire when he said, "Goodnight, Henrietta," in a cold, icy tone. He turned and took two steps toward his beach house before he turned and snarled, "Sweet dreams."

She didn't head for the steps leading to her beach house until he had entered the neighboring one. How could he call that soul-searing kiss his attentions? His thick lips had been so soft on hers. His tongue, rigid and determined, had filled her mouth, and she'd gotten dripping wet. Her genitals still pulsed and ached with desire.

She climbed the back steps and went straight to her bed where she tore off her soaked panties. Then she stretched out on the bed and spread her legs. Her fingers slid up and down her center. Her breaths quickened until she came.

Oh, he'd wanted her alright. She'd seen the naked desire in his eyes, as well as the disappointment at her refusal. His hard dick had pressed against her belly, and she wondered if he'd masturbated, too. *Stop it. Stop it this very minute. Don't even think of making love with him. Making love? No. Screwing.*

* * *

A sexually frustrated Bradley entered the beach house. His dick was painfully hard as he strode directly to the bathroom, tearing off his clothes on the way there. Inside the shower, the hot water sprayed onto his already heated body. He leaned against the wall and began to stroke his penis slowly. His teeth clenched, and his eyes closed as he quickened his pace until he came, imagining he was inside of Henrietta. His head barely moved from side to side. *Face it, man. This is not nearly good enough. You want to slide into her and slam into her over and over again... until she clamps her nether lips around your cock and milks the life and breath right out of you.* Yeah. That's what he really wanted.

Judging from her kisses earlier, she'd wanted him. He ached to make love to her all night long. What made her back away before he'd even gotten to kiss her breasts and tease them with his tongue? He'd wanted to when he had felt them flatten against his chest.

He slid naked between the sheets, still aching for her touch.

Sleep finally came. And with it, dreams of a naked Henrietta in his arms… on the sand… her blue eyes darkened with desire… straddling him… riding him wildly… her breasts rising and falling with each movement… her hair flying in the breeze.

He woke when he came hard. He was in his bed, and there was no Henrietta. It was just a dream. Now, he'd have to wash the damn sheets. "Shit!"

This obsession with Henrietta had to stop. Now. He didn't do relationships because of his ugly divorce. Since then, he had treated women like stamps. He licked them, stuck them, and sent them on their way with no concern about consequences or repercussions. He would continue to live by his mantra. And no matter what, he would not kiss Miss Henrietta Blanchard again.

Chapter 12

On Thursday, Henrietta awakened at dawn. She pulled on her old jeans and a faded t-shirt. After slipping into her beach shoes, she grabbed a denim shirt and tied it around her waist. With an ear bud in each ear, she selected Rod Stewart's *Maggie Mae* to pace her walk on the beach. Humming along and singing the words–when she remembered them–she made her way up the beach. The music switched to Steve Winwood's *Roll With It*. She'd forgotten how much she liked that song and stopped to dance to the recording. She pressed the back button to repeat it and made her way back. Her walk ended to the sound and rhythm of Tim McGraw's *Real Good Man*. Reckless streak... mile wide... wild ride. Was Bradley a real good man?

She looked up. The son-of-a-bitch was seated on her back step. There was no way to avoid him. "You're up rather early," she barked.

He snickered. "I see you're in a wonderful mood again this morning." Then he laughed out loud.

His laughter lit a fire up her ass. Her lips pressed together, and an angry flush warmed her face. Her hands snapped to her hips. "What the fuck are you doing on my steps?" Her head turned to the neighboring beach house, and she pointed at it. "Is there something wrong with those?"

He didn't move a muscle for a moment. "Not a thing," he answered. "In fact, I was sitting here waiting for you."

She smirked. "What on earth for?"

"I'm going for a ride in the woods to take pictures and I thought you might like to come along."

Henrietta had not noticed the camera hanging from his neck. "Will you walk there?"

"No. It's too far. We'd go on the Harley."

Her eyes widened. She stiffened, and her hands automatically grabbed her waist. "You. Have. Got. To. Be. Kidding." Her head bobbed and punctuated each word. "I wouldn't be caught dead on one of those damn things. They are as dangerous as all hell."

"Jesus Christ, Henrietta. I never figured you for a big chicken. It's not as though we'd be riding down a busy freeway. Look around you. Do you see any tourists? No. The only people here are the folks who call this island home. Just how dangerous do you think going four miles would be?"

Henrietta chewed her bottom lip. He made clucking sounds and laughed. Damn if she'd let him win this round. She'd have to go. "Do you have another helmet?" She smiled, sure there was none, and she'd be saved from riding on that *infernal machine*.

"Yes. There are helmets inside. Would you prefer a red or black one?"

Shit. "Red. But so help me God, if we have an accident, I will kill you, Bradley Graham."

He moved off the steps. "Go inside and empty your bladder unless you want to bare your ass in the woods to pee. And grab a bottle of water."

She frowned before heading up the steps. "Hell will have

frozen over the day you get to see my bare ass." He had the nerve to laugh!

After the bathroom break, Henrietta grabbed two bottles of water, locked the door, and met Bradley by the demonic machine he already had purring. He handed her the red helmet, and she strapped it on.

His voice sounded inside the helmet, "Can you hear me?"

"Yes. Your voice is in my ears. This is pretty neat."

"Okay. Sit your butt behind me and slide your arms around my waist. I won't go faster than necessary. Just hold on. Let your instincts lead you, Henrietta. You'll be just fine. In an effort to make you feel more comfortable, we'll take a spin on the beach before we get on the highway."

She sat on the seat behind him and circled her arms around his waist. His back warmed her breasts. Ants seemed to crawl beneath her skin. Her heart raced and thumped against her ribs. She wouldn't admit to her fear, however. "I'm ready. Let's go."

Henrietta's heart settled in her throat the moment the bike moved. She tried to swallow her fright.

"Relax. You're fine. How do you like it so far?"

"I don't. I don't feel safe on this damn thing." She hated not being in control.

His words in her ear sounded clipped. "You decided before you sat behind me that you wouldn't like this." The breath he blew out sounded loud. She supposed it was in exasperation. "Why don't you just try to relax? If you can do that, you'll enjoy the ride. You're in no danger with me."

She slid her crotch close to his backside and loosened her hold a tad around his waist. "Okay. I'll try."

He speeded up a bit, and she rested the bottom tip of her helmet on his back. "That's better. One more time on the sand before we move onto the highway."

Three miles from the beach houses, Bradley turned the bike down a lane leading to the Lafitte Woods. He parked the bike in the area surrounded by a split rail fence. "This is mostly maritime forest," he explained, "an ocean coastal wooded habitat on ground higher than the dune areas within range of the salt spray. Some of these live oak trees are older than one hundred twenty-five years. This forest is home to a hundred species of songbirds.

"I'm going to walk about and see if I can snag a couple of photographs." He took a couple of steps forward and stopped. "Oh, look over there, Henrietta," he said pointing at what he saw. He handed her field glasses. "There's a snowy egret. Shit. I have to change the camera lens because I don't want it to fly away." As soon as the lens was in place, he aimed it at the big, white, showy bird. Henrietta heard the clicks of the shutter.

"Wow," she said. "I've seen these birds before, but never got a close-up view until today. It's so beautiful with its long, black legs and bright yellow feet. And the top of the beak matches the feet. I've never noticed those curvy plumes before either."

"That's because it's a breeding female. Come. Let's move on. We should see some brown pelicans."

After a couple of hours in the woods, he asked her to sit on a large, low branch of a mighty oak. "I'll get our lunch."

"I'm not wild about staying here alone while you go buy lunch. There's no telling what's under this blanket of leaves."

He laughed. "I brought lunch. It's in the saddlebags on my *infernal machine*, as you call it. He returned with a blanket and a Tupperware container filled with chicken salad, crackers, and two Cokes. He spread the blanket. His silvery eyes twinkled when he pointed to the blanket and invited, "Lunch, Mademoiselle?"

He'd made lunch. "*Qui*," she replied and moved toward the blanket. Her heart felt heavy with a deep yearning. For what, she had no clue. She sat. "This was sweet of you, Bradley. Thanks."

He sat cross-legged facing her and spooned salad onto a cracker. "I'm a nice guy, Henrietta." His gaze didn't leave hers. "For some unknown reason, you seem uncomfortable with me. I get the feeling that you've been hurt by a man." He loaded another cracker with salad. "Perhaps I remind you of him. Is that why you don't like me?"

Henrietta choked on a bit of salad when she inhaled sharply in response to his questions. Her face flamed. "Don't be ridiculous, Bradley. I haven't known you long enough to either like or dislike you." She took a big sip of Coke. "I don't usually discuss my personal disappointments. My behavior toward you has been to avoid leading you on. I stay away from relationships with men. It's just easier to avoid trouble than to deal with it later." When she noted his searching facial expression, she quickly added, "No, I'm not a lesbian."

He let out a loud belly laugh. "That had not crossed my mind." His gaze moved to his feet before returning to hers. "Not after those really hot kisses we exchanged on more than one occasion. I'd venture to guess you enjoyed those."

Her face burned again. She couldn't remember the last time a man had made her blush. "I did. But I don't want that to happen again."

"You will tell me what or who hurt you so much that you push men who might genuinely care for you away." Her brows lifted, and her lips pursed. "Don't give me that look, Henrietta. I know that for now, it's your big secret. But big secrets never remain hidden. Someone or something forces them out of hiding. I don't know when that'll be, but I do know that you will tell me. I'll try to keep from kissing you, but I'm not sure I'll succeed." He rolled his lips between his teeth. "That's why I said try!"

They returned to the beach houses.

Janet Foret Lococo

Chapter 13

Henrietta cleared her throat. Her hands felt damp, so she wiped them up and down the front of her jeans. She noted a loose thread on her side seam and toyed with it. Unable to recall any time in her life when she felt so conflicted, she drummed her fingertips on her thigh. She sat upright as a librarian once her decision had been made.

She locked her gaze on his silvery eyes and cocked her head to the side once. "You insist that I reveal my inner secrets to you, but what have you revealed to me? Let's see. You told me you were born and raised in Boston; that you're an only child; and that you're an attorney specializing in maritime law. I witnessed your love of a motorcycle and eighteen-year-old Jameson. You've got to admit that isn't much."

He didn't blink. "So what exactly do you want to know?"

She took a moment to consider her question. And in that moment, she grabbed a lock of hair between her thumb and index finger, twirled it, and came to her decision. "I want to know what made your marriage fail."

Bradley's mouth dropped open. It was obvious to her that

this was not the question he'd expected. She saw surprise, then sadness, and finally anger pass over his face. Looking at his stunning eyes, she was certain a battle raged within him–what to tell and what to keep hidden.

He rested his elbows on his thighs and placed his chin in his hands. "*Touché*," he muttered. "You cut to the quick, Henrietta. That probably makes you a damn good lawyer." He dropped his hands to his lap. "You want my entire story, so I'll give it to you although it is not a pretty one."

He closed his eyes and inhaled deeply. His eyes looked sad when he opened them and began, "I fancied myself deeply in love with Saundra and couldn't wait to bring her home to meet my parents. We were invited for dinner on Easter Sunday. Saundra was a little edgy, but I thought that a normal reaction attributable to nerves.

"When Mom and Dad greeted us at the door, she grabbed my mother in a bear hug before they'd even been introduced. My mother's eyes looked worried, but I just smiled and shrugged. Throughout dinner, I caught my mother looking at me and almost imperceptibly wagging her head left to right.

"Saundra was completely oblivious to everything, chattering non-stop about nothing. I couldn't wait to get out of there. My mother called me that night and said that I was making a mistake marrying Saundra. 'I don't trust her,'" she'd warned.

"We married not long after that dinner. My closest friend, Nate, was my best man. After the wedding, the three of us did a lot of things together." He paused to finish his Coke. "Work sometimes kept me from some activities, but Saundra asked Nate to accompany her on those occasions. I was grateful because I wouldn't have to hear the bitching if she'd had to miss anything." He rubbed his hands and clasped them together before setting them again in his lap.

"Three years later, I came home from work early and found Saundra and Nate fucking in our bed. I went into a rage and tossed them out the front door, naked as the day they were born. I was sick at heart, unable to comprehend how I could have been so deceived. And although my mother did not say it, I could hear I told you so in my mind.

"After eighteen months of psychological help, I was still angry. The psychologist told me I would never heal until I could accept what had happened. I looked him in the eye and countered, 'Accept? Fuck you. I'm out of here.' I never went back.

"After a while, I decided I would not allow Saundra and Nate to ruin my life any longer." He raked his fingers through his hair. "More than a year after our divorce, Saundra appeared at my office saying she wanted us to try again. I let out a loud Jack Nicholson crazy person laugh and told her to get the fuck out. She must have thought I was crazy because she ran out of my office almost as fast as the Road Runner in the cartoons." He cracked his knuckles. "So there you have it. The entire story." He rolled his lips together again. "Except for the part that I decided I would never marry again or have a one-on-one relationship."

"Wow," Henrietta said. "What a shame. You are a nice guy and deserve to find a good woman with whom to share your life. You have a lot to offer someone, Bradley. You're smart, interesting, probably laid back like I wish I were. You shouldn't rule out a relationship. Who knows, it might even work out."

He chuckled. "I don't see you rushing into one. So don't encourage me to do so. It's best to leave well enough alone."

"Perhaps. Thanks for sharing your story." She pulled her bottom lip through her teeth. "And you're right. One of these days, I'll share my deep, dark secret with you. But not today. " She stood. "Do you want to take more pictures or leave?"

He grabbed his camera and snapped several of her. "We can go now if you want."

"Had you something else in mind?"

"I'd like to take you for a ride over the Leeville bridge on my bike, but I'm sure you won't agree to go any further than back to the beach house."

She hated it when people assumed what she would or would not do. It always made her angry, and she usually did just the opposite of what they expected. How could someone presume to know what she'd do or how she'd react when a lot of times she didn't know what her reaction would be.

"You're on," she barked. She started to pull on the helmet. "Let's go." She snapped the chin strap in place and started toward the bike. When she peered over her shoulder, he was still seated. "As John Wayne would say, we're burning daylight."

He rose, gathered up the blanket and empty containers, and strode to the Harley. "You don't have to do this, Henrietta," he said as he placed the things he'd gotten together in one of the saddlebags. "It's not a dare." His gaze studied hers. "I shouldn't have made such a suggestion knowing how you feel about motorcycles. We can go back home."

She placed her hands at her waist. "I said I would go, Bradley. So shut up and sit your ass on this seat so I can climb on behind you. Come on."

He straddled the Harley and sat. She slid on right behind him and circled his waist with her arms. He turned on the contraption. Vroom. Vroom. Vroom. She could feel the vibrations of the motor between her legs.

"Ready to roll?" he asked.

"Yeah. Hit it."

She was feeling comfortable by the time they neared the bridge. She trusted him not to take chances with their lives. She couldn't remember why she'd been so adamant about these machines. This was fun. "Can you go faster?" She whispered in the helmet mike.

"Are you sure?"

"Yes. This is kind of thrilling."

He kicked up the speed so that by the time they got on the approach to the bridge, they were more than likely up to the speed limit. "It feels like we're flying. Oh, my God. Look at all the water from here. This does not compare to crossing this structure in a car."

"Better or worse," he queried.

"Better. Much better."

When they returned to their houses, Bradley asked, "How about having dinner with me?"

"I'm not sure we should."

"Why not. Are you afraid I'll kiss you again? I won't. I just hate eating alone."

She didn't answer at first. Should she or shouldn't she. She nodded and said, "Okay."

Chapter 14

B radley showered and styled the stubble on his face with his clipper. Then he slid into his cargo shorts and a slim white tank undershirt and slapped on a little Giorgio Armani cologne. He'd never worn any other scent.

Vacuum-packed steaks had been shipped from piedmontese. com and arrived the day after Christmas. Before leaving this morning, he'd taken out two of the ribeyes from the freezer. He was happy Henrietta had agreed to dine with him.

He recalled the time he'd spent with her earlier as he prepared the ingredients for the salad and set the potatoes to bake. He couldn't believe how easily she'd gotten him to reveal everything about his divorce, but had held on to her own deep, dark secret—as she called it. Whatever it was, she'd been deeply wounded. He'd at least learned some things from the fucking psychologist during his sessions, so the conferences had not been a total waste of his money.

He would love holding Henrietta in his arms while she purged herself of the hurt and shame. *Whoa. Whoa. Whoa. Where did that come from? Are you nuts?* He closed his eyes.

All you want to do is fuck her. Remember that. None of that wanting to listen to her hurts or shame. You were fooled once. Don't make the same mistake. Feed her dinner and send her on her way.

By golly, he knew what he wanted. And of even more importance, he knew what he didn't want. No more one-on-one relationships. Fuck 'em and leave 'em. No matter how good they looked. He readied the coals though it was a little too early to light them.

* * *

Henrietta showered and shaved her legs and underarms. She kept her pubic area clipped, not shaved, to avoid the prickles when the hair grew out. Not that anyone would see that part of her–certainly not Mr. Bradley Graham. She'd remain in her space, a good distance from him, and would not allow any kisses. She let her hair air dry and refrained from makeup except for a little lip-gloss.

She grabbed a bottle of Tomassi Ripasso and headed next door. "I come bearing a small gift for the cook," she said as she entered and handed him the bottle.

He studied the label. "I've never had this wine before, but since it must be one of your favorites, we'll have it with dinner." The coals burst into flame as soon as he touched the charcoal lighter to them. "There is an art to this. The trick is to sear the meat while the flame is high. Then you remove it and wait until the coals are covered with ash before setting them back on the grill."

He ran up the steps and returned with the steaks and a glass of Alpha Omega for her. "How do you like your steak?"

"Medium rare."

"We agree then. I hate overcooked meat and vegetables. Three minutes on each side. The potatoes are done and being kept warm in the oven. I would ask that you season the salad. All the fixings are on the counter."

Henrietta went inside and peeked into the oven. *Hmm.*

74

Twice-baked potatoes. Good choice. She smacked her lips together and dumped the salad ingredients into the large salad bowl. She had just tossed the salad and served it as he entered the kitchen with the steaks.

"Yum," she said. "They smell delicious."

He served the ribeyes, and then uncorked the bottle of wine she'd brought and poured a small amount in his glass. He sniffed, swirled, and finally tasted it. "I like it. The label shows it's brewed in Italy. I've always been a little partial to Italian reds." He poured the wine.

"I like Tomassi wines. I get some from Spec's Liquor Store in Houston. J.J. drove to Houston specifically to buy wine for entertaining guests here. I accompanied him, of course, so he wouldn't get lost and helped him with his choices. He has accumulated quite a nice selection."

The conversation was lighthearted during their shared meal. The steaks were done to perfection. "These are good; close to the steaks at Pappas Steakhouse at home."

He lifted his glass in her direction. "If I came to Houston, would you take me there?"

She raised her wine to her lips and sipped. Her heart skipped inside her chest, and a shiver raced up her spine. Would Bradley consider coming to Houston? His silvery gaze pinned hers without blinking as he waited for her response. "Of course," she answered. "But it would be my treat. Can you live with that?"

He rubbed the stubble on one side of his face. "It's almost 2011, and I consider myself a modern man. Although I would prefer being your host, I'll do whatever it is that you wish."

She shot him her widest smile. "Deal," she said.

After dinner, they cleaned up the kitchen together. "Grilling makes cleanup easy. Your mom called me today and invited me to a New Year's Eve celebration at her house."

"And…"

"I won't go if you prefer that I don't accept her invite."

"Don't be ridiculous. It appears as though my family has adopted you, so if you want to come, then you should."

"Then I'll come." He served her Port wine and Jameson for himself. "Why don't we sit on the screened porch with our drinks and enjoy the Gulf breeze? Afterward, we could take a short walk on the beach. "

She nodded and followed. An hour later, they were on the beach. Henrietta slipped her arm through his as they walked. The night was clear. Moonlight shimmered on the water and stars filled the sky. The breeze smelled of salt and sea life.

The smell of his cologne wafted to her nose. She wanted to bury her nose in his chest and breathe his enticing scent. She took a few deep breaths.

"Are you short of breath, Henrietta?"

She let out a hearty laugh. "No. I was enjoying your cologne. It's the same one you've worn every time we've gotten together."

"It's the same I wear all of the time. Like it?"

She took in another breath. "Ooh, yes. I love it. It's not at all like that heavy musk so many men wear. It's light and elegant with–she sniffed his chest–mild citrus notes and maybe a little woodsy. What is it?"

"It's Armani. *Acqua di Giò*. So what are your plans for tomorrow?"

"I thought I might do a little touristy thing like a ride to Caminada-Cheniere. I have not come home very often since I settled in Houston. I always felt like I'd outgrown Cut Off. And then there's Mama always trying to pair me off with someone. She doesn't get that I have no desire for a husband and a family. I keep telling her, but she keeps trying." Her eyes widened, and she smiled. "That's my soliloquy for today."

He chuckled before asking, "Want to go on the Harley?"

In the moonlight, although she could see that he had schooled his facial expression–she presumed so she wouldn't know just how much he wanted her to say yes–his silvery grey eyes couldn't hide his eagerness to take her for another ride. "Have you previously explored that area?"

He nodded.

"Will you be just as careful as on our previous ride together on that *infernal machine*?"

Now his broad smile revealed his snow-white teeth. "Of course," he replied and winked. "We'll need to get an early start since I want to take you everywhere."

Henrietta pulled in her chin and scrunched her brows. "How early?"

He eyed her cagily. "Nine."

She blew out a breath. "I can manage that. I feared you'd say around seven. I do so hate to get up early on my days off."

He walked her to the back steps, leaned over, and kissed her cheek very close to the corner of her mouth. "Goodnight, Henrietta."

"Goodnight." *Till in the morning.*

Janet Foret Lococo

Chapter 15

Inside the beach house, the corner of Henrietta's mouth tingled. She'd wanted more than a goodnight peck on her cheek. *I did tell him not to kiss me again. That's true.* She toyed with a lock of her hair. *But I didn't mean it. I wanted him—at the very least—to make an effort. He didn't even give me the opportunity to say no. Jesus! This man totally confuses me.*

Her heartbeat throbbed in her genitals, and her panties were moist. She imagined his tongue slowly making its way between her legs. *I want to screw him. Nooo… I want him to make love to me. Nooo… I don't know what I want.*

Her inner voice sounded in her ear, "You know alright. You do want him, and for the first time in your life, you want to make love to a man."

Her heart ached, and her eyes filled with tears she couldn't hold back. Crying, she ran into the bathroom and stripped. "No. No. No. That can't be right," she moaned. "What I need is a hot shower." *I'd like to use my dildo, but it's so quiet out here that I'm afraid he'll hear the hum it makes. Stick to your fingers.*

She set the water to hot and stepped under the stream. One by one, each muscle relaxed. She leaned against the wall, closed her eyes, and rubbed her slippery hands up and down her torso, imagining her hands belonged to Bradley. His were large with long fingers and dark hair on the tops. She wondered if his chest had hair. If it did, she hoped it was not a forest like the actor in *The Forty Year Old Virgin*. She teased her nipples into hard buds before sliding her hands down her torso again.

Her fingers slid up and down her center before finally settling on her clitoris. Her breaths turned to gasps as she neared her orgasm. Her body convulsed in hard spasms when she came–whispering his name, wishing he were deep inside her.

Her inner voice spoke into her ear, "You'd better chill out before tomorrow morning when your hot muff is hiked up against his fine ass and the vibrations of the motor on the seat tickle it. Don't you go begging for it, woman, even though a hard man is good to find."

She could almost hear her partner Gloria saying, "Jesus H. Christ, Retta. I never thought I'd ever see the day you'd put off fucking a guy." Monique, her other partner, would agree.

"Well, you're seeing it now," her inner voice chimed in her ear.

"I most definitely will not fuck him… or… make love to him. There. I said it. Now get the fuck out of my ear so I can go to sleep."

* * *

Bradley's heart banged against his chest. His dick was as hard as the granite countertop of the beach house. God, he wanted that woman. He'd kissed her cheek when he'd wanted to plunder her mouth and drill his tongue down her throat. He'd drowned in those big blue eyes rimmed with lashes and brows that were a darker shade than her hair–hair that was the same color as a tow-headed youngster. It cascaded in waves down her back. Her small, straight nose sat above a full mouth he so wanted to possess. Absolute perfection. That's what she was.

He'd wanted to ram his dick inside her until she came with abandon and screamed out his name. He headed for the shower to masturbate. It would not feel as good as a real fuck, but it was better than nothing and would provide much-needed relief. He imagined she was in the shower with him and his mind filled with thoughts of her climbing all over him.

Bradley's soapy hands slid easily up and down his penis. At first, his strokes were slow, but he built up speed until he came, spewing his semen all over the shower door while imagining he was inside Henrietta. As his breathing slowed, he realized he'd have to clean the fucking door.

After cleaning the shower and drying his body, Bradley knocked the Jameson back and slid between the sheets with his thoughts of Henrietta.

She was a smoking gun–master of her universe and probably capable of mastering his, too. And he would be happy to allow her to do so, as long as there was no more commitment than fucking. Now, he wished he'd never met Saundra. The bitch had done a number on him and made it impossible for him to trust again.

He licked his lips and imagined they were Henrietta's. He'd never, ever wanted a woman the way he wanted her. And the most frustrating thing about it was that she would never allow him to screw her senseless. Never. Ever.

Always the optimist, he told himself that he still had tomorrow and New Year's Eve at her mother's house. Who knew what could happen? *You are out of your mind, man. Remember that it is always better to be surprised than to be disappointed. Stop thinking about her and go to sleep!*

The Jameson finally kicked in and lulled him to sleep and into dreams of Henrietta.

* * *

On December 29, 2010, Bradley woke as the dark of night began getting lighter. He brewed coffee, filled his mug, and sat on the back steps to watch the sunrise, wearing only his briefs and with his camera hanging around his neck. He turned his gaze east in readiness to catch the sun as soon as it made its first appearance. As he watched, a layer of dark pink became visible, creating a lovely border for the darker water. A shrimp boat was already at work. That would be a nice photo. He pressed the shutter button.

The sky above the pink gradually turned to a deep purple that got lighter and lighter as the pink layer grew. He took pictures with each change until the sun finally made its golden appearance. Snap. Snap. Snap. The sky gradually became its normal shade of blue–the color of Henrietta's eyes.

A slight noise had him turning his face to see what approached. There stood a smiling Henrietta wearing beat-up jeans and a tight, cropped t-shirt. Her hair was in a ponytail, and her lovely face was devoid of all makeup. He looked quickly at his watch. Seven o'clock. He smiled, held up the camera and snapped several shots of her as her facial expression changed from awe to tight-lipped and pissed.

Her fisted hands rested on her hips. "I thought you said we were leaving early, but there you are, seated on the steps in your drawers and taking pictures."

Oh, my God. He wasn't dressed and had developed a hard-on the moment he saw her. He had to get inside and dress. *But she'll see that I'm hard for her.*

He rose and turned to go up the steps. "You're early," he said as he caught her looking at his erection. *Let her look. Let her see just exactly what she's missing.* He hurried up the steps. Once inside the kitchen, he rushed to brush his teeth again and quickly pulled on his oldest jeans and softest t-shirt.

"Since you're very early, I'm fairly certain you haven't eaten breakfast."

"I don't usually eat breakfast."

"Since I haven't prepared anything for lunch, I'll scramble some eggs for you. Help yourself to the coffee. The mugs are in the cabinet above the pot."

They sat and filled up on the eggs and toast. "You're a good cook, Bradley."

He shot her a cagey smile. "That's not all I'm good at." Then he winked.

She slapped his shoulder. "I don't want to hear about it."

After they had finished breakfast, he pulled on his leather jacket and handed her a thick denim one. Put it on. It's still a little chilly."

"Thanks," she said and pulled it on. It was way too large. She pulled on the helmet and snapped the chin strap. "Ready," she said smiling. "And thanks for breakfast."

He straddled the seat of the *infernal machine*. She got on behind him. A vision of him earlier in his underwear and sporting a huge erection filled her mind. She chuckled.

"What's so funny?" his voice asked in her ear.

"Nothing." She laughed again. "Didn't I say ready?" She wrapped her arms about his waist.

Vroom. Vroom. Vroom. The mighty machine seemed to growl. Then he peeled out, and her heart dropped into her stomach.

"We'll go up the Leeville bridge again and exit on Highway 574-1 to visit what the locals call La Cheniere. In 1763, a Monsieur Du Rollin was given a land grant to that parcel of land. He later sold it to Francisco Caminada who gave it his name. The Spanish, during their control of the Louisiana Territory, encouraged colonization, so Grand Isle was divided between four men: Jacques Rigaud, Joseph Caillet, Francisco Anfrey and Charles Dufresne.

"Look down. That's Caminado Pass. Grand Isle is separated from Cheniere-Caminado by that body of water. It was first called *the spit* because the early settlers said 'you could spit across it.'" Her laugh sounded in his ear.

"I do find it a little upsetting that you know more about this area than I do, and I've been coming to Grand Isle all my life. I wish now that I'd have paid more attention to the stories the old folks told. I do know that Grand Isle and Cheniere-Caminada were quite popular with wealthy Louisianians."

"You must have read Kate Chopin's book, *The Awakening*. No need to worry yourself about your lack of knowledge about the history of this area. You might know a lot more about Boston than I do. When you live in a city or town, no matter the size, its history doesn't seem that important. When you visit a town or city for the first time or move there, it's automatic that you want to know the history."

Chapter 16

S he trudged alongside him through La Chenier learning everything historical. They stopped at the iron barrier with a large sign saying Elmer's Island was closed until further notice.

"I would have liked to take you to the wildlife refuge, but it's been closed since the Deep Water Horizon oil spill in April."

She gazed in that direction. "I'm not sure this is an island," Henrietta mused.

Bradley explained, "It is an island because it is bounded by water on all sides, even though the water on the north is a tidal channel and a small bayou named Bayou Thunder which sometimes is silted in at the mouth where it empties into the Gulf of Mexico."

"You sure know a lot about the local area for being a Sassenach."

He laughed. "So you read *Outlander*, too." He paused before adding, I'll bet you loved Jamie. All women do."

"Harrumph."

They headed back home after exploring it all and agreed to have dinner at C Morans on Highway 1 in Fourchon. Bradley said, "The restaurant got good reviews on Internet travel sites, but I've never eaten there. The menu looks good."

"We'll go in my car," Henrietta said.

"Whatever," he replied. "I'm easy... easy as Sunday morning," he crooned.

"Okay, Lionel, what time do you want to leave?"

He laughed. "I'll call and make reservations for six-thirty since they close at nine."

"Fine with me. Not sure reservations are required, especially with nobody but the locals here."

"Better safe than sorry." He pulled out his iPhone and dialed the number. "They're open tonight. It's a go."

Dinner was good though it was a further drive than what she'd thought. He offered to drive, and she accepted. She wore her dressy pants outfit. Bradley's black dress slacks hugged his butt, and his red Polo golf shirt seemed to emphasize his well-muscled chest.

"This is my treat," she said as soon as the left the car. "No arguments."

He shrugged. "Whatever," he snapped. "Must you always be in control and refuse to allow a man to take care of you?" He raked his fingers through his hair. "Never mind."

She didn't allow herself to get pissed at his comment although it was true. She ordered the seafood crepes–thin crepes over-stuffed with lump crabmeat topped with a garlic cream sauce–that were fantastic. The sauce was just right. He had a seafood platter and ordered a bottle of Chardonnay from the wine list.

Afterward, he drove them back while country music played on the radio. She was mellow after a good meal and a couple of glasses of wine and sang along. When they reached the beach houses, he invited her in for some wine, but she turned him down.

He accompanied her to her back steps, kissed her cheek, and whispered, "Goodnight. Thanks for dinner." Then he turned abruptly toward his place.

Henrietta undressed and slipped into her nightshirt. She opened a bottle of icy cold Chardonnay and put it and a wine glass in an ice-filled bucket. She inserted her earbuds and slid her iPhone into her shirt pocket. Clint Black and Wynonna Judd singing *A Bad Goodbye* sounded in her ears. The beautiful song had romantic words that brought on feelings of sadness. She made her way down the back steps, grabbed a folding chair from the storage area, and placed it and the chest near the water. Then she poured some wine into her glass.

The night was clear and the sky filled with millions of tiny stars. She closed her eyes and listened to her favorite country songs and recalled her meetings with Bradley over the last few days. There was no doubt about it. He was a nice man who'd managed to make her want him like no one had ever managed to do before. She wanted nothing more than to lie next to him, in his arms, on a soft bed or even in the sand, and feel his hard dick rub against her thighs on its way up. She wanted to kiss him into obedience to her will... to take him inside her... to make love to him until they were both breathless.

Something brushed her shoulders. She looked up and found herself drowning in Bradley's silvery-grey eyes. He said nothing, just pinned her gaze with his. His desire for her was readily visible and her heart–beating a fast-paced rhythm–rose in her throat. Millions of ant-like feelings crawled beneath her skin. She rose and walked into his out-stretched arms.

His shirtless chest was hot beneath her breasts. God. He smelled good enough to eat. He felt so good it was impossible to resist his mating call. Her nipples hardened into little mountains, and she shamelessly rubbed them against his hot chest. He ground his erection into her belly.

She lifted her lips to his, and he took what she offered and asked for more. His tongue slowly drifted over her lips, and his hand lifted the hem of her nightshirt. Their tongues danced together in a sultry rhythm. His hand moved over her buttocks, up to the band of her bikini panty, and slid inside. She moaned and moved her pelvis even closer to him.

Then, before she knew it, she was shirtless, and her breasts were in his hands. Her genitals pulsed with want. Her heart crashed against her ribs. Her skin ached for his touch. God, she wanted to fuck him… over and over again… until they were completely exhausted.

"You're so beautiful," he whispered. "Your skin is pearl-like in the moonlight." He laved each breast with his tongue. "I want you, Henrietta Blanchard. I want to make long, slow love to you. My dick is so hard it hurts, but I fear you will hate yourself in the morning if you succumb. So I ask you, what is it that you want?"

"Right now, my body calls out to yours. But you're right. I would hate myself in the morning. I'm sorry, Bradley. I didn't mean to turn you on and leave you hot and hard. I wish I could give you what you want, but I think you need to return to your beach house."

He turned and left her. Tears filled her eyes. She had come so close to fucking him. Thank God he'd realized she was mesmerized by desire and had given her a chance to say no. She had so wanted to say yes.

* * *

Henrietta rose early on Saturday morning, New Year's Eve. She would leave for Cut Off by lunchtime. She took her mug of hot *café au lait* to the back steps and sat. The sun had just risen in a cloudless sky that promised a beautiful day.

"Hey," Bradley called from the steps next door. "How about a breakfast of pancakes and sausages?"

She had planned to avoid him, but she couldn't resist the call of the pancakes. He was a terrific cook. "Okay, but I'm leaving around lunchtime."

"Me, too." He called. "Come on over in thirty minutes."

The pancakes were light and fluffy. Delicious. Henrietta helped him clean up.

"I suppose this is goodbye," he said with his gaze burning a hole into hers.

She recalled the words to *A Bad Goodbye*, walked toward him, and kissed his cheek. "Only *au revoir*."

Janet Foret Lococo

Chapter 17

The first words out of her mother's mouth were, "So, did you enjoy yourself?"

Curious pot, Henrietta thought. "Yes, I did." Then she decided to cut to the chase, "Did you know that Bradley was going to be staying next door?"

Her mother's eyes widened, and Henrietta thought she looked a little sheepish. "I did. And before you climb atop your wild horse, I'll explain that I didn't tell you because I thought you might change your mind. I thought y'all might get along together. He's such a nice man."

Henrietta's blood boiled, making her hot all over. Her face burned in aggravation, and she moved her fisted hands to her waist before huffing out a breath. "When will it stop, Mama? I have never been fond of your clumsy matchmaking attempts, and you know it. Jesus Christ. What do I have to do to convince you it's futile?"

The anger in her mother's face was evident. It was red. Her grossly distended neck veins and her facial expression made her look witchlike. "Listen to me, young lady. Did I suggest that you go to Grand Isle?"

Henrietta blushed and hung her head in shame. "No."

"Enough said! I would like to see you happy with a man like I was with your father, but I gave up on that years ago." Her eyes became watery, and she pinched her lips together. After a moment, her face lightened, and she opened her arms in invitation.

Although she was a foot taller, Henrietta walked into the comfort of her mother's arms. "I'm sorry, Mama." She wiped the tears from her eyes. "I assumed you'd tried to get us together. I did have fun. We did stuff together and had a really good time. He's a nice man, but I've never gotten over what happened. Uncle Carl ruined my chances of a relationship with one man. A solid relationship requires love and trust, and I can't trust any man."

"I know. But you must try. Have you considered counseling?" Her hand patted Henrietta's back.

"No," she muttered. "I felt so dirty for so long. Then I suppose I got used to pushing it to the back of my mind."

"I hated him for what he did to you. I'll never forget the look on your face when I opened that closet door. My own brother–God damn his soul! Only God knows how many times I asked myself how he could have done that. For a long time, I felt guilty for asking him to watch you after school.

"Even after he'd died, the hate remained. That bastard ruined my baby. In confession, the priest told me that our Lord expects us to forgive those who hurt us and that I should do so." She lifted her red-eyed gaze to Henrietta's. "I never could, and I'm sorry to say that I hate him still. He'd better be burning in hell. When I die, if he's not in hell, the Lord and I will have a serious talk."

She wiped her face with the sleeve of her dress. "That's enough sadness for the last day of this year. I love you, Henrietta. I always have, and I always will. I'm proud of the woman you've become in spite of everything."

Henrietta wiped the tears from her eyes with the back of her hand and wiped her hand on her jeans. "I love you, too. Let's put away the maudlin thoughts and think party. What time will my brothers be here tonight?"

"The party starts at eight. I've invited a few other folks so it won't be just family. It'll be more fun that way."

"What about food?"

"I ordered a bunch of hors d'oeuvres from the caterer and I've cooked a huge pot of seafood gumbo. We'll use throwaway plates and glasses. J.J. brought over a case of wine and other alcohol for mixed drinks. I'm ready for tonight. There's nothing more to do."

Henrietta turned her gaze toward her mother. "Let's not use throw-away plates or glasses. Did you invite Bradley?"

"Yes, but I invited some others from our office, too."

Henrietta's thoughts turned to Bradley. *I'll wear my red dress tonight. The one I wore to midnight Mass. I'll see if I can knock him over again. I'll have to make sure I'm standing close to him at midnight so that I'll get his first kiss of the New Year.* A thrill skittered up and down her spine. *Stop it! Don't be ridiculous. He's just a man.*

* * *

Her brothers and their wives arrived in one vehicle, J.J.'s Suburban. They brought large containers of potato salad.

"No kids?" Henrietta inquired.

"None. We're childless tonight. Amen! Our kids are all together at Jason's with two babysitters," Johnny Boy replied. "We love them, of course. But it's nice to get away from them for an adult get-together."

Jeremy added, "We came in one vehicle to leave more parking space for guests." He grabbed his wife around the waist and pulled her close. "We're ready to party."

Mary Ann laughed. "Remember when you go back home and get all lovey-dovey not to forget about birth control."

Johnny Boy laughed and said, "Your sons all took care of

that. We got fixed."

"All three of you?" Henrietta asked.

Jeremy's wife, Annie, laughed and announced, "Yeah. We followed Bob Barker's advice and had our pets spayed and neutered."

Debbie and Alice joined in her laughter. "Right on," they added.

Henrietta and her mother laughed, too. "Good move," Henrietta said. "I would think four kids are enough," she added.

Guests began arriving around nine o'clock. Her mother introduced co-workers and their mates or dates to Henrietta. She was sipping on a glass of Chardonnay when Bradley entered at nine-thirty. Her heart began to race as soon as he stepped through the door. *God, he is gorgeous in that obviously expensive black suit and red tie with tiny Christmas trees all over it.* She took a few deep breaths to relax and tried to keep her eyes off him, but her gaze kept returning to him. She couldn't wait to inhale his scent.

She watched as he greeted her mother and brothers. He knew them all by name. He hugged her mother and sisters-in-law and shook her brothers' hands in greeting. Her gaze slowly moved up the length of his body before traveling up to his face. His silvery-grey eyes caught and held hers. His nod was almost imperceptible. Certain that he'd make his way to her, she smiled at him and winked. *Whatever in the world had possessed her to do that?* She was glad she'd chosen to wear her red dress.

One of the men that worked with her mother appeared and seemed to have decided to remain glued at her side. He wore no wedding ring, so she assumed he was single. He was tall and overweight. Nice enough, but couldn't hold a candle to Bradley. His conversation consisted of cliché after cliché. He seemed incapable of an original thought. She excused herself and headed for the bathroom. She hoped someone else would garner his interest.

When she stepped out of the bathroom, Bradley was waiting outside the door with a fresh glass of white wine. Smiling, he handed it to her and brushed her lips with a light kiss. Her heart rate skidded up a notch.

"You look ravishing tonight," he said. "Just like the night we first ran into each other. Sexy. Gorgeous. I love that dress, your scent, your hair, and your face. I'm dying to kiss you, but not in front of everyone. I'm not sure I can wait until midnight."

She took his hand, led him into the bathroom, and closed the door. "Now you don't have to wait until midnight," she said as she turned up her face.

He pulled her close and covered her lips with his. She closed her eyes and leaned into him. He smelled so good. His lips completely possessed her mouth, leaving her wanting more. She opened her mouth for his tongue, and when he entered her mouth with his, she moaned and ground herself against his erection.

He pulled away from her. "We can't stay in here much longer. People will talk."

"I know. You smell just wonderful, and I couldn't help myself."

They stepped out into the hall and remained there. She rubbed her lipstick off his lips with her fingertips. He straightened the top of her dress. "We can stand here for a while and talk," she said.

His darkened gaze locked onto hers. "I would like to visit you in Houston. Would I be welcome?"

She stiffened, and her mouth dropped open. Yes, she wanted to see him again. But she wasn't sure that was a good idea. She didn't do relationships, but she wanted to screw him. She'd bet her car that he'd be great in bed. "You do recall that I'm not into one-on-one relationships?"

"Yes." He studied the toes of his shoes before looking up

95

into her eyes. "Is that a no?"

She sighed. "No, it's not. I would love for you to visit Houston. Just make sure that I have advance notice." They exchanged telephone numbers. "Now I think we need to join everyone else. These down-the-bayou folks are masters at spreading the word, good or bad. It won't bother me since I will be in Houston. You'll be the recipient of it all, so tread lightly."

He took her hand and brought it to his lips. His full lips felt softer than a sponge when he opened her hand and placed a wet kiss in her palm. She shivered. When they entered the living room, Henrietta caught the searching gaze of her mother across the room. It was impossible for anyone to miss her broad smile of approval.

Chapter 18

Bradley sucked in a breath when his gaze lit upon Henrietta. Jesus, she was wearing that hot red dress she'd worn when she'd knocked him on his ass right outside of church following midnight Mass. Had it only been seven days since they'd met? It seemed much longer.

He couldn't wait to get past her family members and head directly to her. Like in the game of Monopoly: *Go directly to jail, Do not pass go, Do not collect two hundred dollars.* His palms got damp and little tremors danced beneath his flushed skin. He wondered about the tall, fat fucker at her side, trying to get her attention. He couldn't remember ever experiencing this bone-deep ache for a woman. Never. He wanted her... naked... beneath him... so he could sink himself deep into her core. He wanted their souls to touch and become one. He needed her like he needed his next breath. *You'd better be careful. You could fall in love with this woman. Remember Saundra. Fuck Saundra! Henrietta is not at all like her. I hope!*

Her gaze remained on him. He noticed when it slid slowly from his shoes to the top of his head. Was that a hungry look he noted in her beautiful blue eyes? Could it be that she felt the same way? That she wanted him as much as he wanted her? If that were true, his life had just changed. He shrugged. There was no way in hell he'd be that lucky.

He smiled recalling the way she'd pulled him in the bathroom to kiss him in private. And what a kiss it was. He'd felt it all the way to his toes.

* * *

Henrietta couldn't recall who'd started the dancing. Her mother had passed out typical New Year's Eve party hats and insisted everyone wear one. Everyone laughingly complied.

She was dancing with Bradley when Jeremy started the countdown. 10... 9... etc. On the count of 1, *Auld Lang Syne* rang out from the speakers, and Bradley's lips covered her own. A thrill shot through her body, and she trembled in his arms. Their bodies were so close that a thread could not have passed between them.

Her mind told her she should pull away and end the kiss, but her traitorous body wouldn't listen. Thoughts bounced around in her head throughout the kiss. What would her mother and brothers think? What would the guests think?

When they finally pulled apart, the room filled with the sound of applause. Completely unaware to them both, her family and guests had formed a circle around them while they kissed. What an embarrassment! Her face warmed. She noticed his was flushed, too, and his lips were swollen. She could tell her lips were also puffed up.

"Happy New Year," she murmured.

"And the same to you, Henrietta," he responded. Then he kissed her again. A sweet kiss this time.

The party finally broke up at three o'clock. Bradley was the last to leave, and Henrietta walked to his car with him.

"I had a good time, Henrietta, and not just tonight. It's been fun sharing my time off with you, and I can't wait to see you again. When do you fly back to Houston?"

"Monday, around noon."

"God, I hate to leave. Do you know how much I want you?"

"I think so."

"But do you want me?"

"Yes, but that won't happen. Now you need to go home."

"Okay. I will call you on Monday night." He brushed a butterfly kiss to her lips. Then he sat in his car, and drove away.

* * *

Henrietta didn't like the thought of going inside, sure there would be another *inquisition*, so she took her time. "Nice party, Mom," she said. "I'll help you put everything away and clean up. I know you won't go to bed until it's all done."

"Yes, I thought so, too, and appreciate your help. Everyone seemed to have a good time."

Henrietta nodded as she stacked the china plates and carried them to the sink to rinse them before putting them in the dishwasher. Her mother put the leftovers in containers. She labeled the containers of gumbo for the freezer.

"Looks like you and Bradley have hit it off."

"Mother!" She rested her soapy hands on the sink's edge and glared. "There you go. Again. Just face it, dammit. Bradley and I have no future. I knew I'd hear this after I came inside. That's why I took my time coming in." She returned to rinsing off the plates and silverware.

Her mother stopped what she was doing and walked over to where Henrietta stood. "Listen here, young lady. I, along with everyone else, saw that burning hot kiss at midnight. There was no mistaking the feelings between you and Bradley. You could not do any better than Bradley Graham. He's a nice man... a good man... with great values. So don't trifle with him.

"His wife did a real number on him. He didn't deserve that kind of hurt, and you didn't deserve the physical and emotional pain you experienced. As a result, neither of you trusts the opposite sex. That's too bad. You both have so much to offer each other." She returned to packing the food containers. "Soliloquy over. I love you, Retta, and I want you happy."

"I know, Mama. Bradley is a nice man. We knocked heads in Grand Isle, but we had fun, too. He has my telephone number and has said he'd come visit me in Houston. You're right. We both have issues with trust. You've always told me there can be no love without trust. We'll see." She widened her eyes and lifted her brows. "Would you believe that I rode on his motorcycle in Grand Isle?"

Mary Ann framed her face with her hands and let her mouth pop open. "I can't believe it."

Henrietta laughed out loud. "Believe it! And more than once!"

"Oh, my God." Mary Ann wagged her head sideways. "I have missed you so much. Please try to come to Cut Off more often."

"I'll try, but don't expect miracles."

* * *

Henrietta dropped off her rental car at Louis Armstrong International Airport in Kenner, Louisiana, at ten-thirty the next morning. She was early. In the V.I.P. lounge, she ordered a Bloody Mary, moved to a booth, and pulled out her iPad. But instead of reading, she allowed her thoughts to wander about her time at home.

Although she'd dreaded returning to her hometown for the holiday, there had been high points on her visit to Cut Off. And most of those favorable factors were related to Bradley Graham in some way. Would he call? And if he did, what would she say? Just thinking of him made her feel weak and vulnerable. She fiddled with her pearls and worried her bottom lip between her teeth. She inhaled deeply to relax.

She slowly sipped her drink and rolled a lock of hair between her thumb and index finger. Would she have sex with him if he showed up? She wasn't sure if she should or not. *That's a first.* She didn't want to ruin their brand new friendship. She'd see. It would be a great temptation. Just thinking about the possibility warmed her.

When her flight was called, she gulped her drink and left the lounge for her gate. As soon as she sat in her business-select seat, she pulled out her iPad. She and her partners, Gloria Babin, and Monique Boudreaux, were meeting in their conference room in the morning. Of course, she would have to tell them about Bradley. What would they say?

Chapter 19

Henrietta arrived first at their office and started brewing the coffee. Gloria and Monique arrived minutes later. They hugged and wished each other happiness for the New Year.

Seated around the conference table, Henrietta drummed her fingers on the tabletop as she wondered how her partners would react to the news that she'd had a great time in her hometown.

Her face warmed, and she automatically reached for her pearls.

Gloria scowled. "So what's got you so nervous this morning, Retta?"

Henrietta glowered. "What makes you think I'm nervous?"

"Well, for one thing, the way you're about to break your pearl necklace. You fiddle with your pearls whenever you're nervous. Something must have happened while you were in Cut Off. So what gives? Do tell."

Henrietta cleared her throat and continued toying with her necklace. "I met a man."

Monique cocked her head and said, "Must've been someone special judging from your agitation. Did you have fun?"

Henrietta tweaked her chin between her thumb and index finger. "I actually had a great time. I'd not expected to enjoy my time in Cut Off." She brought a shaky hand to her forehead. "I met him quite by chance at church."

"Church?" Gloria and Monique asked as one with their eyes wide. "And the roof didn't cave in?" Monique added. "You haven't been inside a church in years."

"It was actually outside of church. My mother insisted I go with her to midnight Mass, and I couldn't refuse since I had not been home in a couple of years and felt guilty. On our way out, I stopped abruptly when I heard someone call my name." Gloria and Monique looked at her like she was crazy. She laughed out loud and continued her story.

"Boom!" She slapped her hands together. "He plowed into me. I felt like I'd run into a stone pillar. He put his arms around me to stop my fall, but when he lost his balance, we both fell to the ground. He dropped onto the cold cement on his back, and I fell on top of him, between his legs."

"Oh, my God!" Monique shrieked. She and Gloria laughed until their eyes watered.

"I fail to see the humor in that," Henrietta barked. "I could have been injured."

Gloria was the first to regain her composure. "Pretty convenient." At her partner's confused expression, she added, "The position, you twerp."

Henrietta narrowed her eyes at them both before continuing, "Do you want to hear this or not?"

"Of course we want to hear," they replied. "Wouldn't miss it for the world."

"Well, when I opened my eyes, I found myself gazing into the most beautiful silvery-grey eyes. They appeared transparent in the moonlight and were framed by long, dark lashes." Her eyes closed, and the corners of her mouth lifted just a little. "He's handsome and tall, and I can still smell his provocative scent. Not sweet or spicy. Hard to describe. His name is Bradley, and we saw each other every night I was home, mostly in Grand Isle."

Monique eyed her partner. "So how long did it take for you to screw him?"

"I didn't." She paused hearing their combined gasps of surprise. "Not that I didn't want to... And not that he didn't try..."

"Oh, my God," they replied in unison. Gloria added, "This must have been a historical moment. So..."

She inhaled and felt her face warm. "He's different from any man I've ever known, and it didn't seem the right thing to do." She sipped her coffee. "He's a maritime law attorney for a huge offshore company and shipyard. Their home office is in Cut Off. He says he's coming to visit me, but I won't hold my breath."

"Sounds like he might be quite taken with you."

"Chill, guys. You both know my secret, but I've never told y'all this. Since then, I've been unable to trust men. Screwing them makes me feel victorious and powerful. I make them moan and groan and come, but I only have an orgasm with my dildo. Am I sick, or what?"

"No," Gloria said drawing circles on the tabletop with her index finger. "You're not sick. What happened to you would cause traumatic stress in anyone. Counseling might help."

"No counseling now. Maybe later. I'll keep y'all informed."

She drummed her fingers on the table and turned her gaze on Gloria. "Did you enjoy New York?"

"Yes." Gloria told them all about seeing Jesse's double almost everywhere she went.

"Are you sure it wasn't him?"

"Positive." Then she showed them the lovely silk scarf sent to her anonymously.

"I know you don't agree, but Jesse should be told he's the father of that baby in your belly. It's only fair," Henrietta advised. "He could've sent that scarf."

"No way! And I don't want to hear another word about it."

Monique leaned her elbows on the tabletop and rested her face in her hands. "I'm sure Retta agrees that we don't want to lose you. So what would you do if you and Jesse did get together? Would you move to Thibodaux?"

Gloria responded, "I don't think so, but I'm not sure." Then she asked, "Are you okay, Mo? It looks like something is bothering you."

She nodded. "I'll be okay. Don't worry about me."

Henrietta gazed into her partner's eyes. "Gloria and I will worry, and you know it. We feel certain that you'll tell us about whatever ails you at a time that is right for you. We love you, Mo. And don't you ever forget that."

Monique nodded and said, "Thanks. Now, let's get down to business. Kathleen gave me a couple of messages from possible new clients. Whose turn is it?"

Gloria tittered. "I think it's yours, but I can take it if you're not up to it."

Monique cleared her throat before admonishing her, "Don't be ridiculous! I'll contact the possible clients. If we get two, you'll get the second one."

The ring of the telephone blared in the quiet office. Henrietta grabbed the phone after its fourth ring. *Where was Kathleen?*

"Babin, Blanchard, and Boudreaux. How may I direct your call?" Her eyes widened, and she gasped. "This is Henrietta," she said. Her eyes got even bigger, and her face warmed. "How are you, Bradley?" Her heart raced like it might fly out of her chest. *Oh, my God. What on earth is happening to me?*

Gloria and Monique eyed each other and left the conference room together. Monique waved her fingers at Henrietta and shot her a dazzling smile. Once in the hall, she whispered, "I think Retta's in love."

"Maybe so… I've never seen her behave this way. You might just be right."

Twenty minutes later, Henrietta found them in the break room.

"So when is he coming to visit?" Monique queried.

Henrietta's hands trembled as she sat and rested her elbows on the table. Her voice shook as she replied, "January 18th." She rose and began pacing the length of the conference table. "Oh, my God. He really is coming to Houston. What will I do?"

Gloria laughed out loud. "I'm sure you'll think of something."

"Yeah," Monique quickly added. "Will you pick him up at the airport?"

"No. He's renting a car and is staying at The Houstonian."

Monique pursed her lips and lifted her brows. "He'll be no more than about twenty minutes away from City Centre. Pretty convenient, I'd say."

Henrietta scowled at them both. "Don't be making more of this than what it is. A visit. That's all."

Monique stopped worrying her lower lip and added, "Hey, I'm not the one pacing. So will you screw him?"

Henrietta's cheeks burned as she stomped to the door, turned, and said, "Fuck you. I'm out of here."

Janet Foret Lococo

Chapter 20

Henrietta was still fuming when she reached her condo, stomped in and slammed the door shut behind her with a loud bang. Her heart pounded inside her chest, and her entire body burned. *What right had her partners to ask if she'd screw Bradley?* She paced to and fro in front of her sofa, her heels clacking on the hardwood floor and her lips tight across her teeth. She couldn't remember ever being so angry at her partners/friends. *Face it. You've asked personal questions of them that were none of your business. They didn't get pissed. And what about the way you brought up the possibility of abortion to Gloria when she first learned she was pregnant? Did she become indignant? No.*

Henrietta kicked off her Louboutin shoes, plopped down on the sofa, and cried. She would apologize as soon as she could stop crying. There was no excuse for her behavior.

When her doorbell rang a few minutes later, she checked the peephole and let Monique and Gloria inside. "We just had to come over and check on you, Retta. Don't be pissed."

"We shouldn't have asked you such a personal question,"

Gloria added. "We were wrong and we are here to apologize."

"Apologize? If any apologizing is to be done, I should be the one doing it. I had planned to go back to the office as soon as I got myself together to do just that." She blew her nose. "I was so stupid, and I'm so sorry for behaving like an ass."

Monique and Gloria hugged her and said as one, "You're forgiven. We love you, Retta, and will always be here for you."

"I love you guys, too. Why don't we stay here until lunch so we can talk about Bradley?"

They nodded and sat on the sofa.

Henrietta slowly paced in front of the sofa. "I think I got angry because y'all posed a question to which I have no answer. I don't even know if Bradley wants to get that close."

Monique cleared her throat. "We have never seen you in this light before, Retta. You've never had problems finding sexual partners."

"Right. And I never got any sexual satisfaction from any of them. I don't know why I feel so different about Bradley. His kisses are enough to drive me crazy. I've never been kissed like that before." She took another few steps before dropping down into her favorite chair. "Never ever."

"Perhaps you subconsciously hope that making love with Bradley is what you really want. Not just fucking," Gloria suggested.

"Maybe."

Monique rolled her bottom lip between her top and bottom teeth. "Perhaps you secretly want to experience your first non-dildo orgasm with him and fear you won't be able to do so."

"Maybe."

Gloria crossed one leg over the other and began to swing her foot. "I think you should stop worrying about what you will or won't do when Bradley arrives in Houston. Enjoy his visit, and if it happens, it happens. Play it by ear. Don't plan anything."

Henrietta blew out a breath. After several relaxing deep

breaths, she replied, "You're probably right. Now if we want to maintain the lifestyle to which we've become accustomed, we'd better get back to the office."

* * *

Bradley whistled through his teeth as he looked at the calendar on his desk. He planned to leave for Houston on January 18th and return on the 22nd. Tuesday through Sunday would be long enough for a first-time visit. His heartbeat picked up speed just thinking about seeing Henrietta again. She's a complicated woman. No doubt about it. And he wasn't sure he was up to putting up with complications. Nevertheless, he had to admit he was intrigued. He hoped they'd get along. He closed his eyes and pictured her beautiful blue gaze studying him. He couldn't help smiling. *Face it, Graham. You can't wait to slide your cock inside her and fuck her long and hard.* He rested his face in his hands and pursed his lips. There was little chance of that happening. The flaxen-haired vixen stirred his heart and his dick, and he would have to keep a tight rein on his desire.

Bradley poured himself two fingers of Jameson and sat at his computer to make flight and hotel reservations, along with car rental arrangements. He'd stay at The Houstonian. An online search for information regarding the hotel revealed that it opened in 1980 and became famous as the designated residence of George H.W. Bush in 1985. Someone had once written, "The Houstonian Hotel looks like something a big-spending Texas oil baron might have built in the old days."

He chuckled and sipped his whiskey thinking, "Texans and their stories." His thoughts soon turned to Henrietta. They'd had fun together in Grand Isle. He recalled their heated kisses. He'd shared his story about his ex-wife cheating with his best friend, but she had not revealed anything of importance about herself. Regardless, he was almost certain she hid a deep, dark secret. He hoped to find out before he completely lost his heart to her.

He rose, grabbed his glass, and paced to and fro in front of his desk. Henrietta was a strong woman. He recalled the way she'd swallowed her fear of motorcycles and climbed onto that seat behind him. He'd felt the tremors in her arms when she'd wrapped them around his waist for that very first ride.

Oh, yeah! Determined. Beautiful. Hardheaded. Long-legged beauty. A no-nonsense woman. Could he grab a handle on all that and survive? He shrugged his shoulders. He wasn't at all certain he could, but he thought he wanted to try.

He closed the cover of his laptop and downed the rest of his whiskey. He set the glass in the dishwasher and padded to his bedroom whispering, "I'm coming for you, Henrietta. Ready or not, here I come." He brushed his teeth before sliding between the sheets. He was asleep moments after his head hit the pillow.

They were in Grand Isle. He watched from his window as Henrietta danced in the sand. She was naked, and her slender body reminded him of a wood nymph right out of Greek mythology. Her long, pale yellow hair lifted in the sea breeze as she spun around in circles. Her graceful arms called him to join her. He slid out of his shorts and ran down the steps, right into her arms.

Together, they danced in circles while he hummed in her ear. Then, without knowing how it happened, he found himself lying on the sand, still warm from the day's sun. She danced around his hypersensitive body like a butterfly before straddling his thighs. He gasped in surprise. His cock was harder than bone. Harder than iron and pulsating with need for her.

She kissed him—a long, sensuous kiss. Her tongue tickled his as she explored his mouth and danced with his. He was losing his breath. Would he die? He didn't mind dying this way. She removed her tongue and sucked his nipples until they were hard as pebbles. God, she was doing everything right. Instantaneously, he found himself inside that hot, wet mouth.

She sucked the thick head of his cock like a heavy-duty vacuum before allowing her tongue to explore the slit and lick up the pre-cum. When she took him all into her mouth, he heard a guttural moan escape his throat. Their closeness felt as though her body had slid into his, and they had become one.

He was begging her to make him come. When she impaled herself onto his cock, he rolled her over to her back. Now he was on top. He slammed his dick over and over into her slick vagina. Their skin smacked each time he was balls-deep.

"Oh, Christ!" She moaned. "I'm so close."

"I know," he whispered. "Look at me. Keep your eyes opened. I want to see your climax in your eyes."

He slid his hand between them and pressed her clit. She shattered around him, her vaginal contractions sucking him dry, as she screamed his name.

His cock shooting semen in long streams into her core woke him up. Oh, God. It was just a dream. It had felt so right and so real. He looked down at the empty bed and the soiled sheets.

He pulled off the linens and put them to wash before stepping into the shower. *What the hell was going on? Wet dreams at his age? Un-fucking-believable.* The steaming hot water was just what he needed. His muscles relaxed, and he scrubbed his skin and his genitals. You have got to get control of yourself. *In fifteen days, you'll be in Houston, more than likely, hoping this dream becomes a reality. God, how I lust for this woman.*

He shoved her away from his mind. He had a lot to do before leaving.

Chapter 21

Henrietta sat at her desk thinking about Bradley. She recalled how Gloria had been surprised by the appearance of Jesse at her door on January 14th with a big diamond ring and a marriage proposal. She and Monique had witnessed their marriage in Las Vegas the next day.

After the ceremony, Gloria and Jesse had gone to Thibodaux, and Monique and Henrietta had returned to Houston. With their baby girl due in mid-March, Jesse and Gloria planned to spend the month of February on his yacht, *Dreamer*, where the child had been conceived. Regrettably, Gloria would not be in Houston when Bradley arrived.

* * *

When January 18th finally arrived, Bradley was so anxious he left his home at five o'clock in the morning for a noon flight. He'd decided he'd just as soon pace at the airport as at home.

Meeting with little traffic on the way to the airport, he parked his truck at Park-N-Fly. He had not even considered leaving his Porsche in the huge parking lot and running the possibility, though minute, of damage to the vehicle he so loved.

He peered at his watch. It was barely past six-thirty in the morning. When the shuttle picked him up at his truck, he marked the parking location on the back of the Park-N-Fly card before taking a seat. No one else was on the bus. He chatted with the driver until she dropped him off at the terminal.

He checked in, bought a newspaper, and headed for the VIP lounge where the hostess greeted him.

"My, Mr. Graham, you're very early today. What time is your flight?"

"Noon to Houston."

"You have a long wait. Coffee?"

He nodded, and a steaming cup of *café au lait* was soon placed on the table. Bradley loved the strong Louisiana coffee and chicory. It had been one of the things he'd had to develop a taste for once he began working *down the bayou,* as the Cajuns called the Larose-Grand Isle area along Bayou Lafourche. He'd learned to like it sweet, too.

Cajuns prepared food completely different from folks living along the East Coast. It was always well seasoned with the spices he'd learned to love. Recipes had been handed down over the years. Before coming to Cut Off, he'd thought–like everyone else–that adding a lot of pepper to food made it Cajun. He'd been dead wrong. The boiled crabs, shrimp, and crawfish were delicious, not at all bland. He smiled as he recalled wondering what gumbo was. Once he'd taken a taste, however, he had lapped it all up and asked for more.

After a satisfying breakfast of bacon, eggs, and grits, he worked the newspaper's crossword puzzle until he became drowsy. He realized he'd fallen asleep when the hostess tapped his shoulder.

"Time to board, Mr. Graham. Have a good trip," she added palming his generous tip. "Thank you."

Seated in first class, he opened his iPad to pick up reading where he'd left off in the latest James Patterson novel. He found it impossible to keep his mind on the murder mystery. However, his thoughts quickly moved to Henrietta.

She would meet him in the hotel lobby at seven o'clock. Again, he quickly glanced at his watch. She'd made dinner reservations at the Piatto Ristorante on West Alabama Street in the Galleria area. She'd said it was one of her favorite places to eat, and she wanted him to try it while he was in town. Of course, he'd agreed. She'd said the restaurant was ten to fifteen minutes from the hotel, depending on traffic.

Bradley had finally been able to concentrate on the murder mystery and was surprised when the captain announced they were making their final approach at Hobby Airport. He checked his watch. They were on time.

Although the distance from the airport to the hotel was slightly more than eighteen miles, it took him almost an hour to get to The Houstonian because of traffic. Thank goodness for the GPS-equipped vehicle.

The hotel website stated the "four diamond hotel was known for comfort, elegance, and exceptional service." Elegant it was, with its fireplaces, rich appointments, mahogany touches, and subdued lighting. His suite was fashionably done in red and gold.

* * *

Henrietta spent most of the morning impatiently checking her watch. Her insides trembled from nervous excitement.

"So, what time does he arrive?" Monique asked.

"His plane lands at one fifteen. He's renting a car at the airport and driving to The Houstonian Hotel. With the heavy traffic, it'll probably take an hour from the airport. I'm meeting him in the lobby at seven and taking him to Piatto. After that, who knows?

Monique chimed in, "I know it's a cliché, but you're as nervous as a fox at a hound convention. You have got to try to chill, Retta. There is no use in working yourself into a dither. It'll go well. You'll see."

Henrietta frowned. "And you have a crystal ball that keeps you informed of what will happen to everyone?"

"Don't be bitchy. You know what I mean. Why don't you go home and pace the floors of your condo? You know you won't get a thing done here."

"You're probably right. Since I won't see you until the 24th, why don't we have a light lunch at Yardhouse?"

Monique agreed, and Henrietta called it a day after lunch. Finally, she headed to her condo with her stomach quivering and her fingers and toes tingling. For the life of her, she could not explain her feelings or her behavior. Could one man possibly rock her world into a full-blown frenzy? It surely appeared so.

She paced the floors of her apartment until she decided to take a walk on the treadmill in the fitness room of their building. She had to stop herself after walking for an hour. She surely didn't want to be worn out for tonight. Her chuckle tickled her throat. She hummed *Tonight's the Night* and wondered if it would be.

She purposely forced her brain to concentrate on lesser issues. What dress would she wear tonight? After mentally reviewing the contents of her closet, she thought about wearing her red dress. She loved it, and the red, black, and white Louboutin five-inch heels seemed to be made to match the dress. But Piatto Ristorante was dressy casual. The red dress would be too much.

She chuckled at what the folks in Cut Off would think of her paying nine hundred dollars for a pair of shoes. Of course, they would find it a perfectly ridiculous waste of money. She lifted her nose in the air. *Well, I love them, and that's all that matters.*

On the way home, she stopped at a liquor store and purchased a bottle of Jameson 18 Irish whiskey. She thought that if she could afford Louboutin shoes, she should be able to pay for the one hundred and thirty dollar bottle for a very special person.

As soon as she entered her condo, she checked to make sure everything was neat and clean in case he decided to come over. After a bath and long soak, she slipped into comfortable sweats and headed to the spa in her building for a massage, manicure, and pedicure.

Now, all she had to do was wait.

Chapter 22

Henrietta ran her fingers through her hair as she paced in front of her sofa. Her stomach fluttered as though it were filled with butterflies batting their wings like crazy to get out. She poured a glass of Chardonnay to relax. She would sip it as she dressed.

First, she pulled up the sexy stockings of sheer black nylon with at least six inches of stay-in-place elastic lace. She managed to get them on without ripping them. She dug into her dresser drawer, grabbed the passion-red lace thong, and pulled it up before getting into the front-closure matching bra. She stepped in front of the full-size mirror to assess her look in the new underwear. If he got to see it, Henrietta knew he'd be pleased with the look. That was a big IF, however. *How can I want something so badly and at the same time fear getting it. He might be just another orgasmless fuck like every other man I've screwed.*

She pushed her thoughts aside and carefully applied her makeup so that it looked light and natural. After parting her hair slightly off center, she let it hang down her back in a pale curtain. Her lipstick would go on last. Her phone rang, and she saw that Bradley was calling.

"Hello, Bradley," she said. "You've changed your mind about tonight?"

"Not a chance. Why don't I pick you up at your place instead of you coming to my hotel to pick me up? Her heartbeat quickened. *That means he'll bring me home, too, and might want to come up.*

"Okay. We're going to Piatto Ristorante in the Galleria area. The dress code is dressy casual. No jacket required."

When she started to give him directions to her condo, he said, "My rental has a GPS so it shouldn't be too difficult."

"Fine. If you get lost, call me. My address is 811 Town and Country Boulevard, #502 on the fifth floor of building #1. Turn right when you exit the elevator."

"I would never admit to getting lost. I'll be there at seven. Will you be ready?"

"I'm never late, Bradley. I abhor lateness."

"In that case, I may be a little early."

She heard his chuckle and couldn't help smiling. "I'll be ready!"

Henrietta slipped into her black Ann Taylor skirt. She topped it with a red, snug-fitting long-sleeved top and sprayed her favorite scent to the sides of her neck. Although she usually wore her pearls, a string of faceted inky black beads made a real fashion statement on her red top.

The last thing she did was to apply matching Taylor Swift red lipstick. She looked into the mirror and smiled.

* * *

Bradley was still smiling when he'd hung up the phone. "Yes!" He hoped Henrietta would invite him in when he brought her home. It was not out of the realm of possibility that he might *get lucky* tonight. He hardened just thinking of it. *Come on, man. Settle down and get dressed. She said she abhors lateness, and you don't want to be abhorred.*

122

He wondered if she'd wear that gorgeous red dress she looked delectable in. He wanted to make love to her tonight, but he was almost certain she'd try to keep him at arm's length like she had in Grand Isle. She'd wanted him. Of that he was certain, and couldn't help wondering what made her push him away. He wondered what her problem was, but wondering about it wouldn't get him any answers.

He showered and shaved before splashing on a little *Acqua di Giò*. She liked his fragrance. She'd said so. It was not overpowering, and he never splashed on enough for people to smell him before they saw him. One of the guys he worked with could almost knock you out with the aroma of his strong cologne before he ever got to your area.

He put on his snug-fitting red stretch silk underwear before putting on his socks and shoes. He slid his arms into his black crewneck cable sweater and pushed his head through the opening. He hoped she'd appreciate the softness of the cashmere. He stuck his feet into the legs of his black trousers and pulled them up before standing in front of the full-length mirror on the bathroom door to check himself out. He nodded. He liked that look and hoped she wouldn't think he appeared to be in mourning. He draped the white and red scarf across the back of his neck and let the ends drop down his chest.

Bradley programmed Henrietta's address into his rental's GPS. He left early to allow for traffic. Following the voice commands, he arrived at her condo fifteen minutes early. His stomach fluttered. *Why does she make me so nervous? I'm a successful man, but she makes me feel like an unsure boy eager to win, but fearful of screwing up.*

He parked under the portico of Building 1 and sat inside the car for five minutes. When he got out, he locked the car, and slowly entered the building. To avoid appearing too eager, he looked around the huge room to kill a little time. Classy. He pulled in a huge breath and slowly let it out as he ambled to the bank of elevators. *Chill, man.* He stepped into the open car and inhaled deeply again before pressing button five. The elevator moved smoothly and silently to the fifth floor. He stepped out, wondering what awaited him as he turned right, stood in front of #502, and rang the bell.

The door opened and there she stood, smiling and so beautiful she took his breath away. Her black skirt hugged her curves and her snug red top accentuated her tits. He stood in her doorway and allowed his gaze to slide from the top of her head to her toes. *Wow.*

Unsure of how to greet her, he stuck out his hand. She took it and pulled him in for a hug.

He smiled, squeezed her close to his body, and planted a gentle kiss on her cheek.

"Ooh," she breathed into his ear. "You're wearing that wonderful cologne. Come on in." She led him to the sofa.

"I'm so glad you came to Houston," she cooed. Her broad smile and twinkling eyes told him she was being honest. She looked so hot he wanted to take her into his arms and kiss her the way he'd done in Grand Isle. "How's your hotel room?"

"Great. I'm in Suite 418."

"Our reservations are for seven-thirty, so we don't have time for a drink here," she said. "I should have told you to get here earlier." She glanced at her watch. "We need to leave now. Although weekday nights are not as bad as weekends, you can never tell about Houston traffic. I'll give you a tour of my condo after dinner."

He nodded his approval. Her remark meant she'd be inviting him in after dinner. He hoped the condo was not all he'd get to see. *Jesus, get a grip.*

When she leaned over the sofa back to grab a shiny black beaded bag from the seat, her ass looked so inviting he wanted to pat it. She slung the strap over her left shoulder. "Let's go," she said and stepped into the corridor first. He followed after pulling the door closed and checking the knob to make sure it was locked.

He helped her into the car and walked around the front to the driver's side. After buckling his seatbelt, he leaned forward to program the GPS.

"No need for that. I'll tell you exactly how to get there. Piatto Ristorante is one of my favorite places. I've gotten to know the owner and his family very well. I think you'll like them." She patted his shoulder. "Turn left at the next street."

Janet Foret Lococo

Chapter 23

A waiter greeted them as soon as they walked into the door. The bright yellow walls and the decorative tiles in the bar area reminded him of Wolfgang Puk's in O'Hare Airport. Large photographs in elegant frames graced the walls.

"Hi, Tony," she said to the waiter that greeted them. "This is my friend from down home, Bradley Graham. It's his first time here."

He shook hands with Bradley before turning to her and said, "You know I'll take good care of him." He chuckled as he led them to their table.

He handed them the menus and asked, "Drinks before dinner?"

"I'll have one of your lemon drop martinis." She turned to Bradley. "Chevas and water?"

Bradley nodded. "Do you have the old stuff?"

The waiter replied, "Yes, sir. We do."

"That'll be fine."

"We'll share one fried asparagus appetizer," she said

before turning to Bradley. "The lightly breaded asparagus with lemon butter sauce and lump crabmeat is to die for. You'll see. It's their signature dish."

The waiter returned with their drinks. "Ready to order?"

"I'll have the spaghetti with one meatball and one Italian sausage, Tony." She turned to Bradley. "Have you decided yet?"

"No, but since you know what you like here, why don't you order for me?"

"Okay. Do you like lasagna?"

"Is the Pope Catholic?"

Henrietta smiled at the waiter. "Bring him the lasagna and a bottle of Tommasi Raphael."

When the waiter returned with the appetizer and the bottle of wine, she slid two of the six asparagus onto her plate with a little sauce and crab meat. "Have a go at this," she said as she slid the plate in front of him.

"Oh, my God," he said after his first bite. "I've never tasted anything like this before. Yummy. You've made a believer out of me already."

He tasted her spaghetti with a bite of the sausage and meatball and practically inhaled his lasagna. "It wouldn't do for me to eat here too often," he said rubbing his belly. "I'd soon outgrow my pants."

The owner approached their table once they'd finished their meal. Henrietta introduced him, and he sat with them while they finished the bottle of wine. Johnny turned to Bradley. "I hope you enjoyed your first meal with us. Henrietta's one of our best customers."

Bradley lifted his brows. "This is no B.S. I've traveled a lot, nationally and abroad, in my work. I've never had better lasagna anywhere. And the asparagus is incredible. Henrietta said it was 'to die for,' and she was right. Looks like I'll have to get down here more often."

"We'd like that," Johnny said. He picked up the empty

wine bottle and pointed to the label. "We've been fans of this winery ever since my family and I went to Italy and visited the Tommasi Estates. It was a most enjoyable trip, and we got to know the winemaker. Learning about the intricacies of wine-making from him was a real treat." He rose and extended his hand to Bradley. "I've got to get back to work. I hope you'll come back to Houston and that you'll return for a meal here when you do. *Arrivederci.*"

Bradley and Henrietta left soon afterward. On their way to valet parking Bradley took her hand in his and said, "Thanks for bringing me here. I loved both the food and the wine. And Johnny seems to be a nice guy."

"I met him when, on a whim, I chose this restaurant after first moving to Houston. He's become a dear friend. His parents, wife, and daughter have all became my friends as well."

Bradley tipped the valet attendant who helped Henrietta to her seat and shut the door while he walked around the back. After locking his seatbelt, he turned to Henrietta and said, "Where to?"

"Home. Do you remember the way?"

"I might." He shot her a seductive smile that caused her belly to knot. "But then again, I might not. So pay attention just in case I miss a turn."

He easily found his way back to her condo and parked in visitor parking. He helped her out of the car, locked it, and led her to the entrance. Hand in hand they ambled toward the elevators. She entered the car first, and he followed. She pressed the #5 button and up they went.

At her door, she handed him the key to unlock it, and they stepped into her open living space. He moved around the large open area, looking at everything.

"This is a great pad, Henrietta. Did you decorate it yourself?"

"Heavens no. I hired an interior decorator. I could never do this." She swept her arm to include everything. She led him to her bedroom. "This is where I sleep," she said. *Your bedroom first? There is no help for you.*

After an awkward silence, he stepped into the bathroom and gave it a once over before turning his burning gaze to hers. "That shower is big enough for two."

He noted the warm blush that crept from her neck to her forehead and wondered if she envisioned them naked in it.

"No comment," she offered.

Bradley was unable to believe she was embarrassed or that he had the nerve to smirk. She quickly moved toward the extra bedroom and bath.

"How about a drink?" she questioned as they returned to the living room.

"Thought you'd never ask," he answered making himself comfortable on her sofa.

"Is it too early for Jameson?"

"Well, damn if I'm not impressed!" He rested his right foot on his left knee and drummed his fingers on his knee. "You bought Jameson for me?"

"Yes, I did." Again, her face warmed in what he assumed was an embarrassed flush. "Don't make a big deal out of it." She brought him the bottle and a Waterford whiskey glass. Then she poured a glass of Chardonnay for herself.

He glanced quickly at the label. "Eighteen-year-old, too. I'm truly flattered." He patted the sofa seat. "Join me."

When she turned on her iPod, Alan Jackson's voice softly singing *A Woman's Love* filled the condo. She slipped out of her heels and sat next to him pulling her legs up beneath her butt. "Now, tell me what you've been up to."

Chapter 24

Warmth radiating from Bradley's thigh onto Henrietta's knee brought on a full body flush and acceleration of her heartbeat as he spoke about his latest project. She couldn't have cared less about his latest undertaking. She wanted him to take her into his arms and kiss her like he'd done in Grand Isle, but he didn't. Instead, he sipped his Jameson and continued talking while he set his glass on the coffee table. She sipped her Chardonnay and put her glass down, too. She quickly decided to grab what she wanted. "Kiss me, Bradley," she whispered. "I want to feel your lips on mine.

His eyes widened in a look of surprise. Henrietta thought it took forever for him to digest her request. She uncoiled her long legs, sat on his lap, put her arms around his neck, and said, "Well?"

Bradley covered her mouth with his and moaned. "Oh, God, Henrietta. I wanted to do this the minute I walked in," he murmured against her lips before taking complete possession of her mouth. He sucked her lower lip before thrusting his tongue inside.

She pulled her mouth from his and asked, "So why didn't you?"

"I feared you would push me away and I just couldn't bear that." He kissed her eyelids and slid his lips down her cheek to her ear and down the side of her neck. Her heart pounded within her chest. His hot breath made the hairs at her nape stand on end. She ached for him as their tongues mated in a sensuous dance. He tasted of Irish whiskey and smelled delicious. She couldn't remember ever wanting a man the way she wanted this one, but she feared disappointment again. *What if she had to resort to her dildo after he left? Better not to risk it.*

Slowly, she slipped off his lap, picked up her glass, and sipped her Chardonnay.

Bradley's gaze burned into hers, and he blew out a breath. "Did I do something wrong?"

"No. It's me."

"Want to tell me about it?"

"No. Not now, at least."

Bradley shook his head from side-to-side before resting it in his left hand. His grey eyes were darkened. "I don't know why you do this to me all the time. You answer my kisses and get me hot and hard for you only to stop any further activity from occurring. Why, Henrietta? I want to know why."

"Not now. Not now, at least." Her hands fisted at her sides. Bradley stood and walked to the door. "I refuse to play stupid games, Henrietta. We're both too old for them. I enjoyed dinner. Thank you and goodnight."

When he opened the door, walked out, and pulled the door closed behind him, all Henrietta could do was gape in wonder.

What is wrong with you? You wanted him. He wanted you. But you pushed him away. You should have told him why you behaved the way you did.

She didn't try to stop the tears. She let them flow until there were no more. Then she brushed her teeth, washed her face, and went to bed. When sleep didn't come, she called Monique and asked her to come over.

Monique arrived in her pajamas and robe no more than ten minutes later. She took one look at her partner and said, "Oh, my God. Bradley's gone. What happened?"

Henrietta began to cry again. "He left, and it's my fault. Shit. Shit. Shit."

Monique got two wine glasses from the breakfront and poured them each a glass. "Come on, Retta. Sit on the sofa. You'll talk, and I'll listen."

Through her tears, Henrietta told Monique about her earlier date with Bradley. "Everything went well. Dinner was great, and we came up here afterward. I fixed him a drink and myself a glass of wine and asked what he'd been up to." She twisted her hands together. "Then I told him to kiss me." She closed her eyes. "His kisses are breathtaking. Shit. Shit. Shit. God, I wanted him. He wanted me. Then I stopped it all."

She grabbed a lock of her hair and began twirling it between her thumb and index finger. "He told me we were both too old to be playing games, thanked me for dinner, and turned around and fucking left. He didn't even slam the door on his way out."

"So why didn't you fuck him, Retta?"

Henrietta wailed, "Because I didn't want just to screw. For the first time ever, I wanted to make love. I wanted to climax with him inside me."

"So, call him right now. Invite him to dinner here at your condo tomorrow night."

"Mo, you know I'm a terrible cook. Why would I do that?"

"To get him here, Dumbo. And if you don't screw him, I will!"

"That sounds so pathetic." She rolled the stem of her glass between her fingers. "I'm tempted to go to his hotel right now and fuck his brains out."

Monique fisted her hands at her waist and snarled, "You haven't got the balls to do that, Retta." In a softer voice, she continued, "Work on preparing yourself for tomorrow night. If you'll be okay, I'll go back home." She looked sheepish when she added, "I left someone waiting for me in my bed."

"Go on. You should've said something. I'm so sorry to have disturbed you. Thanks. Now go."

After Monique had left, Henrietta thought more and more about going to Bradley's hotel. Did she have the balls to do it? She wasn't sure. She wanted to.

After a surge of courage, she decided. "Dammit, I will."

She grabbed her London Fog coat, slipped it on, and fastened the belt closed. She didn't bother with makeup before sliding her feet into her Louboutin heels and heading out the door with her heart knocking hard and fast inside her chest.

Her hands shook on the wheel as she drove to The Houstonian. He'd said he was in Suite 418, so getting up there would be easy. It was only eleven o'clock. What would she do when she got up there? She'd play it by ear.

After valet parking her car, she walked into the hotel and headed for the elevator and pressed number four. Smoothly and silently, the car moved up. Creepy crawlies danced under her skin and her heart beat in a wild tattoo. *It's now or never.*

She found his suite and knocked on the door. She swallowed the lump of fear and nerves in her throat.

The knob turned, and he opened the door a crack. "Who is it?" his voice asked through the opening.

"Room service," she answered in a deepened voice.

"Do you know what time it is? I didn't order anything!" The door opened. Bradley stood in his robe, barefoot. "This is a mistake."

"Perhaps it is," she answered in her own voice.

He looked up. His eyes widened, and he asked, "What are you doing here?"

"If you'll let me in, I'll tell you."

He stepped aside to allow her entry.

Chapter 25

Bradley picked up the phone and dialed. "Room service. Please send up a bottle of your best chilled Chardonnay."

Her turned to Henrietta. "Want to take off your coat and stay a while?"

"I'm not sure."

He wagged his head and held out his hands in a pleading gesture. "And why am I not surprised?"

"It's not at all what you think, Bradley. I left in a hurry before I'd have time to change my mind. I'm in my sleep shirt."

He unfastened her belt and unbuttoned her coat. "You'd look good in anything. You're gorgeous, even without makeup." He helped her off with her coat, and she slipped out of her shoes. He led her to the small table at the window. "Sit," he ordered. "Relax. I won't do anything you don't want me to do. You're safe with me, Henrietta."

A knock sounded on the door. Bradley smiled at Henrietta. "That's really room service," he said and opened the door. The attendant set the wine and the glasses on the table.

"It should be icy cold, sir."

"Thanks," said Bradley and palmed the tip in the attendant's hand. Then he poured them each a glass and sat across from Henrietta.

She took a sip. "It's good." She took in a deep breath and blew it out. "The first thing I want to do is to apologize for my behavior earlier. I shouldn't have led you on and then turned you off." He started to say something, but she stopped him. "Don't stop me as I might lose my nerve and clam up. Do you want to hear a long, sad story?"

"I want to hear whatever you wish to tell me for however long it takes."

"I'll probably cry while telling you, but just ignore my tears. I want to tell you things that only my partners know. My mother knows the first part, but not the rest. Just bear with me."

Tears flowed down her cheeks, and her voice cracked when she told him about her uncle raping her when she was only seven years old. Bradley's eyes filled with tears. "I want to hold you while you tell me. Dear God in heaven. Please let me hold you."

She rose and straddled his hips. "I want to be able to see you while I tell you about it. I don't want to repeat my earlier action. Is it okay with you if I sit this way?"

He nodded and kissed her cheek.

"My mother was forced to give up teaching after my father died because he'd not had enough life insurance to provide for his family. Her new position at a large, local offshore and shipbuilding company kept her working until five o'clock, so she usually arrived home around five-thirty. Although Grammy always stayed with me after school, Mom asked her brother to babysit me that day because Grammy had a doctor's appointment.

"Uncle Carl was glued to the television while I read my book, *Thomas The Tank Engine*. He called me saying, "Come see something, Henny Penny."

"When I went to him, he pointed to his swollen penis that was sticking up out of his unzipped pants. I recall making a face and telling him it was ugly and that showing his *pee-pee* to people was nasty. His face got so red that I was afraid. That's when the bastard picked me up and impaled me on it. My screams must have scared him because he pulled me off of him and quickly shoved me into the closet. After jerking off on my dress, I thought he'd peed on me, he locked the door and left me crying in the dark closet.

"I remember the pain to this day and being taken to the emergency room. Can you imagine being seven years old and having to show everyone your *pee-pee* and having to answer the same thousand questions over and over again to different people?"

"No, I can't." He handed her the glass of wine. "Take a sip, Babe. You don't have to say any more. Recalling this is too painful." He hugged her to his solid chest. She could hear his heart beating beneath her ear. "I could kill the son-of-a-bitch."

"He's already dead. He died in prison right before he completed his fifteen-year sentence. God is indeed just. I barely remember the trial–again more questions. Grammy disowned him and donated his body to science. She didn't want him buried in the family tomb. Is it sick to think it would have been nice if he could have felt the fire turning his body into ash?"

"No, it's not." He hugged her close. "Nobody deserves that, and least of all, a seven-year-old little girl."

She framed her face with her hands and rolled her gaze toward the ceiling, as though she'd find her answer there.

"I hope he's burning in hell for what he did. I wish I could make all of this go away for you."

"Enough about that sad time in my life. I've not been an angel, Bradley. I lost my virginity for the second time when I was in the tenth grade, and it was my idea. I figured I'd been ruined anyway, so I might as well try it. My girlfriends all said how wonderful having sex was, and I was curious to know what it was like. Making that boy come and hearing his moans and groans made me feel strong and powerful, but nothing else. I've never trusted any man since I was seven years old. Whenever I've had sex since then, I've had that same feeling of power over a man."

Bradley brought her glass to her lips, and she sipped a big swallow. "Are you saying that you've never had an orgasm?"

She laughed at the look on his face. "Oh, I've had orgasms. But they've all been self-induced at home."

"So why did you turn me off tonight? Didn't you want me? Or was it lack of trust? I want to know."

"I was afraid of being disappointed again. I wanted you, Bradley. I wanted you in Grand Isle. But it's never been good for me."

"So you've been in search of the little death or *la petite mort* that is not self-induced."

"Yes, I think so."

He took her face in his hands and pinned his gaze to hers. "You are worthwhile, Henrietta. You have so much to offer a man, but you see yourself as damaged goods. I want to make love to you, Henrietta. I want to make you climax while I'm *balls deep* inside you. But not before you're ready to do more than fuck and run home to your dildo or your fingers."

She threw her arms around his neck and kissed his cheek. "Oh, Bradley. You are wonderful. I do want to try making love to you. Why don't we plan to do that tomorrow night? We could fix dinner at my place. We'd have to go to Central Market to get whatever we want to cook." She frowned. "I wish I were a good cook just for you."

"We'll do it together. What would you like us to eat?"

"Since we have reservations on Friday night at Pappas Brothers Steakhouse, we might want to do seafood. What do you think?"

"Yeah. We could do that. Why don't you spend the night here? I'll sleep on the sofa. I don't like to think of you driving home this late after pouring your heart out."

"Don't be ridiculous. You're too tall for the sofa. You take the bed."

"You will not sleep on the sofa. You'll share the bed with me. I promise to be on my best behavior. You can trust me, Henrietta."

She sighed. "Trust has to begin somewhere, doesn't it?"

He nodded. "And this would be a good time to begin."

Her gaze found his and held it. Moments ticked by. Finally, she said, "Okay. I'll share your bed and trust you to keep your word. Since I'm not driving, why don't we finish the wine?"

They watched a funny movie and went to bed around one in the morning. When they woke up the following morning, they were spooned together, and Henrietta could feel his erection against her thighs. *Big... Hard... Tempting...*

He whispered into her ear. "I know you feel it. I didn't plan it. Have no fear. I always keep my word."

She turned to face him. "I do trust you, Bradley. I slept like a baby. What time is it?"

He slid one arm under her waist and the other on top. He pulled her close and kissed her cheek. "Eight o'clock. Can you tolerate a morning breath kiss on the lips?"

"If you can, so can I. If I'd known I'd spend the night, I would have brought a toothbrush."

They kissed. It was a soft and sweet kiss this time. "You can use mine," he said.

"You'd share your toothbrush with me?"

"Yes, I would. You can even use it first."

"You're saying all the right things. I'm thoroughly impressed with Bradley Graham."

"Good. Brush your teeth while I order up breakfast. What would you like?"

"Surprise me."

Forty-five minutes later, the breakfast arrived. Pancakes, bacon and sausages, along with a pot of coffee."

"Yummy," she said. "I do so love pancakes."

"I remembered." He shot her a sexy smile. "And I had them boil the milk so you could have your *café au lait*."

"You are truly wonderful. I can't believe you're not taken."

I was taken–in more ways than one. I've been waiting for you all my life, he thought. But he kept those thoughts to himself. *Don't go falling in love with her or you'll be terribly disappointed. Remember Saundra.*

Chapter 26

After breakfast, Henrietta put on her coat and shoes and left the hotel. All eyes in the hotel lobby seemed aimed in her direction. *What else did you expect? You're leaving a hotel in your sleep shirt and London Fog coat. Perhaps your discomfort is imagined, the result of embarrassment at being caught in what you see as a compromising position.* She hummed the theme from *The Pink Panther* to herself. She told herself she didn't care what folks thought.

Bradley would shower and shave and head for her place. On her way home, she called Monique to tell her she was okay and had somehow found the balls to go to Bradley's hotel room. "I don't have time to tell you about it. I'm on my way home now to shower and dress. We'll be together all day, and we'll fix dinner at home."

"You're cooking? I'm not sure what's come over you, Retta. First church, now cooking." She laughed out loud and added, "Do you even know how to cook other than making chicken soup?"

"Okay, wiseass. I do know how to cook a few dishes. I

must admit that I do have a tendency to overcook some foods."

"Overcook! You mean burn don't you?"

"Come on, Mo. I don't have to cook because Bradley is a wonderful cook."

"Okay. Okay. Just ribbing you. Y'all have fun. Be sure to consider doing the nasty."

"Jesus, Mary, and Joseph. Cut it out. I called to thank you for coming to my rescue. And no, we did not have sex."

"You'd do the same for me. I'm glad you called because I was worried about you."

Henrietta showered and dressed in a pair of her well-worn jeans. She topped it with a big melon-colored sweater before pulling on her black Lucchese python-skin western boots. The only makeup she wore was lip-gloss–the same color as her sweater.

Fifteen minutes later, Bradley arrived. *He looked so hot and sexy in his jeans, dark Hunter-green sweater, black leather jacket, and black alligator cowboy boots.* When he put his arms around her and kissed her lips, his cologne teased her nose and made her heart ram against her chest.

After kissing her and holding her close, he pushed her backward and eyed her from the top of her head to her fancy, expensive boots. "Wow! You look awesome, Henrietta." He kissed her again before asking, "So what's first on our agenda?"

"I thought I'd take you for a ride to Kemah. It's about an hour away. It's something I wish they'd do with Grand Isle. We can have a light lunch there if you'd like. What do you think?"

"Sounds like a good plan to me. When we get back, we can shop for whatever we decide to do about dinner. What's interesting about Kemah?"

"Well," she fondled her pearls, "it was originally a small fishing town that has become a tourist destination for the area's restaurants and attractions. There's a boardwalk leading to hotels, rides for adults and children, shopping, and restaurants.

It's pretty neat."

"Picturesque," he said when they arrived and found a parking place close to the boardwalk. "This would be a neat idea for Grand Isle, but I doubt that'll ever happen. People in Grand Isle do not like change." Hand in hand, they strolled the length of the boardwalk and decided to grab a bite at The Flying Dutchman Restaurant. Bradley's hand was big and warm, and she thought of how those hands would feel on her naked skin. A thrill shot up her spine making her shudder.

"Are you cold?"

"No." She wasn't about to tell him her thoughts.

"Thinking about tonight?"

Henrietta was not about to admit that. Blood rushed to her face, and she figured it was beet-red. "Are you always this swell-headed?"

"Never. I just call things the way I see them. What else would make you blush?"

"Never mind." She pursed her lips for a moment. She ordered a cup of clam chowder and a salad, and Bradley ordered a cup of alligator bisque and a salad.

After lunch, they explored the shops along the boardwalk as they headed back toward the car. When they got there, he took her face in his hands and planted a sexy kiss on her lips that she answered willingly.

"I had fun," he said and winked.

She didn't approve of public displays of affection but kept that information to herself. They stopped at Central Market for fish and side dishes for their dinner. "Have you got a grill?" Bradley asked.

"Yes, a small one on my balcony."

"Then I suggest grilled salmon filets. I'll do the grilling." He laughed. "Do you have charcoal and a lighter?"

"Yes, smart ass," she whispered in his ear so no one would hear. "An un-opened bag of MatchLight."

"I'll bet you don't have a maple or cedar plank."

Her brows furrowed. "For what?"

"Well, you soak the planks for at least an hour, but two to four hours is even better. When the coals are hot, you place the planks on the grill and heat them till they begin to smoke. Then you put on the seasoned salmon filet, cover and cook for about eighteen minutes."

"Sounds good. How about sautéed spinach in garlic and olive oil? I can do that, salad, and garlic bread."

Bradley insisted on paying for everything. At three o'clock, on their way to the car, he asked, "Have you ever used your grill?"

"Yes." She stumbled when she turned her gaze to his for a sassy remark. "I've managed to burn a couple of things on it." She pinched his arm. "Satisfied?"

"No, but I'm hoping to change that later."

Her face burned. Tonight would be here before she knew it. *And what's with the blushing? It's not like you're a virgin!*

He toted the bags in and set them on the table. He put the planks to soak before putting the cold stuff in the refrigerator.

"I'll take off my boots and I'll be right back."

* * *

He pulled off his boots, and silently padded to her bedroom door. She was seated on her bed, trying to remove the first boot. She looked so good on that bed that he hardened. "I'll help you," he said, as he stepped in front of her.

Her hands flew up, and she dropped back onto her bed. "You startled me. I didn't hear you come in."

He made short work of removing her boots and massaged her feet. Judging by the dreamy look on her face, the work of his strong hands was appreciated. Afterward, he took both her hands in his and pulled her into his body. He slid his hands down her back and her buttocks. Dear God, how he ached for this woman. It was obvious she wanted him just as much when she ground her hips against his throbbing erection. His heart fluttered. *I want to make love to her, but I don't want to lose my heart. I couldn't possibly deal with another broken one.*

When Bradley sank his tongue into her hot mouth, Henrietta sucked it hard–like she wanted to swallow him whole. In and out–they thrust into each other's mouth. He heard her whisper, "I want you, Bradley. Now. Please make love to me."

"Are you sure?"

"Yes."

They sank onto her bed.

Chapter 27

Bradley slipped his fingers along the edge of Henrietta's sweater and let his hands slowly creep up her torso from her waist to right below her breasts. His heart rammed his chest wall so hard and fast that he thought it might fly out. The pads of his fingertips felt the goose bumps rise on her satiny skin. Her cologne was a delight for his nose.

"You smell so good," he whispered before covering her lips again with his. He moved his hand up the side of her neck to her nape and teased her lips open before sliding his tongue inside her burning mouth. Her body was pliant against his, her willingness for more unmistakable. So hot... so everything he'd ever wanted in a woman. His dick thrummed with desire for her. And she wanted him.

"I want you to touch me all over," she moaned before grabbing the bottom of her sweater and pulling it off, over her head.

Enraptured, he couldn't tear his gaze away from her breasts in her lacy bra. "There is nothing I want more than to have your naked body pressed against mine, Henrietta. I want to feel the heat of your skin, the warmth of your embrace, and the desire radiating through your body that words can't possibly explain."

He reached for the front closure of her sexy black lace bra, quickly undid the clasp, and allowed her beautiful breasts to fill his hands. She whimpered when he kissed her nipples and sucked first one, then the other, into his mouth. They rose like small mountains beneath his lips. Her whole body shuddered.

He dragged his index finger down the center of her torso and reached for the closure of her jeans. Soon she lay before him, gloriously naked. His eyes feasted on her beauty. He touched the clipped thatch of blonde hair at the juncture of her thighs. She moaned. He leaned down and kissed her there, inhaling her feminine scent. *Control yourself. Go slow. Make sure she reaches a climax.*

He dragged his fingertips up her inner thighs–from her knees to the juncture–slid himself off the bed onto his knees on the floor and spread her legs. Her genitals glistened with moisture. When he slid his tongue between her nether lips, she trembled and moaned.

When he sucked on her clit, she whispered, "Oh, God. Oh, God. Oh, God. Oh, Bradley."

He peeled off his clothes in record time, reached for a condom from his wallet, rolled it onto his turgid shaft, and slid himself deep inside her. The hot walls of her vagina felt like a heating pad at its highest setting wrapped around his dick.

"Oh, my God," she whimpered as he relentlessly thrust into her. He reminded himself to hold back. *Make sure she comes first.* She met each of his plunges. "Oooooh, Bradley. I can't believe this. It feels so wonderful. I think I'm going to climax if you don't slow down."

"Is that what you want? For me to slow down?" He whispered against her lips swollen from his kisses.

"No. Oh, my God. Don't stop, Bradley. Oh, sweet Jesus. I'm coming," she screamed.

Her convulsive tremors and the sucking motion of her vagina quickly brought on his orgasm. He thought he'd never stop coming as she milked him dry, and he could have sworn he saw stars.

Concern over the tears flowing down her cheeks robbed him of his breath. Was she sorry she'd given in to him? "Why the tears?" he asked catching his breath. "Did I hurt you?"

"No. These are happy tears. Oh, Bradley." She patted his chest. "I'm sorry I caused you to worry. It's just that right now, I feel like a virgin. I didn't know sex could be this good. It's impossible to explain with words. We just shared something very special. When you entered my body, it was as though a wave of emotion crashed over me, and our souls connected."

"That's because we made love, Henrietta. We didn't just fuck."

After they'd cuddled for a few minutes, he heard her stomach growl. "Are you hungry?" He asked.

"I'm famished, but I'd like to shower."

"Me, too. Mind if I join you?"

"Not at all." Her lips turned up in a mischievous smile. "I was hoping you would. Perhaps we could bathe each other."

He rolled his eyes at her. "I'd like that, and I'd make sure you'd like it, too."

"Enough said," she replied. "Follow me and bring a condom."

His brows rose. "You're ready for another round already?"

"We'll see. Now that I got the hang of it, I think I love screwing."

"Lovemaking," he corrected. "Not screwing."

They stepped into the shower, and she turned on the hot water. He placed the foil packet on the soap holder. She shampooed his hair first. Her fingertips massaging his scalp were delightful. After lathering up her hands with a clean smelling body shampoo, Henrietta rubbed it into his chest. She spent an inordinate amount of time rubbing the soap on his nipples and his shaft hardened.

"Ooh, lookie! Clarence is ready to play again."

"Clarence?" He frowned. "That's a terrible name for a penis."

"So, do you have any suggestions?" She asked as her soapy hands moved to wash his privates.

"How about Woody?" He gasped when she rinsed off the soap and massaged his balls. "Jesus, Henrietta. You'll make me come if you keep that up."

"That's what I want, Bradley." She said dropping down to her knees and taking him in her mouth. He gasped. Then he moaned a guttural sound that resounded in the shower enclosure.

"Oh, my God," he muttered as she took all of him into her mouth and sucked. "You'd better stop or I'll come in your mouth."

She spoke around his dick, "Go ahead and come. Your seed will serve as my appetizer."

With that, he shattered. "Dear God in Heaven," he moaned as she swallowed.

She wiped her mouth with the back of her hand. "I didn't think you'd have any semen left."

He chuckled and replied, "Well, I've been storing it for a long time."

He shampooed her hair. His fingers on her scalp were like an aphrodisiac. "Ooh, that feels so good."

Henrietta moved under the showerhead to rinse off the shampoo. "Okay, It's your turn to wash me."

Bradley squeezed body shampoo onto her chest and soon there were lots of soapy bubbles clinging to her beautiful body. Her breasts filled his hands as he spread the lather. "Your breasts are lovely. He rubbed the nipples and squeezed the rock hard tips.

"Oh, Baby," she moaned. "I feel that inside my vagina."

He rubbed his hands down her torso and back. *I can't*

believe I'm hard again. She may be the death of me. He grabbed her buttocks and squeezed before he twirled his finger around her rectum.

"I want you inside me, Bradley. Hurry." She grabbed the foil packet from the soap dish, tore it open with her teeth, and rolled it on. "Now," she said as she impaled herself onto his shaft and began riding him."

He leaned her back against the shower wall, let her have her way with him, and couldn't believe it when he shattered again, this time with her. It took a while for them to catch their breath.

"Don't move," she whispered. "I want you to remain inside me for a moment."

She kissed him with wild abandon as she controlled the action. Her tongue danced with his, and she sucked his until he thought he'd die from the pleasure. "I'm starving now. My stomach feels like I haven't eaten for a month. Thank you, Bradley, for a most invigorating and exciting shower." She smacked him lightly on his lips. "Out we go."

They dried each other. She slipped into a terrycloth bathrobe, and he wrapped his towel around his waist. She dried his hair before taking care of hers.

"I want to watch you dress, Bradley," she declared.

His brows rose. "Why?"

"I don't know why. I just know I want to," she breathed.

Bradley reached for his underwear and pulled it on. His socks followed... then his sweater... and lastly, he pulled on his pants.

Henrietta stood on tiptoe and brushed a light kiss on his mouth. "I love being with you, Bradley. You keep me on my toes and make me smile."

"What about lovemaking?" He cocked his head to the side and pursed his lips. "Is an answer to that question forthcoming?"

Her face and neck reddened. He couldn't believe she

was embarrassed. "You're a wonderful lover, Bradley." She lowered her head for only a moment before lifting her gaze to his. "And we will make love again while you're here."

"Promise?" He didn't wait for her answer before adding, "I can't even imagine never making love to you again, Henrietta. Now that I've had that taste, I want a lot more."

"I promise to give you more." Her face flushed again. "I'm famished. So why don't we fix dinner."

While waiting on the balcony for the coals to get hot, Bradley allowed his thoughts to wander. She had pushed him away so many times in Grand Isle that he wasn't sure she'd even want to make love. He'd feared she'd be a cold fish. Humph! He had doubted she'd be uninhibited. But she was hot, great and wanted it as badly as he did. He like her clipped pubic hair.

He wanted to shout out to the rooftops that he had given Henrietta her very first non-self-induced orgasm. That had to mean something. He wished she'd invite him to spend the night. That would really make his day... in her bed... holding her in his arms... feeling her breath on his face... and sinking again and again into her hot, wet core. Making her come over and over again. Hearing her purr his name as she shattered. He shook his head. *Come on, Bradley, that ain't about to happen.*

Chapter 28

They cleaned up the kitchen together and settled onto the sofa to watch a movie. Seated so close to his warm body with her head resting in the crook of the arm he'd placed across her shoulders brought Henrietta comfort and peace. He rubbed his thumb in tiny circles along her shoulder and neck. She closed her eyes and allowed her feelings to take her from the present to a world of endless possibilities. Her skin prickled beneath his fingertips, and she experienced a floating sensation. She'd never felt this way before and didn't know what to do about it. Best to ignore it. It was somewhat magical. *Do nothing to give away your feelings. Take a few deep breaths and allow your body to relax. He's just a man.* She rolled her eyes. *That had to be the understatement of the year.*

Henrietta–who had not graced the interior of a church in years–considered it extremely fortunate her mother had insisted she attend midnight Mass on Christmas Eve. She would never have run into Bradley otherwise. *He's different from any man I've ever met, but what do I do with him now?*

He would be in Cut Off, and she'd be in Houston. She didn't want a relationship and was pretty sure he felt the same. A great sexual experience didn't mean two people were destined to share a life.

Your bottom line is that you don't trust men. And Bradley doesn't trust women. Perhaps they could occasionally get together, maybe even travel together. Henrietta enjoyed seeing new places but didn't like traveling alone. *What in the world are you thinking, woman? That is not going to happen.*

When the movie ended, Bradley pulled her onto his lap, wrapped her into his arms, and kissed her with all the fire and passion of deep desire. His slightly stiffened cock rested against her thigh. She considered fondling it but refrained. "What would you like to do tomorrow?" He muttered against her lips.

"Since you enjoyed Kemah, I thought we might drive to Galveston. It's only an hour away, and we don't have dinner reservations for tomorrow night."

"What's there to explore?"

"Although I'm not at all religious, Grace Episcopal Church is interesting. Built in 1894, it has beautiful stained glass windows. You might enjoy the Lone Star Flight Museum. Then there's the Bishop's Palace, also known as Gresham's Castle, an ornate Victorian-style house from the late 1800s. If you like trains, we could go to the Railroad Museum."

"Any idea about where to eat lunch?" He dragged a finger up the side of her neck. She shuddered. "I've not eaten there yet, but I've heard a lot of recommendations for the Saltwater Grill. But there are lots of other places, too."

"We can try the Saltwater Grill." He moved his hand to her nape and kissed her again. "I love being with you, Henrietta."

Her face and neck flushed. "I like being with you, too. But if we want to get an early start in the morning, it's time we call it a night. We should leave around eight. I'll drive and pick you up at your hotel." She rose from his lap, took his hands in hers, and encouraged him to stand. "Today was fun and I do look forward to tomorrow." She stood on her tiptoes and kissed him lightly before leading him to her door.

* * *

Well, so much for spending the night. His mind whirled as he drove from her condo to The Houstonian. He'd hoped she'd ask him to spend the night after they'd finally made love. God, she was hot and passionate. Their day had been fun-filled. He thought they were very compatible.

It was anybody's guess what tomorrow would bring. He would enjoy her company and, hopefully, Galveston, too. He would take whatever she gave. A serious relationship was not what he or Henrietta wanted. They'd both been burned by life experiences that had somehow managed to change them. Saundra had been his Waterloo, and he would never be able to forget that. And because of that miserable bitch, he'd never be able to trust any woman. What a shame.

His mother's face suddenly filled his mind. All she'd ever wanted was for him to have a happy life. She would have liked Henrietta. *What's not to like?*

The car in front of him stopped suddenly, and Bradley almost plowed into it. His nape hairs rose, and he was almost certain the hairs on his chest did the same. When the vehicle didn't move forward again, he turned on his emergency flashers, stepped out of his rental unit, and marched to the offending car, ready to yell at the person for stopping without warning.

But there was no one to assault verbally. He felt guilty for his earlier thoughts. The driver's head was slumped onto the steering wheel. Bradley dialed nine-one-one and reported it. He told the person on the phone he would remain where he was until help arrived.

The ambulance materialized approximately three minutes before the police. The EMT first checked for a carotid pulse on the driver. Then he checked again. "He's dead," he told

Bradley and the police.

Bradley was allowed to leave after telling the police the little he knew. *Jesus, the guy bought it while driving on a busy Houston thoroughfare.* His mood was somber as he entered his hotel room. He looked at his watch. It was too late to call Henrietta and tell her about it.

In bed, he thanked God he'd been able to stop in time to avoid a shitload of trouble. Bradley deliberately thought about Henrietta trying to forget the victim's face. What a beauty she was… in her sexy bra and panties… naked on her bed.

His thoughts brought on a semi-erection as he thought of sliding into her. *Okay, man. Wake up and smell the roses. Go to sleep. Don't allow her to possess your thoughts or your dreams. Nothing will ever come of this.*

Bradley pulled the long pillow into his arms and finally slept.

* * *

Henrietta lay in her bed with her eyes closed and pictured Bradley in his soft green sweater. Then she mentally removed his sweater and admired his muscled torso. She'd been pleasantly surprised that a man with dark hair had only a small amount of hair across the top of his chest and around his nipples that narrowed down to his dick. She hated hairy men.

She imagined his hands caressing her body and sliding between her legs. She wished he were here now holding her in his arms. *Don't allow this man to lead you astray. Men are NOT trustworthy. Remember that.*

Chapter 29

Henrietta picked up Bradley at his hotel at eight. She watched him walk toward her, one hand in his pants pocket, and his camera bag slung over his left shoulder. He looked really hot in his black pants, white shirt, and red sweater topped with a grey suede jacket. When he let himself into the passenger seat and leaned over to kiss her cheek, his understated scent teased her nose.

She turned on the radio to a country music station before driving off. Garth Brooks was singing *Friends in Low Places*, and they both sang along. When it ended, they both laughed. "I've always liked that song," she told him.

"Me, too. I don't know why, but I do. Maybe it's because I feel raunchy when I sing it instead of feeling like the staunch Yale attorney my mother was so proud of." He shrugged. "So, where are we headed first?"

"After you left last night, I surfed the Internet about tourist attractions in Galveston. Moody Gardens is a really neat amusement park, but it would be better to explore during an early spring weekend since many of the attractions are not yet open. Have you ever been on an offshore drilling rig?"

"Yes."

"I should have known that. Nix a visit to the Ocean Star Offshore Drilling Rig and Museum at Pier 19. I wouldn't want you to be bored. If you had never been, I would have liked to go."

"I've been on rigs in the Gulf of Mexico and the North Sea, but I don't mind going with you. The ride out there is probably scenic, so it's good I brought my camera."

"No. No. The Lone Star Flight Museum is close to the airport and near Moody Gardens. Want to try it?"

He dragged his index finger from her ear to her collarbone. "I think we should."

She scowled. "Are you even listening to what I'm saying, or is your mind stuck on a hidden agenda?"

He chuckled. "Yes, I'm listening. And don't scowl at me. I'm not stuck on anything, and my agenda is not at all hidden. I'll have you know that I'm capable of multi-tasking."

She smirked. "Okay. Okay."

They decided to visit Seawolf Park on Pelican Island to tour the World War II submarine, a destroyer escort, and other military hardware. Then they would visit the vast Railroad Museum. This would take a lot of their time.

"Once we leave the area," she said, "I suggest the ornate Bishop's Palace. It's built of colored stone, rare woods and has unbelievably beautiful stained glass windows. I've been there but don't mind going again. It is truly magnificent. There are other famous old homes, but I don't think we'll have time for more than the palace. I don't think we'll even have time to visit Grace Episcopal Church."

"Put it all down on your mental list for the next time I visit." He placed his hand on her thigh and lightly squeezed. Her blood raced through her veins. "What about dinner tonight? Any ideas?"

"I've given it some thought. There are two Seasons 52

restaurants in Houston. One is two-and-a-half blocks from my condo. The other is on Westheimer. I suggest we make reservations for the one close to my place."

"I'll look it up and make the call. Is seven-thirty good?"

She nodded. "The flatbread is terrific. It's a popular restaurant and usually a bit crowded and a little noisy, but it still manages to feel cozy. I like it."

He made the call and said, "We're on."

From one tourist attraction to another, Henrietta thoroughly enjoyed seeing it all with Bradley. He seemed to enjoy it all, too. He held her hand throughout their explorations. She liked that.

They had lobster bisque and salad at Willie G's for lunch. From there, they spent a couple of hours at the Railroad Museum. As they stepped out of the museum, Bradley pulled her into his body and planted a sexy kiss on her lips.

Although Henrietta didn't approve of public displays of affection, she couldn't help but respond to his sensuous kiss. His tongue danced in and out of her mouth. *Oh, my God. What's happening to me? This man turns me on like putting a match to a log in a fireplace.*

"I enjoyed that so much," he murmured into her ear.

"The museum or the kiss?" She grinned.

"Both. Thanks for allowing me to visit."

Then it was on to the Bishop's Palace before heading for her condo.

"What's the dress code for Seasons 52?" he asked.

"Dressy casual. You're fine just the way you are."

The ride to CityCentre was slow with the snarled traffic. She drove up to the entrance to her building saying, "I'd like to freshen up," she said. "How about you?"

They stepped into the elevator, and she pressed her floor number.

He cocked his head to the right. "I have nothing to freshen up with."

"I want to brush my teeth and I do have a still-in-the-packet extra toothbrush."

They entered her condo. He continued, "So you're not willing to share your toothbrush?" He wagged his head from side to side and followed her into her bathroom.

"Of course I'll share if that's what you'd prefer." She handed him her brush. "And you can use it first."

He laughed, took her brush, cleaned his teeth, splashed his face with water, and dried it. He ran his fingers through his hair. "All freshened up and ready to go." He kissed her cheek. "Your turn."

He watched her brush her teeth, apply lip-gloss, and brush her hair. Ready."

* * *

They sauntered into Seasons 52 at seven twenty-five and were seated without a wait. After the hostess had handed them menus, she asked, "Something to drink now?"

Bradley said, "I'd like to look over the wine list before ordering." He studied the selections for a couple of minutes and motioned to the waiter. "I'll have your New Old Fashioned. Henrietta, what'll you have?"

"I've always wanted to try the Pearfect Storm. Tonight's the night. And bring us a lobster and mozzarella flatbread."

When the drinks and flatbread arrived, Bradley took a bite and said, "I know I'll want another flatbread. This is seriously good stuff. I could make a meal on just this."

"Then why don't we? We can feast on appetizers and flatbread and skip an entrée altogether. I do this all the time."

"Sounds terrific." They inhaled the flatbread, and Bradley called for another one. Mushrooms stuffed with crabmeat, roasted shrimp, spinach, and Ahi tuna tartare came next. He also ordered a bottle of Cakebread Chardonnay.

Henrietta laughed. "I love eating like this. It's like sampling several options. I like this wine though it's a bit expensive."

He shrugged and sipped from his glass. "Nothing is too

good for you, Henrietta."

"I appreciate that, but tomorrow night at Pappas Brothers is my treat."

"We'll see."

Henrietta twirled the stem of her wine glass. "When you say that I think you don't agree but are not willing to say so." She took a sip of wine. "Bradley," she said capturing his gaze with her own. "I want you to spend the night with me."

Startled at her request, he almost choked on his wine. "I'd like that." He wanted to hoop and shout. Yes! Just keep it together. "Since we're close to your place, and since I've been in these clothes all day, why don't you pack an overnight bag and spend the night at my hotel?"

"Okay."

Chapter 30

They got back to her car, and she drove to The Houstonian where she gave the valet her keys. He carried her bag and took her hand as they entered the lobby and strode to the elevator. Alone in the car, he kissed her cheek.

Once inside his suite, he dropped the bag to the floor and took her into his arms. When his mouth covered hers, she opened and let him in. His eager tongue explored all the recesses of her mouth, and she melted against him. Her heart beat a furtive tattoo and desire rushed through all the veins in her body while her tongue danced with his.

"I want you, Bradley," she breathed, "but I want to be clean and fresh when we make love."

He backed away from her. "The bathtub is huge–big enough for two. Are you okay with us being in that tub together?"

"More than just okay," she answered and began removing her clothes. "Please join me."

She finished undressing and almost ran into the bath. He loved the look of her sweet ass as she leaned down to turn on the water.

"Are you okay with a bubble bath?" She asked.

"Yeah. I'm okay with anything that involves you."

Naked, he poured Chardonnay into wine glasses and set them on the ledge of the tub before stepping in and sitting. She got in and sat between his legs with her back against his chest.

Henrietta said, "This reminds me of the scene in Pretty Woman when Julia Roberts and Richard Gere are in a tub about this size."

"I recall that scene," he answered, "but he was seated in front." His hard dick rested against her back. He took the bar of soap and rubbed it against her breasts.

"Ooh, I like that. And I like sitting in front of you. Now lose the soap and use your hands."

"Like this?" He asked as he rubbed her breasts and circled her nipples.

"Yes, just exactly like that." A liquid fire of desire raced through her body. "I can't believe how hot I am with you. It's like I'm in heat. You'd better stop for a minute or two. I don't want to come until we're in bed." She pushed away from him and turned to face him. "Now you're going to pay for getting me all hot and bothered, Bradley Graham."

She soaped and fondled his erection and scrotum. "Got to make sure you're clean before I take you in my mouth." His dick twitched in her hands. "I've changed my mind. I don't want to wait. I want you in this tub." She checked the water level. "I'll let out some water, so we don't get water on the floor. Then she straddled him.

"Wait!" He snarled. "I didn't bring a condom."

"I'm on the pill and I trust you to be disease-free. I've never had sex without a condom, so don't you worry."

"Then bring it on," he ordered.

"Yes, sir," she said as she impaled herself on his harder than nails penis." She rode him like a bucking bronco at a rodeo.

Breathless afterward, he moaned, "Death by bareback

sex."

"What did you say?"

"I said this feels so good that I'm afraid you and your bareback sex will be the death of me. You feel so good without a condom."

"This is my very first experience, and I must say it's really good to feel your velvety skin inside of me instead of latex."

As they lay in bed cuddling and listening to soft music on her iPhone, Bradley's cellphone rang. "Might be work," he said grabbing it. He frowned at the screen and said, "I don't recognize this number and the name is blocked. I'll ignore it." After ten rings, it stopped.

"Maybe you should have answered it," Henrietta mused. The words had hardly left her mouth when the ringing began again.

"Bradley Graham here," he said. Then his face froze into a mask of horror. "How the fuck did you get this number? I blocked your calls." He listened for a moment. "I have nothing to say to you except fuck off." Then he hung up.

He turned toward Henrietta. "Believe it or not, that was Saundra." He switched to a falsetto voice and said, "Ooh, Bradley. I was so stupid. I want to see you. When I told her I'd blocked her calls, she told me she buys a throw-away phone to call me and pitches it afterward."

"So she didn't remain with your friend, Nate?"

"Not for very long. She bugs the shit out of me every time her latest lover splits. She's such a bitch. She deserves to be with your Uncle Carl."

Henrietta pulled her mouth into a tight circle. "You shouldn't let her bother you so much. She probably calls because she knows it pisses you off. And she succeeds. She knew you were angry."

"Maybe I should let you talk to her next time she calls."

"Perhaps so."

Bradley's phone rang again a few minutes later. He glanced

165

at the screen and handed it to Henrietta. "Get it. Whatever you say is fine with me."

Henrietta tapped the screen and said in a breathless voice, "Hi, Saundra. This is Henrietta Blanchard. Bradley and I are in bed at The Houstonian, but is there anything we can help you with?" No response. "Are you still there, dear?" Still nothing. Then a dial tone indicated she'd disconnected.

Bradley laughed and laughed as he slapped his pillow several times. "Boy, was she taken completely unaware! I'd have paid good money to see the look on her face."

"I guess I did get her goat, but enough about her. Would you like to go to The Galleria tomorrow or would you prefer driving somewhere?"

He shrugged. Then he dragged the tip of his tongue from her ear to her collarbone. "Doesn't the Texas Hill Country have wine tours?"

"Yes, but I find the cost prohibitive. And it would take all day. Don't forget our reservations at Pappas Brothers Steakhouse. We could sleep in and visit Hermann Park. We could ride the train, and grab lunch at the Pinewood Café."

"Okay, you've sold me on the idea." He yawned.

"I'm tired, too." She leaned over and kissed him. His stubble scratched her face. "Goodnight," she said before turning on her side.

"Goodnight. I had a good time." Then he spooned his body against hers. He draped his arm around her waist and held her breast in his hand.

I could get used to this.

Chapter 31

Bradley's stiff dick poking her butt woke Henrietta. He dragged his tongue along the side of her neck. *Waking up with this woman is something I could easily become accustomed to if I were looking for permanence. But I tried that and got completely fucked over. No can do.*

"I have to pee and brush my teeth," she said stroking his chest.

"Me, too. You can go first."

He watched her splash cold water on her face through the open bathroom door. *She is so fucking hot in bed. The sex is unbelievably good... unbelievably frequent.* His dick thrummed with desire.

She brushed her teeth and pulled a brush through her hair and left the bathroom calling out, "Next."

He rose from the bed and headed to the bathroom sporting his tremendous erection. When they passed each other, Henrietta said, "Morning, Woody. I'll be waiting for you."

He made short work of washing his face and brushing his teeth before calling out, "Hey, babe. Do you want me to shave?"

"No. I like you with that sexy stubble."

"Sure? I don't want to scratch you while we make love."

"Forget the razor, Bradley, and get your ass here now."

After two rounds of hot sex and showers, it was nine o'clock before they left for Hermann Park. They drove to the park and opted to visit the Houston Museum of Natural Science. He fancied a gander at the Foucault Pendulum and explained how it demonstrated the Earth's rotation.

"I don't understand that stuff at all," she huffed.

He pursed his lips. "You don't understand or you're not interested? There's a big difference in the two."

She straightened her back, appeared ready to strike at him verbally, but relaxed her posture when she realized he was right. She lifted her brows and pierced his gaze with her own. "Perhaps a little of both."

He laughed and cocked his head to the side. "Thanks for being truthful. Maybe we should explore a girl thing–the minerals and gems section and jewelry."

Her fisted hands moved to her hips before she scowled and huffed into his ear, "That is not at all funny. I'm capable of understanding much more than that!"

He pulled her into his body. "I know. I wanted to see how you looked when you're pissed. Come on," he said as he loosened his grip and took her hand. He held the museum map in his other hand and perused it. "Let's go to the Hall of Minerals and Gems, and then the Smith Gem Vault. After that, I'd like to go to the Isaac Arnold Hall of Space Science."

"Agreed."

The museum visit completed, they watched all four shows at the planetarium. Afterward, Henrietta dropped him off at his hotel with instructions to meet her at her condo at seven o'clock.

* * *

After showering and drying her hair, Henrietta slipped into

her lacy red garter belt and matching bra. No panty or thong tonight even though it felt weird. She sprayed on a little Oscar cologne before pulling on silky black stockings and attaching them to the belt. She detested garter belts, but would wear it strictly for Bradley's benefit. He would be leaving the next day, and she wanted to make this last night together a memorable one.

The red dress slipped over her head easily and slid down her matching taffeta slip. She checked herself out in the full-length mirror. *Yes, he's going to love it.* She applied minimal makeup and finished her look with the sexy red, black, and white Louboutin five-inch pumps.

At exactly seven o'clock, she attached the string of pearls around her neck as her doorbell rang. She let him in, her heart beating hard and fast.

He whistled as he entered. "I hoped you'd wear that dress. I love it." He kissed her lips. "You're stunning."

She thought he looked handsome in his expensive black suit and red tie that matched her dress perfectly.

At Pappas, they snagged a table in the cocktail lounge and ordered drinks. In the background, the pianist played a medley of old songs. Bradley scoped the dimly lit room with its dark furniture that more than hinted of the good life. "I've never seen a display of ready to cook steaks, lobster tails, and steamed rock crab before in any restaurant."

Before she could respond, they were greeted by her usual waiter and seated. Henrietta introduced Bradley. Roy smiled and shook Bradley's hand before turning to Henrietta and saying, "I'm going to show you both some love tonight. I see you already have drinks from the bar," he added handing them menus, "so I'll give you a few minutes to decide on what you'd like to enjoy tonight." He turned toward Henrietta. "It's been too long since your last visit!"

After he had left, Bradley said, "Wow! Do they always treat you like a queen?"

She snickered and tapped her finger on the menu. "Pretty much, although Roy is my favorite waiter. My tip is always generous. Don't forget that this is my treat, Bradley. The prime rib-eye steak melts in your mouth. I'll have the eight-ounce filet mignon, medium-rare, with fresh asparagus. We could split a salad and a side of their skillet potatoes."

He nodded. "I'm okay with that and you know I want my steak medium-rare, too. And I'll have the creamed spinach. What about wine?"

"I usually have Roy pair the wine, but we don't have to do that. Whatever you prefer."

"Have you ever been disappointed with his choices?"

"Never."

"So be it."

After a wonderful dinner and a shared dessert of delicious *Crème Brulee*, they headed to her condo. She invited him in for an after dinner drink.

* * *

Bradley wanted more than a drink. He wanted to spend the night with her, holding her in his arms, and making love to her until they were both breathless. He hoped she wanted the same thing.

He took the glass of Jameson from her and took a sip. She sat next to him on the sofa with a glass of Port. "I've had a really good time these past four days, Henrietta. I'd like to come again when I can string some time together." He brought his glass to his lips and sipped. "Would I be welcome?"

"Of course." Her eyes searched his. "As long as you realize I don't want a relationship."

"I know." Again, he brought his glass to his lips. "I don't, either. I do enjoy doing things with you. I think we're compatible." He winked. "I won't mention how good the sex is."

She moved close to him and took his glass from his hand. Then she set it and her wine glass on the coffee table. His arms moved around her waist, and he pulled her onto his lap. He kissed her eyes first, then her cheeks, and her ears. He watched the goose bumps rise on her arms and guessed they'd probably risen over the rest of her body. "Stay with me tonight," she whispered. "We have only tonight, and I don't want us to spend it apart."

"I was hoping to hear that."

He kissed her softly, but his kiss became heated as their tongues mated. She was sure he could feel her heart race against his hand on her chest. She'd said she had never wanted any man, but he knew she wanted him. And he wanted her.

"I want to make love to you until we are completely worn out," he muttered against her lips. Then he picked her up and carried her to her bedroom. "I want to undress you, Henrietta."

He set her down on her feet. She pressed her body into his. He knew she was wet and hot.

"Okay," she breathed huskily. "Then I'll remove your clothes, Bradley."

He unzipped the back of her dress, pushed it off her shoulders, and let it slither to the floor at her feet. He did the same with her slip, leaving her standing before him in her bra, garter belt, and stockings. *Jesus, Mary, and Joseph. No panties or thong.* He sat on the side of her bed and devoured her with his eyes from head to toe. Had he known she was without panties, he wasn't sure he could have gotten through dinner.

"You like?" She queried.

"Oooh, yes." He closed his eyes for a moment before saying, "You take my breath away, Henrietta. You look so sexy and wild without panties."

She started humming *The Stripper* song and began undulating right before his eyes. He all but consumed her with his eyes. This seemed to inspire her to continue writhing, bumping and grinding in the exotic lingerie he knew she'd purchased for his enjoyment. She undid the snap on one of the front dangling straps, still humming. She turned in time with the music coming from her mouth. She undid the second snap on the second dangling strap.

He turned her back to him and unclipped the back straps before placing her down on the bed. Slowly, he rolled each of her stockings down her leg and pitched them onto the floor. Her moisture was visible on her genitals. Her rubbed one finger up between her nether lips and brought them to his lips. "You are so beautiful, Henrietta, and you're dripping wet just for me. Now I'm going to fuck your brains out." He took a deep breath before adding, "And maybe mine, too."

"I want you, Bradley. Make sweet love to me." She spread her legs and took him in.

Chapter 32

They'd made love for most of the night. To Henrietta, it seemed as though neither one could get enough of the other. She never thought she could have one orgasm without her dildo, much less experience several orgasms with a man in one night. But she had and didn't relish the thought of him leaving. They showered together, and he prepared breakfast. His pancakes were the best she'd ever eaten–even better than her mother's.

As she dreamily sipped her *café au lait*, she asked, "Do you have to leave today? Since it's only Saturday, can you remain one more night?" *I can't believe I asked him to stay. This is so not like me. Heat rose up her neck to her face. Oh, my God. My face feels like it's as red as a beet. This is not high school!*

He gulped some of his coffee. "Unfortunately, I can't. From here, I go to the North Sea on business." He leaned over and kissed her lips. "I don't want to leave, but I have to. These four days have been wonderful. Through you, I rediscovered the fun of doing simple things."

She tasted the coffee and maple syrup on his lips. His silvery eyes darkened as they captured and held her gaze. "Me, too," she answered. "How long will you be out there?"

"At least a couple of weeks… probably more. I'm never sure how long I'll be in one location. Not until I learn what's happening. This offshore platform is off the coast of Scotland."

"Ooh." She wiggled her shoulders. "Reminds me of Jamie Frazer in *Outlander*."

He kissed her again. "Damn. I really wish I didn't have to leave today. I will be calling and texting you when I can." Again, his lips brushed hers. "I could be your Jamie."

"Be real, Bradley."

The corners of his mouth turned down in a small frown. "I was being real."

They cleaned up together before he grabbed his overnight bag and left. Henrietta couldn't help the lump from forming in her throat or the tears that dripped down her cheeks after the door closed behind him. She'd had such a wonderful time. She would miss him.

* * *

Bradley stepped out of the elevator in Henrietta's building and strode directly to his rental unit. *She asked me to stay one more night.* His brows lifted and his eyes rolled heavenward, and for someone who didn't want a relationship, he'd wished he could've accepted her invitation. *Just get over it. She doesn't want more than a good fuck either.* He found it hard to believe he'd told her he could be her Jamie. Not! Jamie had truly loved Claire. He didn't love Henrietta. He liked her and lusted for her. That was all. There was no way he'd ever make a commitment to one woman again. People should learn from their mistakes in life, and he'd certainly learned from his.

Bradley grabbed his larger bag from his hotel room and dragged it into the elevator and down to the registration desk to check out. He turned in the rental at the airport and took the shuttle to the terminal.

The long flight to Edinburg would be exhausting. First of all, his non-stop flight would last five hours from Houston to New York. At least his seat was in first class on both flights. He could be cramped in coach with a screaming child close by.

After one night in the company apartment in mid-town Manhattan where he'd enjoy a good meal and full night's sleep, he'd embark on the ten-hour flight from New York to Edinburg, Scotland, and move into the company suite in the Balmoral Hotel for the duration of his stay. He hoped he could finish his business quickly, but doubted that would happen. One advantage of this trip would be enjoying a steak at Maloney & Porcelli on East 50th Street. His stomach growled at the thought.

While he sat in the VIP lounge the next day, an image of Henrietta in her lovely red dress came to mind. *She's beautiful... bright... hot in bed... What more could a guy want?* He pushed the image and thoughts from his mind, and like always, recalled the beginning of his troubles–Saundra, his pain in the ass ex-wife. It pissed him off that she'd called him again–and while he was with Henrietta.

When boarding for his flight was announced, he ambled to the airport gate, not at all anxious to leave. A small smile lifted the corners of his mouth when he recalled the way Henrietta had answered his phone at his request. She'd been calm, cool, and collected. He was pretty sure she'd be that way in court, too. She was head and shoulders above Saundra.

He dozed off and on during the long flight to New York. He was tired from the marathon sex with Henrietta the night before. He chuckled, sure she was feeling the same way. He tried to read but to no avail.

Before he knew it, the flight attendant woke him. "We're making our descent now. Did you have a good nap?"

"I sure did. I was so worn out. I hope I can sleep as well on the flight to Scotland tomorrow evening."

The attendant smiled. "Rest well for tomorrow, Mr.

Graham. Thank you for flying U.S. Airways."

Bradley left the plane and headed for the apartment. After unloading his bags in the bedroom, he freshened up and walked to Maloney and Porcelli from the Waldorf Astoria. The air was crisp with a stiff breeze. As always, he marveled at the beauty of the city at night.

Two hours later, Bradley entered the suite, stripped and slid between the sheets. He was asleep almost instantly. The next morning, since he had all day before his overnight flight, he hoofed it to Saks Fifth Avenue to purchase a memento for Henrietta. *Don't get carried away. Purchase just a little something to imply friendship.* In the jewelry and accessories department, he purchased Dior over-sized sunglasses and had them shipped to her address.

Back in the apartment, he called Henrietta at work to thank her again for a great time.

Midnight, six in the morning in Scotland, found him in his first class seat for the nine-hour flight with his thoughts on Henrietta. She would probably be asleep. Would she dream of making love with him? He ordered Jameson, swallowed two Benadryl tablets, and slept like the dead.

It was colder than a well digger's ass in Montana when he got off the plane at three o'clock in the afternoon. It looked like evening, however, since Edinburg has only two hours of sunshine daily. January was always extremely cold with average temperatures reaching only forty-three degrees Fahrenheit and dipping down to freezing or below overnight. Rain occurred on seventeen days out of the month. It was a dreary place, and most folks remained indoors. So would he after he reported to the company's office to order a helicopter to pick him up from the helipad on the hotel's roof.

It would be tomorrow before a chopper would pick him up due to a massive storm brewing in the North Sea. By the time he'd been given the details of the problem on the rig, it was six o'clock.

He hailed a cab to take him to the company suite at the Balmoral Hotel on Prince's Street. With each visit to Edinburg, he realized how the luxury hotel with its modern interior looked much more like a cathedral from the outside.

After settling in his suite and freshening up, he moseyed to Number One, one of the restaurants in the hotel. He had Scottish crab soup, Orkney beefsteak with vegetables, and a white chocolate praline for dessert. The Tempranillo, Lopez Cristobal 2009 was superb. He was bushed and returned to his room.

He glanced at the clock on the night table. Nine o'clock p.m. in Edinburgh meant it was three o'clock a.m. in Houston. *Should I or shouldn't I? Fuck it. I need to hear her voice.* He dialed the number.

"Hello," her voice sounded sexy in his ears. That adorable voice quickly sounded angry when she uttered, "Do you know what fucking time it is?"

"Yes. I'm in Scotland and marooned in town until a humongous storm in the North Sea abates tomorrow. I was thinking of you and just had to hear your voice." He cleared his throat as his mood quickly went downhill. "I'm sorry I woke you. Go back to sleep and call me whenever it's convenient for you, regardless of the time. Goodnight." He hung up.

His shoulders slumped, and he sighed. *You shouldn't have called her knowing it was so late in Houston. You've probably cooked your goose with her. Jackass.* He shucked off his clothes and stretched out between the sheets. The heavy quilt added warmth to his chilled body.

Just as he was beginning to doze after gulping his Jameson, his cell phone rang. It was Henrietta. His heartbeat thundered in his ears as his heart rammed against his ribs. His body warmed, and he kicked off the covers. *She's returning my call. Yippee!* He let it ring three more times before answering. "Hi, Henrietta. I'm sorry I woke you. You could have waited to call me."

He heard her yawn. "Once I woke up, I knew it would be quite some time before I'd fall asleep again. So what are you up to? Are you okay?"

"I'm okay and not up to much. The wind is so damn bad that I have to wait to take a helicopter to the offshore platform. It's so fucking cold and dreary that I can't wait to leave. I don't know why people want to live here." He sniffed. "You can bet I'll be finishing up this business as soon as humanly possible. I would never come here during winter if I had a choice. Can you imagine living in a place that sees only two hours of sunlight daily?"

"No. That makes the Texas and Louisiana heat and high humidity sound perfect." She yawned again. "I've got a new client since you left. She's fifty years old, married for thirty years, and her millionaire ex-husband threw her aside for a twenty-two-year-old bimbo. She's an absolute delight, and I'll see to it that the bastard will have to pay through the nose for his new babe."

"He deserves to be screwed financially. I'm thankful I had Saundra sign a prenuptial agreement before we married. I hate thinking about what could've happened without it.

"Any more calls?"

"Nope. You must have scared her off."

"I surely hope so. You don't need reminders of what she put you through."

"Right, but I'm afraid she's ruined me for life regarding relationships with women. I find it impossible to get past what she did me. It took me forever to get over it."

"I don't think you're totally over it. You must get over the anger before you can move on."

"Not sure that will happen. It's kind of like your inability to trust men after what you suffered. Are you saying you've forgiven your uncle?"

"No. I'm not sure I'll ever be able to do that."

He chuckled. "My mother would say that we're a matched

set of cufflinks."

She laughed out loud. "We'll never know what she'd think of me."

"I know she'd love you. Remember that you are most definitely worth loving."

Chapter 33

Henrietta found it impossible to go back to sleep after Bradley called. She closed her eyes and conjured the feel of his soft lips, and her lips warmed. She loved the way his tongue found its way into her mouth and danced with hers and the way his hard dick filled her with delight and satisfaction. She would have to be very careful not to lose her heart to him. He didn't want a relationship. And hadn't she told him she didn't want one either? *Watch your step, girl.*

At the gym for her spinning class, Henrietta spent a tough but fun seventy-five minutes. The fast-paced music boomed throughout the room while a huge television screen played scenes of bike-riding trails. She could have sworn she was riding through open land, forest trails, and up and down hills. Burning the nine hundred calories and feeling the high that came from endorphins secreted during exercise was a big plus. Henrietta kept fit with spinning classes three times a week and Pilates classes on Tuesday, Thursday, and Saturday. Sunday was her day of rest.

After her workout on the bike, she returned to her condo,

sopping wet with sweat. After a hot shower and a quick shampoo, she dressed in her Ann Taylor suit and walked to her office. Monique had already arrived and was at work on a file. Henrietta entered her office and called out, "This place feels empty without Gloria here."

"Gloria is here." When they heard her voice, their heads turned toward her office. She stepped out of her office into the hall.

"Oh, my God! Your belly is huge. Is it uncomfortable?" Monique asked.

"Yes, especially when Jessica kicks around during the night."

"What are you doing here early? Henrietta queried.

"I've been having Braxton-Hicks contractions and Dr. Santini ordered my return. He thinks Jessica might be early. I don't agree. She's still way up high. Everyone says I'll know when she *drops* into position for delivery. I'm kind of scared, and Jesse is a nervous ninny. He watches my every step and wants to wait on me hand and foot. Jesus. I feel like I'm being smothered."

Henrietta laughed out loud. "And I thought that's what you wanted." She looked around, "Where is Jesse?"

"Here," echoed a voice from Gloria's office. He stepped out and stood next to Gloria and rested his hands on his hips. "She'll have to put up with it. I'm not letting her out of my sight. She wanted to come to her office, so I brought my laptop hoping to get some work done. Instead, my ears have been inundated with the sound of gaggling women."

"Gaggling? Get back inside my office, Jesse. Now."

* * *

As Jesse and Gloria walked to their bed in her condo on March 14th, Gloria stopped in her tracks and yelled, "Oh!"

"What's wrong? Time to go?" He quickly grabbed the suitcase from its spot next to the doorway.

"No. Jessica dropped into position for birth a couple of

weeks ago. I had a contraction just now, but I'm not sure when my labor will begin. It could be tonight. Don't be nervous. Everything will be fine." She hoped she didn't appear concerned.

He paced in front of the sofa until Gloria thought he'd wear out the floor. "Stop it, Jesse. Chill out." When he didn't stop, she called her partners. "Come on over," she said. "I need some help with Jesse. I think I'm going into labor, and he's freaking out. She bit her lip with a hard contraction that lasted a full minute. Looks like Jessica might be on time."

Henrietta and Monique hurried to Gloria's condo. They tried to calm Jesse, but they were only slightly successful. They watched him pace to and fro.

When Gloria's contractions were five minutes apart, Jesse notified Dr. Santini who told him to bring Gloria to the hospital. "I'll be there to check her as soon as you get there."

In the elevator going down, Henrietta ordered, "Jesse, get your ass in the back seat with Gloria after you put her bag in the trunk of the car. There's no way you're going to drive to the hospital. I'll drive, and Monique will ride shotgun. You'll tend to Gloria in the back seat." At two o'clock in the morning, Houston traffic was light. Gloria moaned with each contraction. Jesse was as nervous as a pig in a bacon factory.

In labor and delivery, Jesse hovered over Gloria like a mother hen over her baby chicks. He fed her ice chips, mopped her face with a cool, wet towel, and whispered how much he loved her while rubbing her belly. He insisted on remaining in the room when Gloria had the epidural catheter inserted. He relaxed a bit when he saw her facial lines soften even with a hard contraction. He put his mouth near her belly and sang a lullaby to his babe.

At six-o-three in the morning, Jessica entered the world. The nurse quickly cleaned her up and wrapped her in a pink flannelette blanket. She slipped a matching stocking cap onto her head. Gloria was worn out. Jesse was ecstatic.

"Oh, my little princess. You're absolutely beautiful, and I love you." He called his parents, her mom, and his son, James, with the good news.

Monique and Henrietta got to see their niece again through the nursery window. "Hi, Jess," they called, "Smile for your aunties." They hugged. "Isn't she precious?"

* * *

Jesse insisted on buying them breakfast in the hospital cafeteria. They drove to their office building later in the morning.

"Have you heard from Bradley?" Monique asked as she entered her office. They were tired, but still excited over the birth of their niece.

"Yes. As a matter of fact, he called me while Gloria was in labor."

"Good thing you were awake. If you'd been sleeping, that would have been a big mistake on his part. I know how you don't like being awakened during the night. Did you tell him that Gloria was in labor?

"I did. Poor baby is freezing his ass off in Edinburgh and can't wait to leave. He's been there much longer than he expected."

Monique leaned back in her chair. "I think you like this guy. He just might be the one for you."

"Don't be ridiculous, Mo. I do like him. He's a wonderful lover. But it's lust we feel for each other. Not love." She moved into her office and shut the door.

* * *

Two weeks later, Jesse took Gloria and Jessica to recuperate on his yacht, *Dreamer*, docked at Southern Yacht Club on Lake Ponchartrain. She would return to work in six weeks. Their departure left Henrietta and Monique with heavy hearts.

On Friday, April 13th, while Henrietta was in the middle of research for her new client, she was not happy when her intercom buzzed. "Yes, Kathleen?" She asked, well aware of the sharp sound of her voice. A stab of guilt pierced her mind, but she'd left specific instructions she was not to be disturbed.

"I know you don't wish to be distracted, Henrietta, but there's a woman here demanding to see you. I offered to set up an appointment, but she insists she must see you now. What should I do?"

"Did she tell you her name?"

"She said her name is Saundra Graham."

Henrietta's stomach lurched at the same time she gasped. She had nothing to say to the woman who'd once been married to Bradley. *What the fuck was she doing here anyway? What did she want?* She inhaled deeply through her mouth and exhaled through her nose. There was no getting out of this, so she replied, "Escort her to my office." Again, she breathed deeply and straightened in her chair. *It was probably time she met the woman.*

Saundra sauntered in as though she owned the world. She was much shorter than Henrietta, and her hair was a mousy shade of brown. Beady eyes, almost black, sought Henrietta's gaze. Her hands were stuffed into the pockets of a pricey blood-red three-quarter-length jacket. Henrietta did not rise to meet her. Instead, she pointed to the chair facing her desk and said, "Want to sit?"

"No. I'd rather stand."

Henrietta shrugged. "So what can I do for you?"

The woman giggled nervously. "I remember your saying those exact words when I called Bradley the night you were with him in his hotel room. It pissed me off when I heard a female voice. You had no business answering his phone. I was calling him, not you."

Henrietta's anger began to simmer, but she kept it under control. She'd handle this like she handled court cases. "I answered his phone because he asked me to. Is there anything else you want to know?" She noted the flush on Saundra's face and figured her fists were clenched inside her coat pockets.

The woman snarled, "Are you fucking him?"

Henrietta bounced out of her chair to her feet. She lifted her brows and looked down her nose at Saundra before answering, "I don't think that's any of your business, and I don't have to listen to any crap from you. Don't come here again." She pointed to the door.

The popping sound of a gunshot surprised Henrietta. At first, she thought Saundra had shot herself. But when a burning sensation that hurt like hell–as though red-hot metal had been shoved into her left chest–she knew she was the victim. That's when she saw the gun Saundra was holding and fell back into her chair. As the bitch dropped the gun and made a run to escape, Henrietta screamed, "Kathleen! I've been shot. Call nine-one-one and security."

Monique ran into Henrietta's office, cast a quick look at her partner, bolted into the bathroom and grabbed a towel. She slid Henrietta onto the floor, put the towel over her wound, and pressed down. Her heart raced, and her body trembled in fear. She tried to sound positive when she assured her partner, "EMTs are on their way. Hold on, Retta. Just hold on."

Those were the last words Henrietta heard before dropping into a dark abyss filled with pain. She wondered if she was dying as she slipped even deeper into the darkness. *Oh my God, I'm heartily sorry…*

Chapter 34

EMTs arrived along with the police. They quickly placed Henrietta on a gurney. One EMT started an I.V. while the other took her blood pressure and pulse and applied a pressure bandage over the wound. They secured straps around her body and hurried to the elevator the police had locked open when they had arrived. Monique followed.

Kathleen told the police about the woman and what had transpired before she'd entered Henrietta's office. She told them she heard the gunshot. The quick-thinking security guard turned off the other elevator, leaving Saundra trapped, and took the elevator the EMTs used to bring Henrietta to the ambulance.

Monique hailed a cab and told the driver to follow the ambulance blaring its siren on its way to Memorial Hermann Hospital. The cab driver turned on his flashing emergency blinkers and did as she requested. Within fifteen minutes, they were at the hospital emergency department entrance. She gave the cab driver a fifty-dollar bill and ran inside behind the gurney.

* * *

By now, a detective had arrived at Building #1. His brown suit looked like he'd slept in it. His grayish hair was longish, and he chewed gum methodically. He stood in front of the locked elevator with his gun in hand. He asked the two policemen with him, "Are you ready to wrestle her to the floor when the doors open?"

They answered as one, "Yes, sir."

The detective nodded at the security guard. "Turn it on," he ordered.

The elevator numbers indicated the car was on its way down from the seventh floor. One by one, the detective called out the numbers. When the number three lit up, he snarled at his men, "Get ready for action."

The door opened. The detective's face reddened like a beet. "What the fuck is the meaning of this? The car is empty. Where is the shooter?"

The policemen didn't answer. They probably feared to speak. The tall and slender blonde man straightened and swallowed. "Sir, she must have taken the stairs."

The detective turned toward him with an angry scowl. "No shit, Sherlock! Any other ideas?" He shook his head before muttering, "Son of a bitch. Now we'll have to search for her. Shit! No telling where she is."

* * *

In the Emergency Room, Monique remained at Henrietta's side as she clung to life. All kinds of monitoring devices emitted beeps when something needed immediate attention. Henrietta's blood pressure was dangerously low while her heart rate was extremely high, indicative of shock. Within forty-five minutes from her admission into the E.R., she had been readied for emergency surgery and whisked off to the operating room.

Monique was taken to the surgery waiting room, her mind awhirl with questions. She would have to notify Henrietta's mother first. She inhaled deeply. How was she to tell Mrs. Blanchard? *Stop worrying about how to do it. There was no way to avoid making the call. Just do it.*

After only two rings, the telephone at the company where Marlene Blanchard worked was quickly connected to Monique.

"This is Marlene Blanchard. How can I help you?"

"Mrs. Blanchard, this is Monique Boudreaux, one of Henrietta's partners."

"Yes, dear. You sound breathless. Is something wrong with my Retta? Is that why you're calling me?"

"Yes, ma'am. A crazy woman came to our office and shot Retta in the upper left chest. She is presently in surgery at Memorial Hermann Hospital in Houston. I'm with her and will remain at her side."

Monique could hear the tremors in Mrs. Blanchard's voice after her initial gasp. "She's not going to die, is she? I don't know if I could handle another death."

"No, ma'am. I don't think so. This hospital is a top trauma center and the surgeons are unbelievably talented. I will call you as soon as the surgery is over."

"I'm coming!" Mrs. Blanchard cried.

"Look, there is no way you'll make it here in a few hours. Try not to worry. You'll hear from me as soon as the surgeon comes out to talk to me, and you can make arrangements to come to Houston after I call you."

"Who would do such a thing?"

"It was Bradley Graham's ex-wife." Monique heard Mrs. Blanchard shriek into the phone. "She showed up unannounced at the office. Retta agreed to see her. For no reason at all, the bitch–excuse my French–shot Henrietta and ran out. I'm hoping she's already been caught."

Monique heard Mrs. Blanchard's sigh. "Well, I am going to notify Bradley Graham about what has happened. I'm sorry now that he ever met my Retta, and I'll tell him so."

"Don't tell him you're sorry he ever met Retta. He's not

even here. He's in Edinburgh, Scotland. From what I can tell, I think they care for each other. He spent four days in Houston before leaving. Henrietta seemed happier than I've seen her in a very long time. Tell him about the gunshot, but nothing more. You can give him my cell phone number if he wants more news. Are you going to be okay?"

"I suppose so. I'll be praying and burning candles at church in hopes that my Retta will be okay. She's much too young to join her father. You be sure to call me as soon as you talk to that doctor no matter what time it is. Promise?"

"I promise I will."

Time seemed to stand still. Monique paced the length of the waiting room, sat for a while, and resumed pacing. Over and over, she repeated this pattern of action. When her cell phone rang, she answered it.

"Monique, this is Bradley Graham. Do you have any more news?"

"I take it Mary Ann called you."

"Yes. I'm afraid she blames me for Saundra's action."

"No more news yet. I will call you and Mrs. Blanchard as soon as I speak to the surgeon."

"I can't believe that my crazy ex-wife shot Henrietta. Do you know if the police apprehended her?"

"I don't. I followed the ambulance taking Henrietta to the hospital and have been here the entire time. I want her caught, but Henrietta's condition is of utmost importance."

"I'm at the Edinburgh airport boarding for my nine-hour flight to New York. It's three o'clock in the afternoon here. It'll be seven in the evening, Eastern Central Time when I land in New York. I have a connecting flight to Houston. I should be there around midnight tomorrow. I'll call you as soon as I reach New York City."

"Okay. I won't be able to meet you at the airport." She sniffed up tears. Retta didn't deserve this."

"I know. Her mother is not happy with me right now, but

how could I even guess that Saundra was capable of doing such a thing?" She sensed Bradley was crying as she ended the call.

Monique resumed her pattern of pacing and sitting. Her insides trembled. She'd have to call Gloria. She longed for a drink as she sat to make the call. Gloria answered on the second ring.

"Hey! What's up Mo? Everything okay?"

"No. Remember the man Retta told us she ran into after midnight mass?"

"Yes. She said he's hot. I know he went to Houston for four days and that they had a great time."

"True. Well, he has an ex-wife."

Gloria interrupted. "Please don't tell me something has happened to what's-his-name."

"Bradley Graham is his name, and nothing's happened to him. His fucking ex-wife walked into our office and shot Henrietta."

"Jesus H. Christ! Retta shot? Oh, my God! I'm coming back to Houston."

"No, Gloria. You have to think of Jessica. How is she?"

"She's great. Jesse is unbelievably stupid about her. He even gets up at night with her. You call me when she's out of surgery. In the meantime, I'll get our little family ready to return to Houston."

"No!" Monique snarled. "You and your little family need to stay put. Jesus! Jessica is not even six weeks old. Don't make me call Jesse, Gloria."

"I suppose you're right. I'll stay put. But you'd better keep me informed daily."

Chapter 35

Monique pulled up a chair to face the one she occupied and propped up her feet. Maybe this would result in less pacing. She wondered if the police had apprehended the witch. She'd like to dress her up in a Joan of Arc costume, tie her to a stake with a shitload of small branches surrounding it, and light the fire. She could easily watch the flames lick her ass and hear her screams.

Monique lost track of the time. When she checked her watch, three hours had passed. She told herself that no news was good news, that Henrietta was still alive. She finally allowed her tears to flow. *Please God, help her. Let her live.*

Another hour had passed before the surgeon moved briskly toward her. *I hadn't noticed before how hot this guy is. He wasn't holding his head down so it might be good news.* She ran to him. She knew her eyes were red. "Please have some good news for me, Doctor."

He took her hand in his. "Your partner is in the recovery room beginning to awaken from the anesthesia. She's lost a lot of blood, but the bullet missed her heart and lodged in the upper part of her left lung. We removed it successfully–along with a small section of damaged lung tissue–but she should be okay. You can see her in a few minutes since she'll be in recovery overnight. Don't be frightened when you see the tube connected to a suction machine to remove blood from her chest cavity. It will maintain negative pressure and allow her left lung to re-expand. She will be attached to monitors for her heart, respirations, and blood pressure. After you see her, I suggest that you go home.

"I understand."

"Tomorrow, your friend will be moved to the Intensive Care Unit for at least twenty-four hours. When all is well, she'll be transferred to a regular room. I'm Jeffery Hansen, by the way. Call me Jeff." He stuck out his hand. "Any questions?"

She took his hand. "I'm Monique Boudreaux. No questions at this time. Thank you for saving my partner who is like a sister to me. Now, which way do I go?"

"Follow me."

A hard to describe medicinal smell greeted Monique the moment she entered through the double doors of the recovery room. Pings and buzzes rang out in the overly bright light. Jeff led her to Henrietta's cubicle. *Oh, my God. She looks so pale.*

"She's waking up, but we'll be keeping her pretty well sedated," he explained. "I know it looks scary to see her in here, however, keep in mind that she's a strong woman. Why don't you get up close and talk to her? She might respond to a familiar voice."

Monique's stomach trembled as she moved toward the bed where the medicinal smell was even stronger. "Retta," she whispered as she patted her hand. "Retta, open your eyes for me. It's Mo. Come on. Try to open your eyes."

Henrietta's eyes fluttered and finally opened. Monique smiled, "Hey girl. Dr. Hansen says you're going to be okay. It will take time, but you will be back to one hundred percent. How do you feel?"

Her voice only a whisper, she replied, "Terrible. Everything hurts. Call Mama, Gloria, and Bradley. Tell them to stay put." Her eyes fluttered closed.

"I already did. Not sure that your mother and Bradley will stay put. Gloria will, or I'll sic Jesse on her."

Henrietta slowly opened her eyes again. "I feel like warmed over shit." Her eyes closed once more before reopening. "You need to go home, Mo. Get some rest. I'm so tired. I just want the pain to go away so I can sleep."

"I'll be right here with you. Bradley is already on his way here from Edinburgh. I'll call your mother to let her know you're okay, but she'll probably come down tomorrow. I called Gloria. She wanted to head back to Houston immediately, but I told her to stay put on *Dreamer*. I will call everyone after I leave you. Understand that we are all hoping to see you well again. So go back to sleep. You'll be okay. They'll take good care of you. Just be patient and do whatever they tell you to do. I love you, Retta. Concentrate on getting well."

Henrietta nodded and closed her eyes. Monique headed to the nurse's station and left her cell phone number along with instructions for the nurse to call her, regardless of the time, if there were any changes in Henrietta's condition.

Monique drove home feeling a little better than when she first saw that Retta had been shot. Her partner would be well taken care of, and all she could do was wait. She peeled off her clothes as soon as she entered her condo and entered the shower. What a day this had been. She realized she'd not eaten a thing since breakfast. She called for Seasons 52 to deliver a flatbread and a salad. She mixed an old fashioned and almost inhaled it. Her stomach felt like she hadn't eaten in a year.

Chapter 36

Mary Ann Blanchard arrived at the hospital around noon with a small bag in hand and the weight of the world on her shoulders. She found Monique in the Intensive Care Unit waiting room and gave her a huge hug. "How is she this morning?"

"She's doing as well as expected. They just transferred her into the Intensive Care Unit and are getting her settled. They're keeping her pretty well sedated. She has a tube in her chest so her lung can re-expand. And of course, the usual monitors. I'll take you in to see her now."

Mary Ann supported herself on Monique's arm "You must be so worn out. I do so appreciate your being here for her."

"Mrs. Blanchard, you know the three of us are as close as sisters. Gloria is recuperating from delivering a fine baby girl on her husband's yacht in Lake Ponchartrain. She wanted to come down here as soon as I called. I told her to stay put. She will, now that she knows Retta will be okay. I figured you would not be willing to remain home. You can either stay with me or in Retta's condo. You packed a bag, right?"

"Oh, yes," she answered. "I left a larger bag at the admission department. I'll stay at Retta's until she's discharged and gains some of her strength back. I don't want to be in your way. My boss told me to take all the time I need, but I don't want to take advantage of their good will in giving me the time off with pay. They're good to me, you know."

"Yes, Retta told me. I already notified our firm's private driver, and we'll pick up the tab. His name is Rick." She wrote the driver's cell number on the back of one of her business cards and handed it to Henrietta's mother. He'll be waiting outside the main entrance for you when you decide to leave. He'll recognize you from the picture I sent of you taken with my phone."

"Now, let's go see Retta." Monique took Mary Ann's arm in case she needed support. Seeing Retta so pale and weak might be a huge shock. It was a relief to see that the overhead light in the cubicle was turned off. In the dimmer light, Retta didn't look quite as pale and lifeless.

Henrietta was quiet with her eyes shut when her mother neared her bedside. Mary Ann tenderly brushed her fingers down one of her daughter's cheeks. "Retta. It's Mom." Henrietta's eyes fluttered open when Mary Ann bent down and touched her lips to her daughter's forehead.

"You should have stayed at home, Mama," she said, her voice barely above a whisper. "Now I'll have you to worry about."

"Oh, sweetheart. Don't worry about me. Surely you must understand that I had to see with my own eyes that you were going to be all right. I love you so, my baby." I'll be staying in your condo, and Monique has arranged for your driver to take me back and forth."

"One week, Mama." She took a deep breath before continuing, "Then you need to go back to work. No ifs, ands, or buts." The sky blue eyes closed and didn't re-open.

Monique warned Mary Ann, "They won't let you see her

except for ten minutes every four hours. That's an awful long time to be sitting in this waiting room. Retta needs to rest. Why don't you go to her condo now? You can come back this evening for the eight o'clock visit."

"Okay." She wagged her head. "Perhaps I should not have come, but I just had to see for myself. I'll call the boys to let them know how she's doing as soon as I get to her place."

Monique led Mary Ann out of I.C.U. to the row of elevators and handed her the key to the condo. Mary Ann hugged her. "Thanks. My Retta's lucky to have friends like you and Gloria."

"We love her, too."

As soon as the elevator began its descent, Monique returned to Henrietta's cubicle. As soon as she reached the side of her bed, Henrietta opened her eyes and muttered, "I know you couldn't keep her away."

"Just like there's no way anybody could keep me away. So rest. You're doing okay. Your mom will return for the eight o'clock visit. I'll be in the waiting room." She didn't mention that Bradley Graham was on his way to see her.

There was no way she'd leave before speaking to Bradley when he'd arrive late tonight. She told the nurse she'd be in the waiting room until eight o'clock.

Around seven, she ordered pizza from Papa Johns–enough for the unit staff. She gobbled down two large slices of bacon and hamburger pizza after realizing she'd not eaten anything all day. *No wonder she was hungry.*

Mary Ann didn't come to visit that evening. She texted Monique saying she was worn out and would return in time for the first morning visit. Monique elevated her feet on a chair. She had nothing to do but wait until Mr. Graham arrived.

She didn't realize she'd dozed off until the sound of the double doors closed behind a tall, handsome man. He moved almost silently toward her saying, "Which one of her partners are you?"

"I'm Monique, and you must be Bradley. Brand new mama

Gloria is in New Orleans."

He nodded. "I just have to see her. When can I go in?"

His eyes were red from lack of sleep, and there were deep circles beneath them. *Not a very pleasant sight for Henrietta to see.* She hoped Retta would realize his haggard appearance was due to his concern for her.

"They stick to the visiting rules; ten minutes every four hours and only two people at a time." She glanced at her watch. "I'd guess they'll call me in within ten minutes. It's lucky you arrived when you did. We'll go in together."

He shook his head from side to side. "I can't believe that Saundra shot Henrietta. It's not like we were recently divorced. I'm so thoroughly disgusted. I could easily put a bullet between her eyes and watch her drop without a single regret." He rubbed his eyes. "Just when Henrietta and I were getting along." He closed his eyes and took a deep breath. "I was even beginning to think we might have a serious relationship."

Monique felt sorry for him. He looked so sad and worried. The nurse stepped through the double doors and gazed at Monique. "You may come in now."

Chapter 37

Bradley's heart ached as he gazed upon Henrietta's pale face. The circles beneath her eyes told a sorrowful story of pain and suffering. She looked so thin, and her eyelashes appeared much darker than usual against her colorless cheeks. At least she was breathing easily. He wished he could take her into his arms and tell her everything would be okay. He carefully took her hand in his and brought her fingers to his lips.

She stirred and opened her eyes just a crack, but they soon widened upon recognition before narrowing. Her lips clamped down over her teeth. If looks could kill, he'd surely be dead.

"Get out!" She ordered her voice slightly above a whisper. "I don't want to see you," she hissed and pointed to the door. "Get the fuck out of my life."

"You can't really mean that," he murmured. His heart ached to think she was sending him away. He didn't budge, unwilling to leave her. But then, she'd added the clincher.

"I never want to see you again, Bradley Graham." She took a shallow breath. "Ever," she added.

"But we're so good together," he pleaded. "You can't possibly mean that," he argued.

"Were." She took a breath. "Past tense. Now get out."

Not wanting to upset her any more than she already was, Bradley slowly turned away from her bed and moved toward the door. He turned and looked at her again right before opening the door to leave. Her eyes were like side-by-side gun barrels aimed at his as she pointed again to the door. He walked out and dropped onto the sofa in the waiting room. He rested his elbows on his knees and held his face in his hands as he wept. Huge racking sobs. His chest ached with what could only be described as agony. How could he live with this?

How could Henrietta blame him for what his crazy ex-wife had done? It was unfair. But who ever said life was fair? He recalled his mother's words, "Life is not fair, and the sooner you learn this, the better off you'll be." Why did this have to happen just when he thought he'd found someone he could trust and maybe even come to love?

Monique stepped out into the waiting room. "I'm so sorry, Bradley," she said patting his shoulders. "I don't know why she reacted that way. It's obvious to me that you care about her. And she spoke so glowingly about you before this." She rubbed his shoulders. "And to think you hurried here from so far away only to get sent away. I'm sorry now that I called you."

He lifted his gaze to hers. "Don't be. I do care for Henrietta." He breathed deeply. "Perhaps even more than I realized. Neither of us wanted a relationship when we met, and we both fought it. Then, when we finally hit it off, we agreed to a fun and sexual relationship only. Jesus, Mary, and Joseph. I don't know what to do. Should I stay and hope she agrees to see me, or should I leave?"

Monique played with a lock of her hair before anchoring it behind her right ear. "I'm afraid she'll not come around any time soon. It would probably be best for you to go home. I know it's not what you want, but I know how to reach you if she changes her mind."

Bradley rose, feeling the weight of worry and fear on his shoulders. "Thanks for being honest with me. I'll leave even though I want to stay close by. All I ask is that you keep me posted on her condition while we wait and see if she changes her mind about seeing me."

"I will. Take care of yourself and thanks for coming."

Bradley made reservations for two nights at The Houstonian Hotel. He asked what his room number would be and let out a breath of relief when the receptionist said, "Room 305." Thank goodness. Suite 418 would have been too tough to handle. There were too many memories associated with it.

Dead on his feet, he stepped into the elevator with his bags, pressed the number three, and leaned against the wall. Smooth and quick, the door opened onto the third floor. With his shoulders slumped, and his gaze lowered, he dragged his luggage to his room, pulled off his jacket and threw it on the floor. His shoes followed the coat. Then he fell onto the bed, and within moments, was fast asleep.

He walked down the back steps of the company beach house just as the sun began its descent for the day and headed toward the water. He liked the feel of the sand between his toes and the Gulf waters lapping onto the shore and his feet. He ambled along the water's edge and felt like he was carrying a heavy burden on his back as he strolled forward. The sky was just beginning to turn into stunning shades of coral that would gradually darken until nightfall. He'd loved watching the sunset with Henrietta when she'd been home at Christmas time.

He had not gone far when he spied her coming toward him in her blood-red bikini. His heart raced with joy, and he held out his arms to receive her. His heart galloped so hard inside of his chest he thought it might burst through his ribs. His heavy burden disappeared like magic. As he held her close, her breasts smashed against his chest before he captured her lips with his. Her tongue danced inside his mouth making him so hard he ached.

She ground her pelvis onto his erection. If she kept that up, he feared he'd come before getting inside her. At the exact moment when he was certain he could take no more, she pushed away from him, smiled as she waved her fingers and disappeared into thin air.

Anguish covered him like a too-heavy coat. He'd only guessed at the real meaning of the word before. A deep pain seared his soul and was like nothing he'd ever felt before. He fell to his knees and prayed. "Lord, please help me. I love this woman with my entire body and soul. Please don't allow her to push me away when I've just found her. I'd rather die than live my life without her."

He bolted up in the bed and noted he was still fully dressed. He shook his head as though to clear it and waited for his heart rate to slow. After going to the bathroom to empty his bladder, he removed his clothes and slipped between the sheets. It had all been a dream, one he was certain had been branded into his memory. But did he love her?

Bradley found it impossible to understand his feelings. After all, he'd once thought he'd loved Saundra, yet had never ever felt toward her anything like his feelings for Henrietta. Yeah, he'd been hurt to find her in his bed with his best buddy, but being pushed away from Henrietta caused his soul to hurt. *I'll never get over this.*

It was a long time before he was able to sleep again in spite of his sheer exhaustion. But when he did, it was dreamless.

* * *

Monique did not return to Henrietta's room right after Bradley left. She used the time to think about how she would approach her partner on the subject of Bradley. How could she tell Henrietta that she did not agree with her decision without pissing her off? Ideas circled about her brain, and the more they circled, the more addled she became.

Who was she to advise her partner/buddy/sister in affairs of the heart? What did she know about love? Zilch. She had not been forthcoming about everything in her life either. For all those years together, she'd kept her secret from Gloria and Henrietta. Yeah, she was from the community of Raceland, but not until she and her mother moved there in time for Monique to begin ninth grade.

She decided it would be best to return to Henrietta's room and not mention Bradley. She wondered if her friend would bring up the subject? If she did, Monique was determined to be truthful about her feelings on the matter.

Henrietta's eyes were closed when Monique tiptoed through the door and eased it shut. The chair at the side of the bed creaked when she sat in it, and Henrietta opened her eyes. She pinned Monique with lifted brows and a glassy stare. Monique stared right back, daring her to bring up Bradley Graham.

Henrietta swallowed and motioned for Monique to come closer. "You think I was wrong to send him away."

"I didn't say that."

Henrietta pursed her lips together and lifted one eyebrow. "You don't have to say it. I can see it on your face."

Monique shrugged. "Oh, so in addition to your many abilities, you now read faces making talk completely unnecessary?"

Henrietta closed her eyes and breathed in a tired breath. "No, dammit. Don't be a pain in my ass. I'm pretty sure, though, that you're taking his side."

"Retta. There is no side to take. This is your decision, not mine."

"But?"

The corners of Monique's mouth turned up in what was not quite a smile. "You know me too well." She wagged her head a couple of times. "He seems so enamored with you. His poor eyes were so red from crying. And you didn't have to listen to the sobs in the waiting room after you put him out. I felt so sorry for him."

"Well, while you're feeling sorry for him, don't forget that it was his ex-wife that shot me." She cleared her throat. "Go on home, Mo. I'll be okay. I'm tired, and I want to sleep."

Chapter 38

The next morning, Bradley drove to the Houston Police Department. His body ached as if it had been run over by an eighteen-wheeler. He found his way to the Detective Division and was finally seated in Detective Lieutenant Patrick Lansing's office.

The detective slouched in his desk chair. His rumpled brown suit looked cheap, but his white shirt was crisp and fresh. He looked bored, maybe tired, as he chewed his gum as methodically as the coach of the Seattle Seahawks.

"I'm Bradley Graham, ex-husband of Saundra Graham–the woman who shot Henrietta Blanchard. I'm close to Ms. Blanchard, and I would like to know if she's been apprehended yet?"

Lieutenant Lansing squinted his small, almost black eyes and pursed his lips at Bradley before allowing his gaze to check him out from head to toe. He straightened in his rolling chair and stopped chewing to ask, "Close to Ms. Blanchard? Just exactly how close?"

"Close. I work with her mother in Cut Off, Louisiana.

I'm a maritime attorney for a large offshore and shipbuilding business there."

The detective drew his lips together, cocked his head to one side, and shrugged his shoulders. "A little hanky-panky going on between you and Ms. Blanchard?" He asked with a sly smile on his face.

Bradley's face burned with a rush of anger he quickly managed to control. His face felt hot, and he was pretty sure the veins in his neck poked out. He was certain he wouldn't get far with this man if he mouthed off. "Look here, Lieutenant, don't try to put a sleazy label on my friendship with the victim. I came here to offer my help in finding the person who did this. She goes by the name of Saundra Graham or Anderson and she's my ex-wife. We've been divorced for three years because I found her fucking my best friend in my bed."

The detective straightened in his chair and fiddled with his tie as though to make sure it was straight. Bradley thought he appeared more interested, so he added, "She's a mean and conniving bitch, and I'm willing to help you find her. So what do you say?"

Lieutenant Lansing leaned his elbows on his desk and clasped his hands. He moved his head back and forth in the tiniest of moves. "So how to do think you can help HPD capture this 'mean and conniving bitch' as you called her?"

"I thought I might be able to lure her into meeting me."

The detective chuckled. "You've been reading too many mystery novels. Why on earth do you think that would work?"

"Because, Detective Lansing, it's me she wants. More than likely, she is without a man at present. Each time she blows a relationship, she calls me and begs me to give her another chance. I've always told her to get lost. I also know her MO." A sly smile turned up the corners of Bradley's mouth. "Method of operation. I learned that from mystery novels, too."

This time the Lieutenant laughed out loud, and his gum fell out of his mouth onto the desk. He picked it up, threw into the wastebasket, and reached for a new slice in his pocket. "*Touché*, Graham, *touché*." He unwrapped the fresh slice of gum, popped it into his mouth, and discarded the wrapper in the wastebasket. "We do have a picture of the perp from security cameras placed throughout the office building where your close friend has her office. Do you have any idea where your ex-wife lives?"

"No. But I would guess her apartment is probably rented under her maiden name of Anderson. She could even be using Nate's last name–Landry–even though they never married. I was taking care of business in Edinburgh when Ms. Blanchard's partner called me with news of the shooting. I have a feeling she will call, maybe even to gloat. I believe she lives here."

"We got a couple of good prints from the gun she dropped in the victim's office and we're running those through AFIS right now. Something might pop. Why don't you go home, Mr. Graham? Leave me your card, and I'll call you if anything materializes."

Bradley handed the detective his business card. "I'll be leaving for home tomorrow. If she contacts me, I'll let you know, Lieutenant."

"Thanks. We'll get her. Attempted murder is a serious offense, and I want to see her put away for a very long time."

Bradley turned away from the desk and headed for the elevator. He would have liked to see her burn in hell, but prison would have to do. He'd check on Henrietta's condition at four o'clock, get some dinner at the hotel, and hit the sack.

* * *

Bradley entered the I.C.U. Waiting Room ten minutes before the four o'clock visiting hour. Monique rose to greet him. "Did you get some sleep?"

"Yes. How's Henrietta?

"About the same."

"I went to the Houston Police Department and talked to the detective in charge of the case. So far, they have nothing.

A couple of prints were on the gun that were sent through AFIS, but I doubt they'll come up with anything. Be careful, Monique. I believe she's still in Houston. I will be leaving for Cut Off in the morning." He handed her his card. "I would like you to call me with a report on her progress every day if that's possible. And if she needs anything, call me."

"I'll call you with reports, Bradley. I know you care deeply for her. I'm hoping she'll change her mind about you as she recovers."

The double doors opened. "I'm going in, too," he warned. "I don't care what she says; I want to see her once more before I leave."

Bradley stood at the foot of Henrietta's bed. Before she could say anything, he held up both hands to stop her words. "I know you don't want to see me, Henrietta, but I'm leaving for home in the morning, and I couldn't bear to leave without seeing you. I've gone to the HPD and met with Lieutenant Lansing. They have not yet captured Saundra. I offered to help them apprehend her. If she calls me, I'll get as much information as I can from her and let the police know. In the mean time, you will be guarded until they find her. No arguments! I'm leaving now, with the hope that you will one day change your mind about seeing me." He blew her a kiss, turned, and left.

* * *

"We spoke in the waiting room before the time for visitation," Monique explained after he left. "He does care about you, Retta. When the I.C.U. doors opened, I thought he'd leave. I had no idea he planned to see you or speak to you. His outburst was completely unexpected. Please don't be pissed at me for talking to him."

Henrietta took a deep breath and closed her eyes. Monique watched a tear find its way down into her ear.

"I'm not pissed at you." Then she broke into sobs.

"Do you want me to call him back?"

She wagged her head from side to side and sniffed. "No,

no."

"So why are you crying?"

"I don't know."

"You don't know or you don't want to say?"

"Not sure. I'll be okay. You can leave, Mo. I feel like being alone right now."

Monique kissed her partner's forehead. "I love you Retta. Your mom will be here in the morning. Have the nurses call me if you need me to come back."

Henrietta sniffed up her tears. "I know. I'm okay. See you in the morning. Goodnight, Mo."

Monique walked out into the hall. She didn't turn around even though she heard her partner crying. She'd said she wanted to be alone. Perhaps a good cry was what she needed.

Janet Foret Lococo

Chapter 39

Henrietta cried for what felt like an eternity after Monique left. Her incision hurt. Her eyes burned. Her throat felt like she'd been in the desert without water for days. But her heart is what hurt most of all. And for once in her life, she had no idea what it was that she wanted.

The nurse came in and quickly made her way to Henrietta's bed. "What's wrong?"

When Henrietta's response was only to wag her head slowly from side to side, she questioned, "Are you in pain?"

Henrietta tapped her chest, near her heart.

"You're having chest pain?"

"No," she said barely above a whisper.

"Man trouble?" the nurse quipped.

Henrietta nodded. "Pain pill so I can sleep, please."

"Okay," the nurse said and left her cubicle.

She soon returned with the medication. "Percocet," she said. "I'm giving you one now, and if you're not asleep in an hour, I'll get you another. You need your rest so you can heal and get out of here."

Henrietta swallowed the pill with a full glass of water. The nurse lowered the head of the bed and fluffed her pillow. Henrietta hoped the pill would have her asleep in less than an hour. She closed her eyes and prayed to a God she'd ignored for a very long time.

Her doctor had said her bladder catheter would be removed in the morning and that she might be moved to a private room. That was good news, and she'd be glad if that happened. It was almost impossible to sleep without being drugged in this hyperactive and brightly lit area where alarms almost constantly warned of an impending disaster of one kind or another. It's no wonder patients in such an atmosphere suffer from sleep deprivation. After all, the patients in I.C.U. were all seriously ill. She was lucky Saundra's bullet had missed her heart. If it hadn't, she'd be history. On a slab in a morgue.

As minutes ticked away, the beeps and buzzes sounded softer and softer in her ears until her eyelids felt as though they were weighted down with steel, and she finally dozed into a dream-filled sleep.

The sun was shining brightly in a cloudless sky as she sat at the end of the pier at her brothers' company beach house. It was hot, and there was no one else around. Even the neighboring houses were empty. She slipped off her bikini top and bottom and smeared on sunscreen before stretching out on the beach towel she'd spread over the wooden slats. She set her iPhone alarm for forty minutes and pulled her rather large straw hat over her face to protect her eyes from the glare on the water. It was so quiet she heard only the slap of the surf upon the pilings beneath her and the shore. Peaceful...

When the alarm sounded, she rolled over onto her stomach and reset it. She plopped the hat over her head. With her ear directly over a space in the slats, the sounds of the Gulf lapping at the pilings lulled her to sleep.

When her alarm rang the second time, she set her hat on top of her iPhone to protect it from the sun's heat. Then she slid naked into the water under the pier. Oooh... The water felt divine against her sun-baked skin. She slid underwater to cool off her head, too. Then with her head above water, she made sure the narrow plastic raft was well secured to one of the pilings and stretched out on it as it bobbed with the wave action. So relaxed...

She dozed in the shade of the pier. Henrietta was awakened suddenly when a strong arm dropped around her waist, slid her off the raft, and pulled her into a hard naked body. Her heart beat erratically in a panic until she opened her eyes and found herself gazing into silvery-grey ones. Bradley.

His cock was as stiff as the mast on a sailboat when he covered her mouth with his. Her tongue ventured into his hot mouth and teased him by pushing it in and pulling it out. At first, he was willing to dance to her tune, but he soon took the lead. God, she wanted him... inside her... ached to come.

He gave her a small laugh. "Aha. You wanted to tease me, but you want to finish now. But I won't allow it. It's time to pay the piper," he warned before taking over her mouth again. When he pulled away, he whispered, "What do you want, Henrietta? Tell me."

"I want you to fuck me until we both have trouble breathing, Bradley."

He frowned. "Fuck you? Is that all?"

She considered her answer. "No. I want you to make love to me. Long, slow love with you deep inside me until our souls touch and dance." Then she impaled herself on his dick. His hands held her hips as she rode him. Slowly at first – like trotting on a horse. Then faster – like galloping. Then even faster – like a barrel-racer getting her horse to go as fast as it could.

The orgasm that had been tightening her insides beckoned. "I'm going to come, Bradley."

"I know. Go ahead. Let go. I'm not far behind."

When she finally broke free in ecstasy, her spasms sucked

his dick until he came hard. "I love you, Bradley," she whimpered.

He closed his eyes and took a deep breath before saying, "Finally! Thank God. I love you, too."

The powerful orgasm that rocked her body awakened her. She looked around and saw she was still in I.C.U. *Jesus.* She hoped she hadn't moaned. That would be so embarrassing in the glaring brightness of the unit. Her gaze moved around the unit. Nothing seemed to have changed. Jesus! She'd had a wet dream in I.C.U. She frowned and wondered if other patients ever had this same experience. It felt so real. She closed her eyes but could not erase the memory of Bradley's silvery-grey ones or his hard body.

Henrietta recalled the dream. She'd told Bradley she loved him. *No way. I do not love him. This has only been a dream, a hot one, but no more than that.* She wondered if the pain medication could have been responsible for it. It seemed as though she'd read somewhere that narcotics could cause hallucinations.

Henrietta noted the shadow of a man seated outside and to the left of her cubicle. She pressed the call button for the nurse. Was this also a hallucination?

When the nurse came in, Henrietta asked, "Is there someone sitting at the door of this room or am I dreaming?"

The nurse nodded in the direction of the man in the chair. "Oh, him. That's your personal guard, dear. HPD gave the okay for his presence. There are two. Each does a twelve-hour shift that coincides with ours."

"What?" She pulled her brows together. "Who's paying for this?"

"I don't know, Henrietta. You'll have to ask Detective Lansing about that. He usually comes to check out the situation in the morning."

Henrietta scratched her head. "Well, you make damn sure he checks with me when he comes in the morning."

"Will do. Is there anything I can get you? Perhaps another pain pill to help you sleep?"

Henrietta thought about it. She didn't want to become an addict, but she wanted to sleep. "Yes, please bring me one."

The balance of her night was dreamless. The nurse awakened her for her bath and vital signs before seven in the morning.

"Why are you waking me up so damn early?" She demanded.

"You must be getting better," she admonished. "This is the first time you've complained about it."

"Are you saying that someone has awakened me this early every morning?"

"Yes."

"Jesus F. Christ! You people give patients sleeping medicines and then wake them up at the crack of dawn to bathe them. That doesn't make any sense at all."

"I'm sure it doesn't, but doctors begin to arrive here around seven and it will be tough getting this done once that begins."

"Okay, but before you start, call that guard into my room. I have some questions for him."

Once the guard entered, Henrietta asked, "What's your name?"

"Watson, ma'am. Leonard Watson."

"And who relieves you?"

"Blake. Thomas Blake, ma'am."

"So who's paying you and Blake?"

"I'd rather not say, ma'am. The man that pays us doesn't want anyone to know."

Henrietta scratched her head in thought. "Perhaps I should call Bradley Graham and tell him I don't want this protection."

Leonard Watson flushed and countered, "I hope you don't do that ma'am. Blake and I need the money."

She eyed him the way she eyed a witness at a trial. Hard. Unforgiving. She'd gotten the information she wanted. Might as well leave the man alone. And Saundra had still not been apprehended. "Okay, Watson. Just keep your eyes and ears open."

"Yes, ma'am." He bowed and returned to his chair outside her door.

Chapter 40

When the doctor came in at a little after seven o'clock, he ordered her catheter removed. "Once you can urinate, you'll be transferred to a private room on this floor," he said. "It's called the *step-down unit*. They provide more nursing care than a regular medical-surgical unit. I'm pleased you're doing well. You are one lucky woman. Once inch lower and the bullet would have killed you. Need anything?"

"No. I know I'm fortunate about the bullet, but I was also fortunate to have been taken here for treatment. Thank you."

"This is not the last you'll see of me, Ms. Blanchard. I'll be in charge of your care until you are discharged. See you tomorrow."

She mused about Bradley Graham paying for her private security. He was not responsible for his ex-wife's actions. Then too, perhaps she shouldn't have been so cocky when she'd answered his telephone the night Saundra had called while they were together in the hotel. She realized she shouldn't have treated him like shit when he'd come to see her. But that was all water under the bridge. Her mother had always warned, "Don't cry over spilled milk." The bottom line was that Bradley's crazy ex-wife had almost killed her. That was not okay. She hoped the police would catch her soon. She would not feel safe until they did.

Her mother walked into her room. "Good morning, Retta. You look much better."

"I am. As soon as I can pee once they remove this catheter, they will move me into a private room on this floor. I'm going to be okay, Mom. You need to go back home and to your job."

Her mother's lips turned up in a sad smile. "Giving me orders is a sure sign you're getting better. Grumpiness will come next."

Henrietta lifted her gaze toward the ceiling, but before she could say a word, her mother advised, "And don't you give me that look. I'm not dumb, Retta. Far from it." She sat in the chair next to the bed. "I'm leaving for home today. My flight reservation has already been made. I was certain you wouldn't be upset to learn I would return to work. Don't know why we've always knocked heads."

"Probably because we're too much alike. You've learned to be independent with Dad's death, but you still want to treat me like the little girl ruined by your brother. I'm fine, Mom. I love you, and I admire your spunk that I somehow seem to have inherited. Now come over here and give me a hug."

Tears filled Henrietta's eyes when her mom pulled away after hugging her and kissing both her cheeks. "I love you, too. And you're right. It is almost impossible for me to lose the image of my baby in tears the day that bastard hurt you. Believe me. I've tried. God says we should turn the other cheek, but I will not. Cannot. Even if I burn in hell for hating my brother, I will never forgive or forget what he did. Now let's talk about something pleasant for the little while I'm here."

The nurse entered and asked Mary Ann to step out for a short time. She pulled the privacy curtain along the glass wall and door. "Are you ready to lose the catheter?"

"Yes."

The nurse tented the covers to expose her genital area. "Spread you legs a little. This won't hurt." She grabbed an empty syringe saying, "I'll remove the saline solution that keeps the retention balloon expanded. Then I'll slide the catheter out. Ready?"

Henrietta nodded and before she knew it, the deed was done. "I just hope I can pee so I can be transferred out of here. You all have been really good to me, but..."

The nurse interrupted, "I know. Patients in here suffer from sleep deprivation because of the constant activity and noise from monitor alarms. Stop worrying. You'll pee and will be transferred out of here right afterward. And tonight you will more than likely sleep like a log. Now can I get you anything?"

"No. Thanks."

Her mother returned after the nurse left and took Henrietta's hand. Words were not necessary between them.

After her had mother left, Henrietta's mind unwittingly turned to Saundra. She'd never forget the look on the woman's face when she pulled the trigger that almost took her life. It would be a happy day when she would be sent to prison for life with no parole for attempted murder. She hoped a big, burly guard would fuck her in the ass every night. *Wait. There are only female guards in the cell blocks housing female prisoners. Shit. Well then, maybe some big ass woman would force Saundra to eat her stinking genitals nightly while shoving something big and rigid up her ass.*

After her mother left and while she waited to pee, Henrietta reminisced about her hot dream of Bradley. She blew out a breath, closed her eyes, and recalled his face. His big silvery grey eyes framed with lashes every woman would die for... such dreamy eyes. She sniffed as though she could smell his signature scent. The soft pads of his fingers always felt so good on her skin. She'd told him she loved him in the dream.

Her eyes popped open. No... No... Not possible! She could never love anyone. She wasn't even sure she loved herself. She had too many faults. And she'd been so promiscuous. Bradley Graham deserved much better. She shoved those thoughts from her mind.

Finally, she had the urge to urinate. The nurse helped her to the bedside commode, and the tinkling sound of her urine stream was music to her ears. *I'm so out of here!*

Monique appeared thirty minutes after Henrietta called. She smacked a kiss to her partner's forehead and said, "Okay. Let's see what we can do to get you out of this noisy place and into a quiet room."

* * *

Back at HPD Central, Detective Lansing was hot under the collar of his rumpled brown suit. He wiped the sweat off his brow with his index finger and wiped it on his desk blotter. "Son-of-a-bitch! Son-of-a-bitch! Son-of-a-bitch!" Two of his best detectives, Briggs and Jackson, had followed up on a lead to find the woman responsible for shooting Henrietta Blanchard and had found her. But then, as they'd moved to make the collar, she'd slipped away from right under their noses. Now the Chief was on Lansing's ass big time. He rolled his head around in an effort to relax. *And his wife wondered why his hours were so long.* Jesus! It would be nice to catch a little break.

Just for the hell of it, and because he knew perps sometimes returned to the scene of the crime, he posted two HPD policemen dressed as security guards at the entrance to Ms. Blanchard's office building that night. Nothing happened.

As punishment for losing the perp, he assigned Briggs and Jackson to the day shift the next day. They'd not been happy to wear security guard uniforms or about their assignment. *Tough shit!*

* * *

Briggs and Jackson took their positions inside the

building's entrance. "Can you believe the Lieutenant has us dressed as security guards?" The lead detective, Briggs, asked his partner. "Makes me feel like an asshole. As if the bitch would return here. She'd have to have shit for brains."

With each passing day, Briggs and Jackson hated their assignment even more. Jackson complained, "We've been on this detail for three days and have nothing to show for it. Fuck!"

While Briggs watched the elevators, Jackson muttered to his partner, "Motherfucker!" When Briggs turned toward him, Jackson pointed two fingers at his eyes and moved them toward the door. He whispered, "Across the street. That's her. Stay cool. Our gold badges are at stake if we lose her again." He scratched behind his right ear. "Looks like our Lieutenant might have hit the nail on the head after all."

"Yeah, follow my lead. I hate it when he's right!"

Chapter 41

Briggs and Jackson watched Saundra walk into the building as though she owned the place. Her expensive-looking clothes made her seem like a wealthy businesswoman on the way to her office in the high rent district.

"Good morning, ma'am," Briggs greeted the woman.

She smiled as she eyed the identification card pinned to his collar. "Good morning, Mr. Briggs. Isn't it a beautiful day?" She frowned and stiffened when he and Jackson entered the elevator with her. "What are you up to Mr. Briggs?"

"My buddy and I have been ordered to escort all unaccompanied females to their offices in the building as a matter of safety. Haven't you heard that some crazy bitch shot one of the lawyers at Babin, Blanchard & Boudreaux law offices?" She visibly relaxed.

"I hadn't heard," she replied scrunching her brows. "I've been out of town for three weeks. Don't worry about me. I'll be fine," she admonished. "You can both remain at your post."

"HPD is combing the city for her as we speak, but she's

nowhere to be found. Probably not even in the city by now, but we have to follow orders. We have wives and kids and need our jobs. What floor, ma'am?"

When she turned her eyes upward, Jackson slapped a handcuff on her right wrist and pulled it behind her while Briggs drew her left arm to her back and snapped on the other cuff. "You are under arrest for the attempted murder of Henrietta Blanchard. You have the right to remain silent," Jackson began reading the Miranda Rights from the card all HPD employees carried.

"Anything you say can and will be used against you in a court of law. You have the right to speak to an attorney. If you cannot afford an attorney, one will be appointed for you. Do you understand these rights as they have been read to you?"

"You two shitheads think you're real smart," she snarled.

Jackson laughed. "Do you understand your rights, ma'am? Just answer the question."

"Yes." She chuckled down deep in her throat. "You two will soon learn how little power security guards have when I sue both of you brainless dipsticks for harassment."

"I don't think so, ma'am. Show her your security guard badge, Briggs."

Briggs pulled out the shiny, gold detective shield from his right pocket and held it close enough to her face that she could read it.

Her mouth dropped open, and Jackson held her up when he felt her knees buckle. Then he whispered in her ear, "I have one just like it, ma'am. Now get moving."

They led her outside, and Briggs protected her head with his hand as he eased her into the back of their unmarked car. "You can call your lawyer once we get you in HPD Central Lock-Up. You should've played nice with Ms. Henrietta Blanchard. If you had, you wouldn't be on your way to jail right now." He slammed the door shut.

He strapped himself into the front passenger seat. "Well

done, Jackson. Well done. I sure do hate it when the Lieutenant is right."

The perp was crying in the back seat as Jackson peeled out into the street. Her tears would not move him or his partner. She had lots to cry about. He hummed the Beatles' tune; *I Should Have Known Better.* Briggs hummed along with him.

* * *

Lieutenant Lansing met them once Saundra Anderson had been booked. Her driver's license proved she used her maiden name and lived in the Clear Lake area south of Houston. The marine attorney had been right about the maiden name and that she was close by. A mug shot was taken; she was fingerprinted, and her fingerprints entered into AFIS. After a DNA sample had been retrieved, Lansing called for a female police officer to do a strip search. She'd been patted down, but he didn't trust that she was weapon-free. She'd been made to empty her purse on a table, but no additional weapons were found. Three cellphones and the rest of her personal effects were bagged and tagged.

Afterward, the suspect was taken into interrogation and left to sit and wait for fifteen minutes. Briggs and Jackson observed through a one-way glass.

Briggs said, "She looks as nervous as a cat in a room full of rockers." He laughed at his own joke.

Jackson told Briggs, "Yeah. I bet you five she doesn't talk."

"No bet. No way she'll say anything."

Lansing entered the room and set a small tape recorder and a telephone on the table before taking a seat.

Before uttering a word, Detective Lansing depressed the record button and instructed, "Our conversation is being recorded. You may call a lawyer before answering any questions. Do you have a lawyer, Ms. Anderson?"

When she wagged her head to indicate a negative answer, he instructed, "You must answer verbally."

"No, I don't have a lawyer," she yelled. "Can you hear me

now on that fucking recorder?" She rose from her seat and glared at the lieutenant.

"Sit down!" His voice boomed.

She plopped down hard onto her chair. "This is a huge pain in the ass for me and you will pay the price." She shifted in her chair. "You've got nothing on me, and I'll be out of here in a flash." Again, she shifted in her chair. "When that happens, you'll kiss your shield and lieutenant bars goodbye."

Lansing didn't respond to her jibes. He continued, "An attorney will be appointed for you. I know you've already been told, but I remind you again. You have the right to remain silent; anything you say can and will be used against you in a court of law. You have the right to speak to an attorney. If you cannot afford an attorney, one will be appointed for you. Do you understand these rights as they have been read to you?"

"Yada, yada, yada. I'm not stupid." She swallowed. "I will not say another word without my lawyer's presence."

Lansing rose from his seat. "That will do it for now, then. We'll meet again once your court-appointed lawyer has had a chance to talk with you. Good day." He left and sent a policewoman to take her to a cell.

The lieutenant nabbed Briggs and Jackson from the anteroom. "Follow me."

Once in his office, he ordered, "Tell me everything that happened from the time she was first spotted."

Briggs spoke up. "Lieutenant, I have to admit that I initially thought our assignment was a waste of time." He looked down as though he was checking out his shoes before continuing.

"I'm sure that wearing security guard uniforms didn't please either of you." He smiled. "I'm also sure it was not easy for you to admit I was right."

Briggs nodded. "Jackson's the one that eyeballed her headed our way. When she entered the building, we fed her a line that all unaccompanied females had to be escorted to their destination. She didn't like it but didn't resist other than verbally. We made the collar in the elevator, handcuffed her and read Ms. Anderson her rights." He looked over at Jackson and asked, "Anything to add?"

"No." Neither mentioned humming the Beatles' song.

"Good job, boys," Lansing said as he shook their hands. "Two of Ms. Anderson's prints matched those on the weapon she dropped to the floor after shooting Ms. Blanchard. She'll do time. I'll put her in a line-up and get the secretary to take a look later today. Finally, the Chief will be off my ass about this, and I'll be off yours. Shit does indeed roll downhill. Now get out of those guard uniforms and get to work."

"Yes, sir, Lieutenant," they replied as one.

* * *

Lieutenant Patrick Lansing dropped his butt into his office chair. The first thing he did was to call his wife with his good news. His next call was to Bradley Graham in Cut Off, Louisiana.

"We've got the 'mean and conniving bitch' in a cell downtown. She's been booked with attempted murder one. I need you to identify her in a line-up."

Bradley blew out a breath. "Thank God! I feared she'd get to Henrietta at the hospital and finish the job."

"That why you hired private guards?"

"Yes. Don't give me any shit about that. Look, I'll make arrangements to have the company jet fly me to Houston. I should make it to the airport in no more than two and a half hours."

"Fine. I'll have an unmarked unit pick you up and take you to HPD Central. They'll meet you on the tarmac where private planes land. Once you arrive, we'll set her up in a line-up and have you and Ms. Blanchard's secretary have a look to make sure. Her driver's license says she lives in the Clear Lake area."

Chapter 42

Bradley experienced an unexpected release of all tension after receiving the call from Lieutenant Lansing. His gaze traveled heavenward, and he prayed a silent thank you. He called Mary Ann with the news before making arrangements for the company jet. He hurried home to pack a bag for the trip. Perhaps Henrietta would be more willing to see him now that Saundra had been captured.

Two hours and fifteen minutes later, Bradley exited the plane and was soon seated in an unmarked police car. Bradley fidgeted in the seat as the driver drove at breakneck speed with siren blaring and lights blinking. Thirty minutes later, they arrived at HPD Central.

"Do you always drive like that?" he questioned the driver.

"No." Then he grinned and added, "Only most of the time. Did you shit your pants?"

"No. Are you disappointed?"

"Nah. Come on," he gestured with his arm. "I'll take you to the lieutenant."

"That won't be necessary. I know where his office is."

"Standard operating procedure, sir. I'll take you there."

Bradley followed.

In Lieutenant Lansing's office, he met Henrietta's secretary, Kathleen O'Grady. The lieutenant explained that they would observe the line-up individually. "I don't want any screw-ups in getting this woman convicted. We will do everything by the book. Understood?"

When Bradley and Kathleen nodded in agreement, he said, "Let's go." They followed his brisk walk to interrogation. He questioned the officer at the desk, "Everything ready for the line-up?"

"Yes, sir. Just waiting your word to herd them in."

"Do it." Then he turned to Bradley. "You'll go in first. Once you're done, Ms. O'Grady will follow."

"Okay." He was ushered into a musty-smelling narrow area with a one-way glass and waited with Lansing.

A small door in the room opened. He heard the instructions the women were given from the ceiling speaker. "Step up, ladies. Stand in a single line facing front." Saundra was the fourth person to enter the room and stand in line.

"That's her," he nudged Lansing. "The bitch." She appeared nervous and jumpy. She kept straightening the badly rumpled jacket of her expensive outfit. Bradley thought it would be nice if she were to shit in her pants. He zoned back to the situation when Lansing asked a question. "I'm sorry. I wasn't paying attention. Would you repeat the question?"

"Are you certain?"

"Yes. I'm so sure that I'd put my neck on the chopping block."

The women were instructed to turn to their left; and after a couple of minutes, were told to turn to their right. "The fourth from the left is Saundra Anderson, Lieutenant. There's no question about it."

The women were taken out. Bradley was led out of the small room, and Kathleen was called in. The door opened, and the officer called out, "Come on in, ladies. Again. You know the drill. Face forward in a single line."

As soon as Saundra entered, Kathleen O'Grady said, "That's her. The fourth woman from the left is the one who shot my boss. I am absolutely positive. I'd know her anywhere."

Nothing more was said as Kathleen watched the women turn left first and then right. "That's the woman, Lieutenant. The woman fourth from the left."

"Take them out," the lieutenant ordered. "We're done."

The lieutenant took them back to his office. "Thank you both for your help. You're free to go now. We'll be in touch when we need you as witnesses."

Kathleen left, but Bradley remained behind. "What is the prison sentence in Texas for attempted first-degree murder?"

The lieutenant scrunched his brows until they almost met over his nose and cocked his head to one side. "Ten years maximum. Tell me you're not thinking about vengeance, Counselor?"

"Not on your life, Lieutenant. That would make me as bad as she is. Ten years just doesn't seem long enough. Does parole follow discharge from prison?"

"Four years."

Bradley massaged the sides of his face between the thumb and fingers of his right hand. "What about bail?"

"It depends on the judge, but I doubt anyone would allow it since Ms. Anderson is charged with a capital crime.

Lansing patted Bradley's shoulder. "Don't worry. Your woman is safe now."

"She's not my woman, and I'll try not to be concerned," he called over his shoulder.

"Are you ready for your ride to the airport?"

"Nah. I'm going to check on Ms. Blanchard at the hospital. I'll grab a cab. Thanks for everything."

* * *

At the hospital, Bradley discharged the guard at Henrietta's door before knocking. Monique stepped out. "Saundra is under arrest at HPD Central Lock-up. Henrietta is safe."

Monique hugged Bradley. "Thank goodness they caught her. I think you should tell Retta this news yourself. Come on. She's too weak to bite," she said smiling.

Bradley followed Monique inside the hospital room. Two big blue eyes locked onto his gaze without blinking. Although still very thin and pale, she looked a lot better. He stopped at the foot of her bed. "I know you don't want me here, but I have news. The police have arrested Saundra, and she's been charged with attempted first-degree murder."

Henrietta covered the bottom of her face with her right hand, and her eyes filled with tears.

He continued, "Her fingerprints match the two found on the handgun. They put her in a line-up, and both Kathleen O'Grady and I identified her. The detective doesn't think any judge will allow bail since she's accused of a capital crime. She doesn't have an attorney, so one will be appointed before she'll respond to any questions. It'll be at least a week before that happens. Maybe even longer."

"Thank you, Bradley. I appreciate everything you've done."

"But…"

Tears rolled down her cheeks. "But I don't think we should see each other again. Please leave."

His heart would burst if he lingered one minute longer. It felt too big for his chest. A heavy fog of sadness enveloped him. He wanted to run to a place where he could grieve in peace. "I'll go. Try to be happy, Henrietta." He turned and quickly made his way to the door. In the hall, he raced to the elevator where he finally broke down. Thank God he was alone in the car.

Chapter 43

Outside the hospital, Bradley hailed a cab and slid onto the back seat. "Hobby Airport," he ordered. "The private jet tarmac." That's when he realized he'd left his small bag in the police car. "Fuck it," he mumbled softly. He reminded himself to hold on until he got home. Then he could let it all out. Until then, he'd remain strong.

It was eight o'clock in the evening by the time he reached his house. Once inside, he strode to the bar, pulled out a shot glass from the cabinet, filled it with Jameson, and knocked it back. He had another before heading into the bathroom.

After a hot shower, he slipped into cut-off jeans and a t-shirt. He turned on the television and grabbed the bottle of Jameson along with the shot glass. He filled the glass and sipped this time. Jameson shouldn't be gulped. What would he do now with Henrietta out of his life? He had nothing to look forward to. He ached to have her in his arms... in his bed... Shit! She was already in his heart, but that's not where she wanted to be. *Was this love?* He hoped not. Lust was so much better. Over and over again, he filled the glass and sipped the smooth whiskey.

When he woke up, the sun was shining through the window, and he was on the floor in front of the sofa with an empty bottle of Jameson next to him. His eyes burned, and his head felt like it might explode if he moved it one iota. He could hear his pulse pounding in his ears. *Jesus, Mary, and Joseph.*

With difficulty, he managed to sit up. The room whirled around him bringing about intense nausea. His mouth was as dry as the Mojave Desert as he crawled to the bathroom and embraced the porcelain god, Kohler. Bradley heaved for what felt like an eternity. The emesis smelled like shit. He thought it might be since he'd probably thrown up his guts.

Covered in a light sheen of sweat and still dizzy, Bradley wasn't sure he was done worshipping the porcelain god. It would probably be better to remain in place for a while. Though he was thirsty, he was afraid to drink water. And consuming any more Jameson was out of the question. In fact, he wasn't sure he'd ever drink his favorite Irish whiskey again.

He wished he could just die. At the very least, he'd be at peace. With no family left, no one would mourn him. Death would be better than life without Henrietta. Still afraid to stand, he rinsed his face in the fresh toilet water and dried it with the terrycloth bathmat off the floor.

He closed his eyes and envisioned his mother's face. She'd be very disappointed in his behavior. She'd never experienced anything like this. So what did she know? Zip.

Thoughts of his mother gave him the impetus he needed to rise and step into the shower. He turned on the water to just under boiling and leaned on the shower wall to maintain his balance. He soaped his body and shampooed his hair. The aroma of the whiskey on his breath was stronger than the clean smell of the soap. Yuk! He balanced himself with his hands against the shower wall and rinsed off. After carefully stepping out, he sat on the toilet to dry himself.

Now in clean clothes and hungry, he made it to the kitchen

without falling. Toast and coffee would do. He didn't even want to think about the pancakes Henrietta loved. If the toast and coffee stayed down, he'd try to eat a light lunch and then head to the office. There he'd have to deal with Mary Ann.

* * *

Henrietta felt like all the air had gone out of her sails. The sad look on Bradley's face when she told him they should not see each other again broke her heart. Poor guy. He'd done nothing to deserve her ill temper. How could she blame him for his ex-wife's behavior?

She recalled meeting him after midnight Mass on Christmas Eve. If she'd not gone to church, she never would've run into him. Literally. She reminisced about the day she'd met him at her brothers' beach cottage in Grand Isle. She'd even gotten up the nerve to ride his damn Harley with him.

But it was here in Houston that she'd discovered his skillful lovemaking. They were incredibly compatible. Sadly, she hated to think about never being in his company again... to think about never being in his company again... enjoying his sensuous kisses... enjoying the feel of his tender touch on her skin... drowning in his silvery-grey eyes... and taking him inside her. Oh yes, Bradley was an expert at pushing her buttons. She should never have told him she refused to ever see him again. *Big mistake.* She'd been taught not to cry over spilled milk, but it was exceedingly difficult not to do so right now.

She finally gave in to her despair and cried until there were no more tears. Crying brought relief although it did not raise her spirit and left her with hiccoughs. Long ago, she'd determined that a one-on-one relationship was not for her. She told herself she preferred a variety of men that she could screw into submission. This agony is what you got in a one-on-one relationship. She'd try to become accustomed to more men again. Perhaps she would succeed. She'd sent the only person she wanted away. Bradley was now out of her life. *Shit. Here come the tears again.*

After the second round of weeping, Henrietta decided she would somehow learn to live without Bradley. *He is just a man. I don't need him to be happy. What I need to do is concentrate on getting well.*

After a week in the step-down unit, Henrietta was discharged to her home on April 28th. She'd been in the hospital for two weeks. It would be great to get home and back into some kind of routine although she would not be able to return to work.

* * *

A month later, Henrietta had regained most of her strength. Her surgeon allowed her to return to her office for half-days of work for a couple of weeks. "We'll decide at your next appointment how much you can do."

Over a cup of coffee in her office, she grabbed The Houston Chronicle and opened it up. Her jaw dropped, and her brows rose when she spied a rather large photograph of herself on the front page. She wondered where the media had found the photo. She'd hoped they'd leave her alone. And if they didn't, she would tell them, "No comment," no matter how many times they asked.

The headline read: Woman Found Guilty of Attempted Capital Murder of Houston Attorney. Henrietta read every word of the article. Saundra drew a ten-year sentence without parole at Mountain View Prison in Gatesville, Texas. It also noted that she had been designated a G-2 custodial level that required her to be housed in a cell for the duration of her sentence.

Her court-appointed attorney had attempted to plea bargain with the District Attorney. He told the DA that Saundra Anderson was willing to plead guilty to a second-degree attempted capital murder. The District Attorney refused. "We have a solid case," he'd replied. "She'll do time. Count on it."

And she would. "Yippee!" she cheered and felt the heavy weight of fear lift from her shoulders. *Thank you, God.* She called for Monique who came running into her office, and handed her the paper.

"I saw it on the morning news. I hope this cheers you up. I miss the old Henrietta. Perhaps you need a change of scenery." She started to leave but turned and suggested, "Think about a month in Jamaica. Maybe you'd get your groove back just like Stella did."

As Monique made her exit, Henrietta hummed the Beach Boys' *Kokomo*. Perhaps she should follow her buddy's suggestion.

Chapter 44

Henrietta thought about Monique's suggestion when she got home. She acknowledged that she did need to get her groove back. Her spark had fizzled and died, and she wanted to find it again. She longed to look forward to each day like she had before Saundra. She was going through the motions of living, unable to enjoy anything. Yes! She'd do it.

After studying about vacation rentals in Jamaica on the Internet, she chose to visit the Sandals Resort in Negril for three weeks of luxury. The price was hefty for a luxurious suite with personal butler service and 24-hour room service on the ground floor of the Plantation Suite Building, but she decided she was worth it. The suite opened up to a lush private garden with a plunge pool and miniature waterfall, and an outdoor shower with a private wall. The adult retreat meant there would be no noisy children to annoy her, but there would probably be numerous honeymooners. *Surely I won't be the only single adult at this resort.*

Without further thought, she made her hotel and air reservations before she could change her mind. She'd tell

Monique and Gloria in the morning at their nine o'clock meeting. They would be envious when she returned with a glorious tan, completely relaxed, and ready to work hard.

Her sleep was deep and dreamless–one of the few nights Bradley had remained away from her dreams. She woke refreshed and anxious to share her news with her partners.

When Gloria and Monique arrived, Henrietta was already seated at the table with papers neatly arranged around her spot at the table. A brewed pot of rich and strong Louisiana coffee along with boiled milk awaited their enjoyment.

Gloria's butt had barely touched her chair when she said, "Okay, Retta. Spill it. What are all those papers?"

Henrietta shot her partners a sly smile. "I have a couple of questions first. Gloria, are you able to carry a full workload?" When Gloria nodded, she continued, "Mo, do you have any plans for the next three weeks that would stop you from carrying a full load of work?"

Monique eyed Gloria before answering, "No plans. What's up?"

Henrietta took a deep breath and began, "For the first time in a long time, I feel the need to get away. You suggested that yesterday, Mo. After you had left, I realized you were right. At first, I thought of spending three weeks in Grand Isle, but summer is the busy season for my brothers' charter services. You mentioned that I needed to get my groove back, and Stella found hers in Jamaica. So that's where I'll be headed on June 1st. I'll be there until my return on June 23rd."

Gloria's eyes rounded, and her smile indicated approval. "Good decision, Retta. I do hope you'll make reservations at one of those pricey resorts and enjoy being waited on."

"And who knows," chimed in Monique. You might meet someone to have fun with."

Henrietta harrumphed. "I'm not going there to meet a man. My reason for the trip is to forget all about one."

Gloria eyed her suspiciously. "You should have told us

you were mourning the end of your relationship with him. We could've helped you."

"Hah hah hah! You really think you and Mo could have accomplished ridding my mind of Bradley Graham? Come on girls. Be real. Gloria, you know what you went through before Jesse realized he loved you. Remember your escape to New York City to avoid seeing him at Christmas time in Thibodaux?"

"Yes, I do," Gloria replied. "And New York City did not erase him from my mind or heart. Jamaica won't do that for you either. The most you can expect is to push him into the back of your consciousness. I believe, however, that Bradley has managed to steal your heart." She shrugged and cocked her head to the right before straightening it. "I know because I've been there."

Henrietta pinched her lips together. "So you don't think I should go?"

Gloria's eyes tightened as though she couldn't believe Retta's question. "Of course you should go. Have fun. Fuck somebody if that's what you want. Just don't expect to rid yourself of Bradley's memory."

"Okay. I'm going. I'll be staying at the Sandals Resort in Negril. I've reserved a fancy butler suite in the Plantation Suite Building. I'll return with a golden tan and an ear-to-ear smile. I'll bring my laptop and iPad just in case I get bored. I'll more than likely be a fan of rum drinks served in coconut shell containers with little decorative umbrellas when I return." She wagged her head and lifted her brows. "I'll be spending a lot of time shopping. Hoping to find bikinis and see-through cover-ups in every color. But for now, it's time to work."

* * *

Bradley had been in a serious slump since leaving Henrietta in Houston. He'd seen her briefly at Saundra's trial, but she'd completely ignored him. Nothing was good anymore. His heart and his soul ached for her. Getting her out of his mind and heart was impossible. If this kept up, he'd go crazy. Getting drunk didn't help either. He prayed she'd come to her senses.

It was with surprise that he received a text from Monique on his cell phone with instructions to call her after eight o'clock that evening. She had news, the message said. "Okay," he replied.

All day long, he wondered what was up. His mind raced about in circles. The hands on the clock didn't seem to move forward. He worried something was wrong with Henrietta. He left as soon as it was five o'clock.

It was his bad luck that the chief executive officer of the company arrived at the elevator at the same time. They shook hands and entered the car together.

Mr. Connelly said, "Bradley, is everything okay?" And before Bradley could answer he continued, "You've been looking peaked for quite some time. It looks as if you've lost weight and you have dark circles under your eyes. Woman trouble?"

"Maybe." He raked his fingers through his hair. "I don't want to be disrespectful, sir, but I'd rather not talk about it."

"Perhaps you need to take some time off. Looks like June will be a slow month for your department, so why don't you plan on a month-long vacation. You've certainly earned it."

"Thank you, sir. I'll think about it."

When the alarm on his iPhone sounded at eight o'clock, he sipped his vodka on the rocks with a slice of lime before dialing Monique Boudreaux's number. His fingers shook, and he could have jumped out of his skin with nerves. *Something had to be wrong.*

"Bradley," she purred into his ear. "I know you're probably anxious to know the reason for my text so I'll get right down to it. Henrietta is okay physically, but she's not been her old self since the shooting. She's despondent and not interested in doing anything. I think she's mourning the loss of your friendship. Of course, she would never admit this.

"I don't usually stick my nose in other people's business, but I know you care about her and maybe even love her. She's leaving on June 1st for three weeks in Jamaica. She's made reservations at the Sandals Resort in Negril in a butler suite at the Plantation Suite Building. I thought you might be interested in this information. Make of this what you will, but NEVER let her know I told you where she'd be."

"Thanks, Monique. I've been going crazy trying to get over her. My CEO told me today that I needed to take some time off. I'll go, but I'll make my reservations for a week before her arrival, so she doesn't get suspicious. I can never thank you enough for this opportunity to make things right with her."

After the call, Bradley felt the weight of the world ease off his shoulders a bit. For the first time in ages, he was hungry. He built himself a large sandwich on French bread. A steak would have been better, but his supply was frozen. Tomorrow would be soon enough for steak. He wolfed down his sandwich with a Coke while reminding himself he'd have to make the most of this opportunity for a second chance with Henrietta. He was certain there would be no other.

He successfully made arrangements to have the suite next to Henrietta's. With a private pool at his disposal, he would have to go shopping for bathing trunks. Then he made flight reservations. His heart felt light. His dick heavy and thick…

Janet Foret Lococo

Chapter 45

May 25th dawned to find Bradley packed and ready to get out of Cut Off. He gulped a cup of coffee, threw his bag in the truck bed, and took off for Louis Armstrong International Airport. His noon flight would arrive in Jamaica five hours later. He consumed a full breakfast in the V.I.P. lounge followed by a couple of cups of coffee. When boarding for his flight was finally announced, he almost skipped to the gate.

He watched the movie, *The Departed,* on his iPad during the flight thinking blood and gore would keep his mind off of Henrietta. It didn't. He shook his head. Anticipation danced in his veins, although he was sure she'd be pissed when she saw him. *Well, what else was new?* He thought it would be a good idea to avoid her on the weekend she arrived. He'd see. He'd spend a lot of time outdoors and would have a glorious tan by the time she turned up. He ordered a vodka martini with a twist of lime to relax.

Bradley's flight arrived at the Montego Bay Airport on time. He grabbed a Joe Cool Taxi to take him to the resort.

Forty-five minutes later, he was at the check-in entrance of his luxurious resort. Before he could step inside, his butler met him, introduced himself as Thomas, welcomed him to the resort, and handed him scented towels to freshen his hands. He led Bradley to a golf cart and placed his luggage on the back of the cart. He outlined all the services he'd provide during Bradley's stay and handed him a cell phone to use to call him for anything.

Bradley was impressed with the ritzy suite. The butler even checked him in from there. He was tired and famished, so he had Thomas reserve a table at Cucina Romano located close to the suites. Thomas drove him to the restaurant and seated him at a table facing the water. He ordered the spicy baby octopus soup followed by tortellini with fresh Caribbean rock lobster tail and ginger scallion dressing along with a bottle of fine Italian wine. He passed on dessert but ordered a cappuccino.

With a full belly, he chose to amble back to his suite. It felt good to stretch his legs. Thomas had unpacked his things, so he showered and hit the sack. No alarm to set. He was asleep in moments, dreaming of making love to Henrietta.

During that first week in Jamaica, his biological clock woke him at six each morning. After cussing about not being able to sleep late, he'd splash water on his face, brush his teeth, and get into swim trunks for a five-mile walk each morning. After a long swim in the Caribbean Sea, he slathered on suntan lotion and toasted beneath the hot sun for an hour on his back and his front. It was good to relax, but Henrietta was never far from his thoughts.

When he arrived at his suite, the butler always had brunch ready on the patio leading to the private pool. He told himself that life was good. It would be much better, however, with Henrietta.

Would she believe the coincidence of them being at the same place? It was, after all, rather far-fetched. Like something you read in a book or saw in a movie. Regardless of what happened when she saw him, he would not snitch on Monique.

* * *

Henrietta shopped at Neiman Marcus for casual clothes and swimwear with an anticipation she'd not experienced before. She wasn't sure what caused the excitement that resulted in her spending a couple of thousand dollars. She believed she would come to a crossroad in her life on this trip and hoped it meant ridding her mind of Bradley Graham. *What about your heart? Can you rid yourself of him there, too?* "Oh, shush," she whispered to herself. *I. Do. Not. Love. Bradley! After all, he was just a fuck.* And who knows. I might meet someone to have fun with in Jamaica.

Her partners came over to ooh and ah over her new clothes. Monique chided, "Boy, that'll put a big dent in your checking account."

Gloria piped up, "Yes it will, but she can easily afford to buy whatever it is she wants. All three of us can." She nodded forcefully once as though to emphasize her statement. "I'm happy you made the decision to take this trip, Retta. You need to get away from everything and have some fun! There's a lot to do in Jamaica." She glanced at her watch. "I'd better go. Jesse asked me not to be too long."

* * *

June 1st finally arrived. Her flight would land at four-thirty in the afternoon, and it would probably take an hour for her to reach the resort. "All aboard," she said out loud as she drove to the airport. She'd Park-N-Fly and didn't relish the thought of lifting her fifty-pound suitcase and the carry-on bag into the shuttle. She generously tipped the driver for his help.

She had a light lunch in the V.I.P. lounge. Thank God she had her iPad so she could read during the flight. Instead, she dozed in her comfortable first-class seat and was surprised when the flight attendant woke her right before they landed.

The baggage attendant led her from the crowded baggage area easily, and she gave him a generous tip. Outside, the sky was blue and cloud-free. He hailed a cab and said, "Enjoy Jamaica, Miss."

She slid into the back seat of a Joe Cool Taxi. During the ride, she admired the lush vegetation in every shade of green imaginable and silently thanked God for seatbelts. She wondered if everyone in Jamaica drove like her taxi driver. Probably. He dropped her off at the registration building for the resort.

Henrietta was tired but excited. Her private butler met her outside the building with scented towels for freshening up. "I am Angelica," she said. "My friends call me Angel. My job is to make sure you have everything you wish," she added as she led her to a golf cart. "I'll take care of everything."

"I didn't check in, Angel."

"No problem. I'll take care of that from your suite." Angel handed her a cell phone. "You will use this phone to call me, no matter the time–day or night. By the way, no tipping is allowed except for butlers–and not until the end of your stay."

Henrietta ambled through the fabulous suite while Angel carried in her bags. Everything was immaculate. She wanted a drink.

Angel suggested she might want to enjoy dinner on her patio. "Would you like a nice, relaxing drink, Miss Henrietta?"

"Yes. I think I would like one of those rum drinks that are widely popular here. And Henrietta is fine."

"Yes, ma'am. While you enjoy your drink, I'll go over a map of the resort with you, and I'll leave it with you. But anywhere you want to go, I will take you in the golf cart. She brought the drink and warned, "Our drinks are made with one-hundred-fifty-one proof rum. Too many will knock you on your backside." After she had reviewed all the restaurants and bars connected to the resort, she hoisted the heaviest bag onto the bag holder. "I'll unpack for you if you like."

"Goodness, Angel. I'm not a queen."

She smiled. "While you're with us, you are. So is it okay

for me to unpack your clothes?"

"Yes. I'm really tired. Could you arrange for dinner from Cucina Romano here in my suite?"

"Of course." Angel turned on the television and downloaded the menu from the restaurant. Look it over while I unpack your things. Make your choices, and I'll see to it." Then she showed Henrietta how to get all information on the TV."

Angel ordered the food. "What about wine? Are you okay with Mondavi?"

"Yes."

"Your dinner will arrive at eight, and I'll serve you. I'll leave you to enjoy the quiet."

And she did although her thoughts were constantly on Bradley. She couldn't stop thinking about him.

After the tasty Italian dinner, Gloria explored the suite and bath while sipping on a glass of merlot. Decorated with dark mahogany furniture and pristine white gauzy curtains leading to the pool area, it was truly magnificent. The bathroom was unbelievably wonderful with its huge Jacuzzi tub and a separate shower large enough for four. An image of Bradley suddenly came to mind. *No. I will not think of him!*

Instead, she called Monique and described her surroundings and the butler services. Mo laughed and told her to have a great time. She reminded, "Don't forget to schedule daily walks if you don't want to balloon out of your beautiful new clothes."

"I take it all is well?"

"Yes. Don't worry about us. Just have a great time. Find your groove again."

"I'll try. I think I'll try snorkeling tomorrow. Can you believe that I was given a cell phone to call my butler day or night? She makes my reservations, takes my dirty laundry, has it cleaned, and returns it. I feel like a queen."

"Wow! Now all you need is a king."

Janet Foret Lococo

Chapter 46

Henrietta slept the sleep of the dead. All night. No dreams. She woke refreshed and full of gusto. There were so many things she wanted to do that it would be difficult to decide what to try first. She tugged on her beach shoes, slid on her sunglasses, and pulled her large-brimmed straw hat over her long hair she'd arranged into a ponytail. After tucking the tail into the crown of the hat, she took off for a long walk on the beach. She called Angel to let her know she'd be ready for a light breakfast of island fruit and coffee by nine. The sky was clear and the briny-fishy smell of the air was so enticing that she decided snorkeling would be her first adventure. She'd have Angel make the arrangements.

About a mile away from the suites, she stopped to watch a man windsurfing smoothly over the water. His hair was dark. His profile and body reminded her of Bradley. Her heart rate accelerated. The life jacket he wore hid his chest. Could it be him? *Don't be ridiculous. This man's legs are a golden tan, totally unlike marine attorney, Bradley Graham. And what would he be doing here, anyway?*

Angel made arrangements for Henrietta to snorkel around lunch. After a shower, Henrietta put on one of her white bikinis before wolfing down her breakfast of island fruit and savoring the Blue Mountain Reserve coffee that was so different from the coffee and chicory popular in South Louisiana.

"Can you arrange dinner at eight o'clock at Bayside Restaurant?"

"Reservations are not required, but you should probably arrive by seven-thirty since it closes at nine. I'll pick you up at seven-twenty and will see that you get a waterside table. I'll leave a cold snack in the refrigerator to tide you over till dinner."

"Sounds good. I'll be ready to leave in five minutes."

Henrietta's guide to the Coral Reef was a powerfully built big, black man. She thought of the movie, *How Stella Got Her Groove Back*. She enjoyed listening to his vibrantly deep voice and Jamaican accent.

Snorkeling was a complete pleasure; the amazing bright hues of the reef and the colorful fish would remain etched in her memory forever. She wished Bradley were here to enjoy the sight. Tomorrow, she would purchase an underwater camera. She completely lost track of time admiring the many species of tropical fish swimming around her and, before she knew it, she and the others were signaled to return to the boat. She would do this again before leaving. Perhaps she should do SCUBA diving if the resort offered a course.

With a pleasant tiredness of body, she returned to her suite. Angel prepared an island rum drink to go with the cold shrimp salad in the refrigerator. "Thank you," Henrietta said. "After you smear my back with lotion, you're free to go until you pick me up at seven-twenty."

Henrietta slathered on suntan lotion on her front and legs and set the timer on her iPhone for forty-five minutes before stretching out face down. She was determined to return to Houston with a wonderful tan. The sun was hot and she didn't want to burn. When the alarm went off, she turned on her back and reset the timer. When the alert sounded, she eased into the pool to cool off. The water caressed her body like the hand of a lover. *Bradley.*

Henrietta dressed in her brand new turquoise empire-waist sundress and flat turquoise and green sandals. She loved the long sarong-like skirt. Angel drove her to the Bayside Restaurant, and Henrietta instructed her to return at nine to take her to Margaritaville. Henrietta balked when Angel insisted on returning to drive her back to the suite from the nightclub. When Henrietta refused to call her late at night, they finally agreed on one in the morning.

Although the popular tourist bar was packed, Angel managed to find her a small table. The crowd was mostly couples, but there were single men, too. She ordered white wine and sipped as she watched everyone having fun. The dancers undulated to calypso, reggae, and oldies music. When the live band played Jimmy Buffet's *Wasting Away Again in Margaritaville*, everyone sang along.

Before long, unattached males made their way to her table and invited her to dance. She gracefully refused. The crowd grew wilder after midnight. She eyed a dark-haired man on the dance floor. His hair and profile reminded her of Bradley. When he turned his partner, she saw his tanned face for only a moment. *Not him, but a lot like him. Shit. I must be seeing things.*

* * *

Bradley's plan to avoid Henrietta was much more difficult to follow than he'd thought it would be. Desperate to see her, he had to fight his feelings as though they were demons. Hoping for a glimpse of her, he'd been windsurfing that morning when she took her first walk along the beach. He'd spotted her solitary figure and had felt her gaze as he glided smoothly across the water. It had required a Herculean effort to keep from turning his head in her direction.

At Margaritaville for dinner at nine o'clock, he had coconut-battered shrimp with sides of potatoes and sautéed squash along with a Red Stripe beer. At ten o'clock, the restaurant closed, and the place became a nightclub. Semi-loud calypso and reggae rang through the rafters. At midnight, a live band appeared on stage to play dance music. The party would probably last until the wee hours before people would stumble to their hotels.

A woman invited him to join her on the dance floor for some hip-hop. It would be impolite to refuse, so he stood and followed her to the dance floor. Out of the corner of his eye, he noticed Henrietta seated at a table facing the water. She was conversing with not one, but two men. And smiling. Her gorgeous turquoise sundress was strapless, and she wore her hair in a ponytail braid. She was simply stunning. Bradley's gut roiled with jealousy. He looked away and left for his suite as soon as the song ended.

By the time he entered his suite, his muscles quivered in anger. Fear of losing her made his chest tighten. He tried to relax by taking deep breaths through his mouth and exhaling through his nose. As slowly as a turtle crossing Highway 1 in Louisiana, his chest loosened, and his muscles relaxed. *What did you expect? Did you think she'd moon over you? Of course guys will hit on her. She's a masterpiece like a Van Gogh or a Renoir.*

Bradley's dreams were filled with Henrietta... together on a windsurfer... tumbling into the aquamarine waters of the Caribbean Sea... stripping off their bathing apparel in the water... and finally mating. He awakened with dried sticky cum on his thigh and in his pubic hair. *Jesus!* Thoroughly disgusted with himself, he hurried to the shower.

This would be the very last day he would remain hidden from her. The fear he experienced had him so dizzy and weak in the legs and knees that he sat on the shower seat and wondered what her reaction would be. He prayed she would not be pissed.

Chapter 47

Henrietta rose at eight on Sunday for an early breakfast. Angel surprised her with a breakfast of pancakes, two strips of bacon, and coffee. "That's too many calories to begin my day," she argued.

"So you say, but you'll burn them during your first SCUBA diving class that begins at eleven o'clock. Now eat your food like a good girl."

Henrietta lifted her brows and cocked her head. "I'm not a girl, Angel. I'm a woman."

Angel turned up the side of her mouth with a slight smile. "So eat your food like a good woman." Then she cackled with laughter.

Henrietta couldn't help but laugh, too. Then she lapped up the pancakes and bacon in short order. With the last bite, she recalled the pancakes Bradley had made for her. These were good, but his were better. Everything is better with him. *Stop thinking about him! You're here to get him out of your head. Right.* But she feared he'd crept into her heart.

Angel drove her to the pool for her lesson. It looked like

she was the only student. Her instructor met her at the golf cart. "Good morning, Miss Henrietta. I am Kymani." Then he turned to Angel, "Since she's the only student today, I'll keep her out longer. I'll call you to pick her up when we're done."

He led Henrietta to the pool where tanks, vests, and breathing apparatus were arranged on the decking. He reviewed each piece of equipment with her. "Are you a good swimmer?"

"Yes, I swim and dive well off a board."

He rolled his lips between his teeth. "Good. We'll get in the pool at the level where your head will remain above water while you're on your knees. Strap on your life vest and listen to what I say. Never, ever attempt a dive without a life vest. Got it?"

She nodded and strapped on the navy blue Body Glove and flippers. She didn't need his help to strap on the tanks or to slide her head between the tubing connected to the mouthpiece. Then she grabbed the heavy-duty goggles.

When Kymani instructed her to put her face in the water and inhale and exhale through the mouthpiece, she complied. It felt kind of funny, and her breathing accelerated. Her heart raced with an adrenaline spike. She deliberately slowed her breathing down. *Ah... that's better. Remain calm and this'll be a piece of cake.*

When Kymani tapped her shoulder, she raised her head. "Good," he said. "Your breathing was too fast initially, but you did well controlling it. Now I want to see you swim underwater to the deep end of the pool."

Floating effortlessly while only kicking her flippers was wonderful. She wondered if this was how astronauts felt when they floated through space. She couldn't wait to try deeper water.

Kymani kept her swimming on the deep end of the huge pool. Her lesson ended at three. It was hard to believe she'd been in the water for three hours. After he had called Angel to come for her, he said, "You're a quick study, Miss Henrietta.

Tomorrow, we'll go out on the open water. I will show you how to get into the water from a boat and will dive with you. Same time. Angel knows where to bring you. Remember that you're not certified to dive without an instructor."

Angel drove her back to the suite, and she chattered about her lesson all the way there. "What about dinner, Miss Henrietta? Where would you like to go?"

"I haven't a clue. I want really good food, and I want to look sexy."

"Why don't you try Barefoot by the Sea? You can look as sexy as you like. You can even go barefoot. Evenings in Jamaica suggest island casual which translates to anything goes. It is located on the sand at the water's edge and is lovely at night. Dinner is served from six to nine-thirty. There's no need to be there before eight."

"Okay. Do it. Try for a table facing the water."

"Will do. You need a snack. Fruit salad with totally different fruit from the one you had earlier." She set the plate on the table near the pool. And along with it, a fancy rum drink. "I'll come for you at seven-forty."

"Fine." Henrietta would eat and then work on her tan.

* * *

From the time he woke on Saturday, Bradley thought the day would never end. Tomorrow was the big day he'd *accidently* run into Henrietta. The meeting would have to be carefully planned. He parasailed in the morning. That was fun but had not taken much time. And Henrietta remained on his mind. After that, he jet skied for a couple of hours. Again, his thoughts were on Henrietta. Now back at his suite, he planned what he'd do tomorrow. Unable to sit still, he paced the floor of the living room. If there was such a thing as a body being on red alert, his was.

He knew Henrietta walked each morning. He'd spied on her with binoculars. Her walks always took her east. Tomorrow, he'd go west and take his field glasses. Just like in the song, he

259

hoped they'd *Meet in the Middle*. Whatever the outcome, he would see her tomorrow. He could wait no longer.

Visions of Henrietta haunted his dreams. If this kept up, he'd lose his mind.

* * *

According to Angel, Cosmo's Seafood Restaurant & Bar was also popular after dark. "It's on the beach and offers recorded music," she told Henrietta. "They play everything from old hits to SOCA–a blend of soul and calypso. You can play pool, drink, and mingle. And you can attend in a bikini," she added. "It's known for wild and raunchy parties. It is not included in the all-inclusive package. Non-guests are required to purchase a US one hundred dollar night pass."

Henrietta's brows lifted, and her eyes widened. That seems a bit steep."

"The fee provides all the food and drink you can consume AND the entertainment, but it's still steep. Action begins at ten-thirty and often goes on until two in the morning."

Henrietta nodded. "You've talked me into going. Can you drive me there and pick me up?"

"Of course. When do you want to leave?"

"Ten is okay. And unless I call you earlier, pick me up at one o'clock. Okay?"

Angel nodded agreement. "You'll have fun."

Cosmo's was packed with people that were almost naked and sweaty from dancing so much. She asked for a seat upstairs. Angel had said it was less crowded and cooler there. As usual, her butler was right.

Henrietta eyed the couples gyrating on the slippery dance floor. She couldn't help but notice the tall, handsome, dark-haired man dancing with a lovely island native. He reminded her so much of Bradley. Same build. Same height. She couldn't see his face, but his prowess on the dance floor was remarkable. He never missed a beat. He had moves she doubted Bradley would ever think of trying. *Chill, woman. It's not him. Why would he be here?* When she searched the sea of people again, the man and woman had vanished into thin air. Was she hallucinating? She didn't think so.

She sipped the sweet rum drink and toyed with the paper umbrella while her thoughts rambled. Tears filled her eyes, but she patted them away with her paper napkin. She'd come here to rid her mind and heart of Bradley, or as Monique suggested, to get her groove back. Henrietta desperately needed something, but she didn't know what it was.

The scene of an old-fashioned revival meeting from a movie she'd seen came to mind. She closed her eyes to recall it. Under a big tent, sweaty attendees clapped their hands together and shouted, "Amen," like punctuation at the end of each sentence leaving the mouth of the traveling preacher. Accompanied by a lot of clapping and singing, the minister had preached about hell, fire, and damnation. "Who wants to be saved?" he screamed.

People started beating their chests and shouting, "Me! Me! Me!" After pausing and looking over the audience, he shouted, "Who wants to testify and be redeemed?" Everyone shouted again, raised their hands above their heads, and stomped their feet.

One woman rose from the audience and walked with her shoulders drooped and her head down in shame toward the preacher. When she reached him, she loudly proclaimed her sins; hate, drugs, stealing, and fornication. The preacher touched her head and said, "You are saved, Sister." She returned to her seat in the back, her posture straight and proud.

That was easy. Without warning, what she needed became crystal clear to Henrietta. Redemption. Not from the fires of hell, but from her inability to trust herself that made it impossible for her to trust Bradley. She would have to learn to trust her feelings and actions. It would not be easy. She decided to begin her positive affirmations as soon as she returned to her suite.

Janet Foret Lococo

Chapter 48

Henrietta crawled out of bed for her daily walk at eight o'clock. She splashed water on her face, brushed her teeth, ran a brush through her hair, and pulled it up into a ponytail. After slipping into her beach shoes and plopping on a sunhat, she headed for the beautiful white sand. The sunglasses from Bradley looked great, kept the glare away, and made her feel like a movie star. She'd headed east every day since her arrival. Today she would follow her habitual route. Her gaze remained on the invitingly beautiful turquoise water. Later today, she was scheduled to SCUBA dive with her instructor. Filled with confidence, she automatically straightened her spine.

Bradley filled her thoughts so much that she chided herself. *You spent all that money to come here to forget him, but he's all you think about.* "Let it go," she mumbled right before she collided with someone walking in the opposite direction. His arms circled her waist to prevent her from falling.

Anger made her face burn. She should have been watching where she was going. Didn't she abhor people who walked around stores and shopping malls with their eyes glued to a cellphone? And here she'd done the same thing except that the sea, and not a cell phone, had her attention. When she looked up, it was into familiar silvery-grey eyes. His arms quickly dropped from her waist.

Speechless, her mouth gaped open and her hands moved to her cheeks. She closed her eyes. *This had to be a hallucination.* When she opened her eyes, though, he was still there. She reached for his arms to make sure this wasn't a dream. *He's real. Not a figment of my imagination.*

Her fisted hands moved to her hips. "What in the name of God are you doing here?"

Bradley cocked his head to the right and tightened his mouth. "I take it that you're not happy to see me." His look became guarded. "Am I right?"

It did not take her long to rally. She pinched her lips before snarling, "I suppose Monique told you where to find me."

He hesitated and appeared guilty as charged. She could tell he didn't want to lie to her. She was certain he knew she'd be pissed. But he'd probably agreed to keep quiet about Monique's involvement. He took too long to answer, sealing his fate.

"You don't have to answer. Your hesitation proves I'm right." She drew in an exasperated breath and shrugged. "I should have known. She preached to me about my behavior toward you while I was hospitalized. She thought I was wrong to throw you out and to tell you I never wanted to see you again."

"I guess you're pissed, but I refuse to lie to you about how I got here. Now Monique will be disappointed, and maybe angry that I did not keep her secret. I've been completely lost since you sent me away. So much so that my boss insisted I take a vacation. He said I looked like shit and asked if I had *woman problems.* I've been here since May 25th, and I leave on June 23rd. So I'm here until then. When do you leave?"

"Another coincidence? June 23rd."

He took hold of her arms and said, "Look, I know you have trust issues. So do I. But I don't want to call it quits with you. Why don't we just concentrate on having fun together while we're here? There's a world of activities to experience." He squeezed her arms, and she gazed into his silvery-grey eyes. "What do you say?"

She inhaled deeply and let her breath out slowly. He could probably see the wheels turning inside of her head. "I suppose so," she responded. "This is mostly a couple environment and single women get hit on at every bar. So okay." This was her chance at redemption, and she'd be damned if she'd miss it. "I have my first SCUBA dive with my instructor this afternoon so we can do dinner. By the way, where are you staying?"

He appeared to be uncomfortable with her question but answered, "In the suite next to yours." He shot her a sly smile. "You could knock on the wall when you're ready to leave for dinner."

"You seem to have thought of everything," she asserted. "My butler, Angel, will have a light lunch ready when I return since I don't want to dive with a full belly."

"At what time is your appointment and where do you meet your instructor?"

"One o'clock at the boat launch where we'll board the boat and go to the dive site."

"Okay. I look forward to our dinner and maybe even some dancing. Is seven o'clock okay?"

She nodded. Her stomach quivered with excitement as she left him to walk to her suite. Damn he looked good with his golden tan. The man she'd sighted at clubs and parasailing had to have been him. *I want him, but I really must try to abstain. Jesus Christ! You haven't seen him for months, and you're already thinking about having sex with him. Wake up and smell the roses, Retta. This is about your redemption. It's about trust, not sex. So don't screw up.*

After her light lunch, Angel took Henrietta to the boat site for her first real dive. She couldn't wait to try everything she'd been taught by Kymani.

Henrietta and her instructor dropped off the side of the boat together. Backward, like she'd practiced in the pool. The underwater world was not silent and much greater than the deep end of the pool. The bubbling sound of her exhalations seemed noisy at first, but she soon tuned them out.

The feeling of weightlessness was the most freeing sensation she'd ever experienced. Kymani had said the trick was to relax and let the water support her body, so she did. Just as he'd taught her, she tried to be as still as possible and enjoy the freedom from gravity.

The loss of peripheral vision at first bothered her, but she quickly got used to it. Kymani had thought of everything, and she became more and more confident. Her instructor had explained she might feel the need to urinate underwater because the body speeds up the synthesis of urine. He'd told it was okay to pee in the water. *Yuk!* She'd just hold it since the dive would last only thirty minutes.

Following Kymani's hand signal, she moved up to the water's surface and climbed the ladder into the boat. An adrenalin rush had her giggling like a teenager. She thanked her instructor for an amazing experience and asked if they could dive the next day.

"Yes," he answered. "Same time, same place. Have Angel drive you. I might have a nice surprise for you."

There's nothing he could surprise me with. In her suite, she ate the mixed fruit salad Angel had left in the refrigerator. Next to the salad was a pitcher of the sweet rum drinks she so enjoyed. She removed her clothing, slathered her body with suntan lotion, and spread out on the chaise lounger for forty-five minutes on each side. She'd be gloriously tan when she returned home. She smiled.

Her thoughts turned to Bradley. What a hunk! And now

with that deep tan, his eyes appeared even lighter. Like you could see through them. *Was he serious about her knocking on the wall when she was ready to leave?* She wasn't sure, but would try it.

When she felt as well done as a slice of toast, she slid into the pool. The cool water eased over her hot skin. Perhaps she'd entered another world and had become a water nymph, like in the classical mythology she'd enjoyed in high school. *Are you crazy? Water nymph?*

She left the pool for the shower and wrapped her body in a thirsty white bath blanket afterward. After filling a glass with the rum drink, she sat at the desk and called her partners.

Chapter 49

Bradley couldn't believe the mighty Henrietta Blanchard had accepted his being at the same resort so easily. She'd appeared miffed when she'd run into him and realized he was the man she'd ordered out of her life forever. God, he'd wanted so badly to kiss her inviting mouth. Unfortunately, that would have to wait until she made the first move.

He made reservations for Kimonos, an Oriental restaurant specializing in exotic cuisines in an interactive way. Dress code was evening resort wear. He'd ask Thomas what that meant.

Anxiety caused a churning in his stomach along with restless legs. He couldn't remain in one spot for long. *Jesus, Mary, and Joseph.* He told himself to chill out, but to no avail. Even fifty laps in the Olympic-sized pool didn't calm him. He dried himself with a towel and headed back to his suite while repeating his mantra, "Don't screw up! Don't screw up! Don't screw up!" He was pretty sure that if he did, he would never get a second chance.

He kept telling himself he didn't love her but admitted he liked her a lot. Much more than a lot. She was important to him... fun to be with... smart... well educated... beautiful... the same profession... not to mention the hot sex capable of setting the sheets on fire. *Face it, Bradley. She's more than important to you. This time around, you could sink deeply into love or die of a broken heart.*

He showered, splashed on a little of the cologne she loved, and pulled up his tan stretch underwear so it wouldn't show through his white linen pants. He slid his sockless feet into leather moccasins before putting on his floral print white-on-white linen shirt from Nordstrom. He tapped his heels on the floor as he sat and waited for Thomas to pick him up.

When Thomas finally arrived, Bradley's heart banged against his ribs in anticipation of seeing the woman he feared he already loved. He knocked on the wall dividing their suites and moved to the entrance of hers.

She was a vision in her strapless white all-in-one pants outfit. Each pant leg had four, wide see-through lace bands. Her hair was in a messy bun on top of her head. Skinny black earrings finished her sexy look. He immediately wanted to drag his lips along her neck and collarbone.

"You look wonderful, Henrietta. One thing is missing, though," he said as he sat her in the golf cart. "And I've got it right here." He produced a beautiful white orchid. "For your hair," he added.

"Thanks. How thoughtful of you. I think I'll put it on the side of my bun, but I'll need your help."

"No problem," he replied and pinned it in place. "We're going to Kimonos Oriental Restaurant with interactive entertainment."

"Sounds good. I haven't been there, and you know I love Oriental food."

When they arrived at the restaurant, Bradley told Thomas he'd call when they were ready to leave. The décor was slightly exotic with an air of mystery. The dim lighting showcased the red accents and mahogany windows resembling the sliding screens of East Asia.

Tepanyaki style eating meant sitting around the table with six to eight people, but Bradley insisted on a table for them alone. The chef would work on the cooking surface preparing various meats and vegetable. He ordered a bottle of Caymus Cabernet Sauvignon.

The chef asked, "What would you like?"

Bradley turned to Henrietta and asked, "Are you game to try anything?"

She puckered her lips before she nodded. He turned to the chef and said, "Feed us. We want to taste as much as we can tonight. If we like it, we'll come back and ask for you. And you'll get a handsome tip."

"Tipping is not necessary. It is in the all-inclusive price."

"Are you going to tell me you can't use more money?"

"No sir, but we are not allowed to accept tips."

"So don't accept it. I'll just slide it into your pocket. Now get with it and feed us."

And feed them he did. The food was incredibly good and the wine excellent. They tried bite-size samples of chicken breast marinated in mirin, sake and served with Teriyaki sauce. Then they ate skirt steak in fried garlic and sesame ginger sauce, plus marinated tiger shrimp in miso lemon sauce, bay scallops in Ponzu sauce, and finally, grilled fish brushed with Japanese BBQ Sauce. Henrietta even tried seaweed salad. They shared a dessert of ginger *crème brulée*. They laughed at the chef's antics whiled he cooked, and he even sang for them.

Bradley kept the conversation light to avoid any chance of pissing her off. She avoided any mention of the shooting, so he didn't bring it up. He couldn't wait to take her into his arms and kiss her with wild abandon. Glimpses of their time spent in Grand Isle popped up into his mind without any warning.

Two and a half hours later, they called for Thomas to take them to Alfred's Beach Palace in the center of the seven-mile Negril beach. The word was that this place showcased some of the best local rock and reggae artists in Jamaica. Thomas told them the stage was set up on the beach and dancing took place on the sand, under the stars.

When they entered Alfred's, they discovered it was not at all a palace. A contortionist was performing. At the end of her act, the Master of Ceremonies announced the limbo contest would begin in thirty minutes. "Want to try it?" he asked Henrietta.

"You're kidding, right?"

He shot her what he hoped was a sexy smile and shrugged. "Maybe, but maybe not."

It was her turn to laugh. "I'm not at all ready to show the world how bad I am at the limbo rock."

He took a big sip from his frozen Pina Colada. "These are delish. Very refreshing."

"You'd best beware if you don't want Thomas to have to pour you into the golf cart. Angel told me these drinks are all made with one-hundred-eighty proof rum."

The live band finally played something they could dance to. Bradley pulled her close and breathed in her Oscar de la Renta scent. She felt wonderful in his arms. He'd waited so long for this moment. *Don't blow it.* When the song finished, he kept her in his arms and asked, "Would you prefer a walk on the beach at our resort or to stay here and dance?"

Her eyes softened. "Definitely a walk on the beach."

He called for Thomas.

Chapter 50

Henrietta slipped out of her outfit and into one of her white bikinis and topped it with her black lace cover-up. When she got to the beach, Bradley was already there.

His gaze warmed her all over, and her nipples rose into tiny steeples. It was impossible to describe her hunger for this man. Stepping into his waiting arms, she realized she'd been yearning for him ever since he'd left Houston. She took his face in her hands and gazed deeply into his silvery-grey eyes. "It seems like I've waited to do this forever," she whispered as she brazenly captured his lips with her own.

It was a blazing kiss. One that made tingles travel all the way down to her toes. His tongue teased hers into mating with his; in and out... sliding against hers... making her wet for him. Her heart banged against her ribs, and she could hear it thumping in her ears.

He pulled his mouth from hers. "So have I, Henrietta, every night and every day. Scenes of you and me on the beach in Grand Isle and of us making love in Houston have haunted my dreams. I felt a deep melancholy when you sent me away. Nothing was good. I didn't care about anything. I went to work each day and left as soon as possible for home, where I was equally miserable thinking of you." He kissed the thin scar left by the surgery to remove the bullet where his ex-wife had shot her. Sooner or later, they would have to discuss this. *Not now.*

"I drank myself into oblivion the night I returned to Cut Off from Houston. The following morning, I woke up on the floor in my living room with an empty bottle of Jameson next to me, and a headache from hell. I feared the top of my head might explode. I barely made it to the bathroom to throw up. I sat on the floor next to the toilet until I was sure I had no more to come up.

People at work began asking me what was wrong, but I couldn't tell them. When my boss told me how bad I looked and that I needed to take a month, I said I'd do just that. But I didn't know where I wanted to go. I just wanted to see you.

"Imagine my surprise when I received a text from Monique asking me to call her after eight that night. I feared something was wrong with you. When she told me your plans, I was flattered she trusted me enough to share that information. She told me where you were staying, and I arranged to arrive a week before you did." He shrugged. "So here we are."

He kissed her again and pulled her tightly against him. His hard-as-nails erection poked at her belly.

She wanted him but felt the need to finish telling him what she needed him to know. Right here. Right now. Before she lost her nerve. She continued, "After enough time passed, and Saundra was safely in jail, I began to examine my life and promiscuous behavior under a microscope." She stopped to gather enough courage to go on. "I didn't like what I learned. After deep exploration and recalling my life's experiences, I realized that I'd never trusted men since Uncle Carl. And even worse, I have never trusted myself to choose wisely." Her face warmed, and she paused. "I'm ashamed to admit that I've used men ever since my first sexual experience as a high school sophomore, but that's exactly what I did. Please kiss me again, Bradley."

Her body melted against his. Her nipples were so hard they were painful. He rolled her across his erection, and she ground her pelvis into it. When she started to pull away, he begged, "Please, Henrietta. Don't push me away. You and I both know that you want me. You surely must know how much I want you. Please let me love you tonight."

"Not here," she replied. "There are bound to be people on this beach even though we can't see them."

He quickly led her to his suite and pulled her toward the pool/patio. He removed his clothing and slipped into the water. Within seconds, she was naked and with him under the waterfall. Skin to skin, they kissed–a long, deep, kiss she felt all the way down to her toes. Her genitals pulsed.

"Shit," he murmured.

"What's wrong?"

"I forgot to bring a condom."

"I'm still on the pill, and I have not been with anyone since you. I've never had sex without a condom except with you."

"Neither have I," he murmured as he slid into her. Since you, I have not been even remotely interested in any other woman. She wrapped her long legs around his waist and took him deep inside.

"Jesus, Mary, and Joseph. It's been so long that I don't think I'll last," he whispered in her ear and stilled within her.

He pulled out of her and began rubbing her clitoris in hard circles and pushing his fingers inside her until she could no longer bear it. *Oh, dear God. This feels so good.* Her respiratory rate rose along with her heartbeat.

"Now, Bradley!" she urged.

He rammed himself into her and rocked back and forth. Deeper and deeper… faster and faster… making waves in the pool with each stroke… She shattered with a monstrous quaking orgasm that sucked him into his own completion.

He kissed her again. "I've missed you so." His hands caressed her body. "You're so beautiful. Can't you see that we just seem to fit together?"

She nodded. "Yes."

"I'd love for you to spend the night, Henrietta," Bradley said after making love to her a second time–this time in his bed.

"No. I don't think I should."

"Why not?"

"Because I don't think I'm ready for that." Although she wanted to stay where she was, she managed to rise from his bed and glanced at her watch. "I know you're disappointed. I have SCUBA diving tomorrow at one o'clock. We can get together afterward if you like." She turned when she got to the door, blew him a kiss, and said, "Good night. I had fun."

* * *

After she had left, Bradley lay in his bed, still naked. Fun? Was that what had just happened between them? Fun? What about the passion that seemed to rock their worlds? Didn't that count for more than fun? He wagged his head. No woman had ever confused him more than this one. He must love her to put up with this shit. His thoughts startled him, but in his heart, he knew he wasn't sure.

He'd best try to get to sleep. Tomorrow was another day and might end up differently. He shook his head slowly and rolled his eyes heavenward. He had to admit that Henrietta was one difficult piece of work. *But worth it.*

There was a lot to explore in Jamaica, and he hoped they could do it together.

* * *

Henrietta let herself into her suite still unsure as to why she'd not accepted Bradley's offer to spend the night. She'd told him she wasn't ready, and she wasn't. "Harrumph." *It was wonderful. They probably would have gotten little sleep.*

They would have to discuss her lack of trust and his. She wasn't sure about when this discussion should take place, only that it would have to for them to move along in their relationship. *Relationship? Was she crazy?*

She stretched out on her bed and pulled up one of the pillows to hug. *It could have been Bradley is she'd agreed to his invitation.* Worn out, she soon was asleep–her dreams filled with Bradley.

Janet Foret Lococo

Chapter 51

Henrietta's steps were brisk, and her thoughts were on Bradley as she walked east. It was already warm and humid indicating the day would be another hot one. She wiped off the light sheen of moisture coating her neck, arms, and legs with a hand towel. The sun glistened on the water. In the distance, she noticed a catamaran moving over the waters of the Caribbean Sea. Up in the sky, someone parasailed. It looked like it might be fun, but she wasn't sure she'd be brave enough to try it.

On the beach, people–mostly couples–were already stretched out on loungers on the beach working on tans. It wouldn't be long before they would have to open their large beach umbrella. Some had taken to the water and floated on rafts. She was happy she'd decided to come to Jamaica. She smiled and thought she might have even started to get her groove back. Monique would laugh at that. She'd call the office when she returned to her suite. Meanwhile, she'd enjoy her long walk.

She was surprised to find Bradley at the boat launch

when she arrived to go for her SCUBA dive. Kymani greeted her with a huge smile on his shiny black face and asked, "So how do you like your surprise?"

She glanced at Bradley before returning her gaze to her instructor. "What surprise?"

Kymani pointed to Bradley and said, "Him. Mister Bradley is a certified SCUBA diver and will accompany you and me on our dive. Okay?"

She quickly turned to Bradley and her eyes widened. "You're certified?" She wagged her head and murmured, "I wonder what else I don't know about you."

"I heard that, and the answer is not much. Now will you allow me to tag along?"

She stuck out her chin. "Yeah, but don't forget that I'm a beginner, and I only pay attention to Kymani's instructions."

Bradley laughed out loud. "Come on. Get in the boat."

The dive was glorious. She remembered all she'd learned and was delighted not to make any errors with Bradley present. Henrietta loved the feeling of freedom she got during a dive and couldn't believe she'd never tried it before. Huge angelfish were close enough to touch. She snapped pictures with her new underwater camera. Colorful tropical fish swam about in schools. Kymani kept her out of the way of a beautiful jellyfish. Coral in so many different colors and textures covered an ocean wreck beneath them. Henrietta took more pictures.

Kymani took them down to the forty feet limit Sandals resort enforced. There was too much to see in too little time. But if she'd learned anything about diving, it was to follow safety precautions. All too soon, Kymani signaled them to rise to the surface of the water.

It was close to three o'clock when they returned to the launch. An endorphin overload had her chattering away about everything she'd seen. She asked Kymani if they could dive on the cliff side of the beach the next day.

"Same time and place tomorrow. Enjoy the rest of your

day."

Angel was waiting in the golf cart. "It's my turn," she said. "Since you two are doing things together, Thomas and I decided to take turns taking you wherever you want to go. Where to?"

Bradley grinned. "We have enough time to try parasailing before it's time to watch the sunset at Rick's Café."

Henrietta frowned and looked over her sunglasses. "I don't think I want to do that."

"Why not?" he questioned as he peered into her eyes without blinking.

She shrugged and lowered her gaze. "I just don't want to."

Bradley howled with laughter. "You're just afraid to try it. Why not admit it?"

"I am not afraid!" She asserted and stomped her foot on the sand. *Jesus. Like a first grader.*

"Yes, you are. Admit that you're a big chicken." He caressed her upper arms. "You'll miss a wonderful experience." Then he put his hands on his hips and flapped his bent elbows up and down and said, "Pok, pok, pok, Parok!"

She hated that he was right. She was afraid but would never admit it. She swallowed and snarled, "Okay. Okay. Okay. I'll go." She continued slyly, "I might even knock your ass out of the seat, so beware."

"You heard her, Angel. Take us to the parasailing launch."

The closer they got to the launch site, the faster her heart raced. She tried to swallow her fear but was not successful when Angel announced, "Here you are. Call when you're ready to head for Rick's."

Bradley took her hand in his and led her to the shuttle boat that would take them to a small boat out in the sea. The crew helped them board and get into life vests before fitting them with parasailing harnesses.

He took her hand and said, "I know you're afraid, but I promise you'll love it. Just keep an open mind. I would never let anything happen to you."

Henrietta nodded. Her insides trembled. As soon as the boat began to move forward, she closed her eyes and gripped Bradley's hand. To her surprise, take off was very smooth as was the boat ride. When she opened her eyes, her muscles relaxed, and she smiled. It was like flying. *Correction. It was flying. Like birds.* Bradley whispered that their sail was almost four hundred feet up.

"I don't want to hear how high we are. Shush!"

The great view of all the resorts lining the Negril coast was awesome. She was happy Bradley had insisted she try this. She turned to him smiling. "Thank you, Bradley, for being insistent."

Their landing back on the deck of the boat was as smooth as the ride. Before departing from the shuttle boat, Bradley paid for photos the crew had taken of them during take off, while they were up in the air, and the landing. In the first ones, her eyes looked as big as saucers.

"I gather you enjoyed this experience."

"Yes. It was not at all what I expected... much more... not frightening... delightful..."

They'd planned to watch the sunset from Rick's Café, but it was packed with people. Instead, they'd told Angel to head for their suites so they could watch the sunset from the beach.

Henrietta carried the large pitcher full of rum drink and two glasses while Bradley spread out a large bath blanket he'd brought from his suite onto the warm sand at the water's edge. They sat and watched as the fiery golden globe slowly slipped into the Caribbean and the sky around it turned coppery red. Ever so slowly, the red turned into molten orange, then to coral, and finally into lavender and the darker purple that came before the sky turned into night.

"The stars will be out shortly," Bradley said. "I've never seen the sky from here. How about you?"

"Never. I love sitting out here, away from a crowd, where

we can relax and do nothing at all."

Bradley sipped his drink. "Why don't we plan to windsurf in the morning? It's pretty neat."

"If we both can fit on one contraption, I'm willing to do it. Otherwise, I'd probably run into you and cause a catastrophe."

"Together is possible. It's called tandem surfing. There are usually two large sails on a really big board."

"I'll give it a try, then. But I don't want to control a sail."

"We'll see if they have a larger board with only one sail and something for a passenger to hold on to. I wouldn't want you to fall off."

"Okay," Henrietta said and stretched out on the towel. Her muscles ached from all the physical activity. But when Bradley leaned down and captured her lips with his, all her aches disappeared into the caress of a light breeze.

Chapter 52

When they returned to their suites, Henrietta told Angel she and Bradley would be dining in her suite around eight. Bradley suggested food from Bayside Restaurant, a French Brasserie. Before ordering, he studied the menu and they made their selections before he returned to his suite to shower and shave. He left Henrietta with a searing kiss that had her wanting more.

At the door, her turned and smiled, "Later, beautiful."

She stepped into the shower, lathered up with the clean-smelling body wash Sandals provided, and washed her hair. She was pleased with the tan she caught sight of in the full-length mirror. After applying lots of moisturizer, she sprayed a little of her favorite scent to the sides of her neck and between her breasts. *Just in case.*

From the closet, she selected a long, sarong-type, multi-colored silk dress with spaghetti straps. She chose to remain barefoot. A knock on the wall let her know Bradley would be there shortly.

Like a dark Greek god, he entered wearing white linen

shorts, a white muscle shirt, and flip-flops. "You look ravishing," he cooed as he kicked off his shoes and spread out his arms.

"You're not bad yourself," she smiled, lifted her brows, and stepped forward. Already, her heart rate escalated. She breathed in his sensual scent and rested her head on his chest. "You smell so good. I could breathe your scent forever."

Their lips had just met when a knock on the door signaled their dinner had arrived. Thomas and Angel came in together, each rolling a cart. "We'll get back to that later," he murmured into her ear. "I'm starving."

"Me, too." She took his hand and led him to the patio. He seated her.

Thomas poured perfectly chilled French Pouilly-Fuissé saying, "For your enjoyment while we get things together for you.

From the kitchen area, Angel added, "Thomas and I took the liberty of adding to your selections some foods we think you'll enjoy. I hope that was okay."

Bradley nodded his approval. The butlers began serving their meal. First up, were bowls of delicious piping hot Bouillabaisse, served with roasted slices of French baguette. It was especially good after their very active day. Henrietta and Bradley lapped up *escargots* in phyllo purses with garlic-parsley butter, crab cakes on a bed of field greens, and followed the appetizers with mussels in a white wine sauce, crispy pommes frites, and French bread. They sipped on wine throughout the meal.

Two hours later, Thomas asked, "How about dessert?"

"No," they said as one.

"Thank you for taking such good care of us," Henrietta said. "There's no way I can eat another bite."

"That goes for me, too. We're staying in, so you both can have the night off," Bradley added.

The butlers eyed each other with sly smiles and rolled the

carts away in short order.

"Goodnight," said Angel.

"Sleep well," added Thomas.

Bradley rose, took Henrietta's hand, and pulled her into his body. "I know what I want for dessert. Let's finish what we started when I first arrived." He captured her mouth, and his tongue toyed with her lips. She opened for him, but he kept up his teasing.

Goosebumps rose all over her body and thrills ran up and down her spine. Her body automatically molded to his. She rubbed herself on his erection pushing against her belly. Finally, he entered her mouth with his feral tongue and investigated every nook and cranny. He tasted of wine and garlic–good enough to eat. Nobody had ever kissed her like this. Never. She was on fire. He drove her wild with his frantic kisses.

He pulled his mouth away and put space between them. "Your dress is beautiful, but I think you have entirely too many clothes on," he said as he slid the straps off her shoulders and found the side zipper. The silk floated down her legs onto the floor around her feet, and his eyes widened. His silvery gaze trapped hers. "No underwear?"

She nodded. "Just for you."

His hands caressed her breasts and slipped down her sides to her buttocks. "Jesus, Mary, and Joseph. Have you any idea how much I want you?"

"Yes, but I want to see you, too."

He pulled his muscle shirt over his head and dropped it to the floor. She unbuttoned his shorts and slid them down over his bare buttocks. He pushed them down to the floor and stepped out of them.

"Aha. I see that you left your underwear home, too. I wonder what you had in mind."

"Socrates said that wonder is the beginning of wisdom." He picked her up and carried her to her bed. "Does the lady say yes to further activity?"

She chided, "The lady would be most disappointed if more action were not forthcoming."

"You just said the magic words. Now we're going to make long and slow love, and you'll come screaming my name. I'm going to…"

She interrupted. "Oh, yeah?" she queried. "*I need A Little Less Talk and a Lot More Action*, like Toby Keith sings in the song."

And she got it… all night long… one orgasm on top of another… until she was blissfully boneless and sated. There would be no long walk in the morning for either of them. They'd burned up the sheets and a huge amount of calories during their amorous night.

It was almost noon when Bradley finally awakened. The smell of coffee wafted into the bedroom from the kitchen. He bounced out of bed, quickly pulled on his clothes, and followed the smell. There was Angel, about to begin preparing their breakfast.

He stopped her. "She loves my pancakes," he whispered and made a list of what he needed.

"But this is my job," she whispered back.

"I know, but I want to make her pancakes. Now skedaddle and bring me the ingredients on the list."

When Angel returned, he got to work mixing the batter and cooking the pancakes and pork sausages she liked.

Henrietta padded silently to the kitchen. Wrapped in a sheet, she found him at the stove. "I thought I was dreaming," she announced. "You made me pancakes. Wow! I'm so impressed. And starving."

When she looked at the clock and frowned, he cautioned, "Don't worry. I already notified Kymani we wouldn't be diving today."

"Thank goodness. I hate missing appointments. Never do."

Later in the afternoon, they paddled around on an aquatrike until it was time to watch the sun sink like a big, golden light over the water.

They had dinner at the Sundowner, feasting on West Indian Wahoo Kebab, grilled skewers of wahoo, bell pepper, and red onions along with yam hush puppies with a spicy glaze and sautéed veggies. And wine.

They called it an early night so they could sail early in the morning and keep their SCUBA diving appointment scheduled for one o'clock. While waiting for their ride back, Henrietta said, "I've had a great time with you."

"But," he asked as he lifted his brows and pinned her gaze with his own.

She lowered her gaze to the ground. "I think we need to sleep in our own suites."

"Did I do something wrong?" He questioned with a show of concern.

"No. You've done everything right. It's me, Bradley."

He nodded his head up and down and dropped his arm from her waist. "You're afraid I'm getting too close, right?"

"I don't know. I'm so confused."

"And fearful," he added and shrugged. "I won't pretend I'm not disappointed. I am. But I will abide by your decision. I am not your Uncle Carl! We'll meet at the boat launch at eight."

She nodded, thankful to see the golf cart approach with Thomas driving her means of escape.

Chapter 53

Bradley pecked her on the cheek and helped her out of the golf cart. She hurried inside and quickly shut the door behind her.

Now inside his suite, he wondered what had triggered Henrietta's decision. When had she made up her mind they should not sleep together? He hoped it was only for tonight. Sleeping had been the mildest form of action they'd experienced the previous night. *Duh! Of course, she didn't mean sleeping.* He didn't even know how many times they'd made love.

He wanted a drink, so he poured a glass of icy cold Chardonnay and took a gulp. Under no circumstances would he become inebriated to put his thoughts to rest. He'd already done that once because of her and could still remember puking his guts up the next morning. Hadn't Socrates said that the wisest man alive knows that he knows nothing? He was not the wisest man, and he was convinced he knew nothing about the woman he wanted more than his next breath.

At the table on his patio, he continued to sip his drink. Feeling sorry for himself wouldn't help anything or solve the problem. Maybe he should just give up on her. His heart ached at the thought. How could he give up on someone who made his heart sing?

Bradley had never in his life been satisfied with *status quo*. Sadly, nothing had changed in his non-relationship with Henrietta. For every two steps he moved forward, she pushed him three steps back. He couldn't win although he desperately wanted to.

He rose and refilled his wine glass. Who was it that said, "The more things change, the more they remain the same?" He scratched his head. *It was a Frenchman in the 1800s.* He impatiently tapped his index finger against his head searching for the name. He snapped his fingers together when he recalled it was Alphonse Karr. That was true of him and Henrietta. "Shit!"

You could be with Henrietta right now. Fucking her over and over again. Maybe that's what I should have been doing last night instead of making love to her... worshipping her... making her come over and over again.

He couldn't stand sitting alone in his suite, so decided to take a walk on the beach. Perhaps the stars would guide him to a decision. He doubted it but had to get outside.

The moon was full. Maybe that's what was wrong with Henrietta. He'd always heard people did crazy things during a full moon. He chastised himself. *Be real, man. Don't blame it on the moon.* She's the only person who knew why she turned him on and off like a light bulb. And he'd been stupid enough to make her pancakes this morning. *Asshole.*

Bradley walked a long way allowing his thoughts to circle about in his mind in no particular order. He sat on the sand and listened as the surf brushed its kisses to the beach. What was she was doing right now? Thinking of him? He doubted it.

It was not about the sex. That was unbelievably good. He loved her quick mind and her sense of humor. He loved her scent... the feel of her skin... her willingness to try something she'd always feared… the look on her face when she approached orgasm… her sky-blue eyes… her long blonde hair… her long legs–especially when they were wrapped around his waist.

"Shit," he muttered as he rose and started walking back. He wasn't sure how it had happened, but it became painfully clear to him that he had fallen in love with Henrietta Blanchard. He tripped on a piece of driftwood and almost fell before regaining his balance. So he loved her. But he'd be damned if he'd allow her to play him like a piano. He'd put up with her indecision until it was time to leave Jamaica. If she made no move to at least discuss their relationship, he would somehow have to find a way to erase her from his heart and his mind. He couldn't remain in *limbo*. Doing so would drive him crazy.

* * *

Henrietta closed the door to her suite and leaned against it. Aware that she'd hurt Bradley, tears welled up in her eyes and flowed down her cheeks. She had not meant to. She wiped the tears away with the back of her hand. But she just couldn't spend each night with him. She wagged her head from side to side. If she did, what would she do once she returned to Houston? They would have to have that talk about trust as soon as she worked up the nerve to bring it up.

She undressed and slid into her bed. Somehow, she'd have to find the courage to enjoy doing fun things with Bradley without the romance he wanted. *Face it. You want it, too.* She didn't know how to balance the two and wasn't sure it was even possible.

She examined her behavior of the night before. She shuddered when she realized she'd started it all by leaving off her underwear, knowing what that would lead to. She pursed her lips as she recalled his expression when he found her naked beneath her beautiful silk dress. But hadn't he done the same?

Well, Missy, you did ask for it, so don't be angry because he did what you asked. She cringed. In the morning, it would be difficult to act as though nothing had happened. Something had happened. The man who completely confused her and made her pulse thunder inside her ears had worshiped her body like it was the Holy Grail. And she had loved it.

Perhaps she should leave for home. No. If she did, she'd have to explain her action to Monique and Gloria. She always played her cards close to her chest, unwilling to air her dirty laundry even with her best friends. Most of all, however, she'd miss being with Bradley.

Was now the time to discuss the trust issue? She gazed heavenward and prayed silently, "I need Your help!" What should she say next? Might as well be honest since He knows everything. "Look, I know I don't go to church and that You probably think I have a lot of nerve asking for help, but I don't know where else to turn. I should begin attending Sunday Mass, but I do not promise anything to bargain for Your help." She probably had not aided her cause with that last statement, but she barreled on. "I would appreciate a little enlightenment. You know I've been promiscuous all of my adult life. I can't learn to love and trust myself without Your help. You see, I'm afraid to love a man like I should because I expect to get hurt again. And just so You will know before making a decision, I still hate Uncle Carl for what he did to me. I've never been one to turn the other cheek, and if that means I must forego the insight I've requested, so be it." She ended her silent prayer with the sign of the cross.

It was done. All she had to do now was to wait for some sort of revelation from God, if indeed it was forthcoming, and to see Bradley in the morning.

Chapter 54

The next morning, she met Bradley where he waited for her on a cat-rigged dinghy. The single sail meant he'd be doing most of the work. *Thank goodness*. He wore no shirt, but already wore his low profile life vest and cutoff jeans. His muscular legs were a deep, golden tan. "Good morning," she said avoiding his eyes.

"Yes, ma'am. It is a beautiful day. Before we take off, I need to ask you a question."

Her heart thudded against her ribs. *Here it comes. Ready or not.* Her palms grew moist, and she wiped them on her shorts. Still avoiding his gaze, she replied, "Yes…"

"Have you ever sailed before?"

She blew out a breath in relief. "Yes, I have, but only a couple of times. And I only sat and enjoyed the ride."

"So you really know very little about sailing."

"You could say that." Then, from out of nowhere, she added, "And don't ma'am me, Bradley Graham. I see no reason why we can't just enjoy doing things together."

"I take it you mean during the daylight hours only."

"Harrumph!" Her face warmed as she recalled the previous night. "Why must you be so difficult so early in the day?"

He laughed out loud. "Maybe I want payback for last night." He laughed again. "We can enjoy today, but I can tell you that we will be having a discussion after our diving expedition. "Now get your lovely ass onto the boat."

She climbed onto the small deck of the dinghy and held on to the mast. He handed her a matching life-vest she immediately put on. It had been a good decision not to wear one of her bikinis. He handed her a strap to attach to her sunglasses so they wouldn't fall off into the water. Then he plopped a baseball cap on her head.

"Sit," he ordered, "and pull your hair through the back opening of the cap to keep it out of your eyes." He pointed the boat into the wind, and they started to move. Pretty soon, they were expertly gliding across the water.

She slathered suntan lotion on her arms and legs. He managed the dinghy like a master seaman. "Where did you learn how to sail so well?"

"Boston Harbor Yacht Club on Dorchester Bay. I spent hours and hours there while I was in high school, Yale University, and Yale Law School. My summers were always spent on the water."

"You owned a sailboat in high school?"

"My father did." He rolled his head from side to side. "She was a sailing yacht. A real beauty." He got a faraway look in his eyes. "I lost my virginity on that boat."

Henrietta's eyes widened. "How old were you when that happened?"

"Fifteen and that first time was over almost before I knew it. But Alice had me doing it over and over until I got it right."

She lifted her brows. "Oh, my God!"

"Don't you 'oh my God' me, Henrietta. I distinctly recall you saying you had your first sexual experience in tenth grade." He scrunched his brows together. "Were you even fifteen?"

Tamping down the anger that began to rise, she snarled, "Yes, I was. And it was only once, not multiple times. Enough said."

"So touchy. Chill, my dear. Enjoy the sun and the beauty of the water."

Bradley tacked the dinghy east to directly across the end of the seven-mile beach before turning it around to head for the opposite end of the beach and the boat launch.

"Can I interest you in a light lunch since we have about an hour to kill before diving?"

"Thank you, but no. Angel left me a small salad in the refrigerator, and I have to change into a bathing suit. Since it's daytime, we could go together to meet Kymani."

"*Touché*," he said as the corners of his mouth turned up in a small smile. "Thomas can take us there. I'll knock on the wall when it's time to leave."

* * *

"What a total pain in the ass," he murmured as he entered his suite. *And you were no better.* He quickly showered and pulled up his bathing trunks before eating the sandwich Thomas had left in the refrigerator for him. He consumed two bottles of water and sat to wait until it was time to leave.

He considered how he should begin the discussion he'd told Henrietta would occur after the dive. Where should it take place? It would have to be a private spot. He didn't want others to hear what he had to say. Her patio pool area or his would be the perfect place, but she'd probably think he'd chosen that place to hit on her. Probably should be his.

He knocked on the wall and left his suite to find her already waiting outside. Her black cotton lace cover-up hid nothing of her lovely white bikini-clad body. *Dammit! I will not get hard.* Thank God Thomas arrived in the golf cart. He helped her in and sat in the front seat with Thomas, who eyed him sideways. Bradley shrugged.

Kymani helped her out of the golf cart and shook Bradley's

hand. "You're both ready for fun?"

"Yes," they said together.

"Could've fooled me," he murmured. He helped Henrietta with her tank harness. Bradley needed no assistance.

From the boat, all three of them dropped over the side into the warm water of the Caribbean. Bradley kept a close eye on Henrietta to make sure she remained safe. He noticed Kymani did the same.

Today, they would venture down to forty feet. They came upon Shipwreck Reef at only eighteen feet. Turtles, morays, barracuda, and colorful tropical fish swam around the sunken ship. Golden sponges attached to white coral, and sea whips that looked like colorful, small, leafless trees captured Henrietta's attention.

Obviously enraptured with the scenery, she snapped one picture after another. Kymani floated to her and pointed down. She shook her head to indicate no and pointed to the wreck. She floated all around it and above it taking pictures.

After thirty minutes, Kymani indicated it was time to re-surface. Henrietta climbed the ladder without help, got into the boat, and quickly shed all her equipment. Her adrenalin high had her jabbering away about nothing. The smile on her lips was broad, and Bradley was certain she was not giving even the slightest thought to their scheduled discussion.

Bradley felt like he was standing at the proverbial fork in the road. One fork led to an unexciting existence with a focus only on his work. The other fork led to a happy, work and home life with Henrietta. Was he destined to be lonely or loved… with or without Henrietta? He didn't know.

A hand smacked his shoulder. He looked up into sky-blue eyes. "Are you going to just sit here in the boat?"

He wagged his head, "No. No. Let's go."

"Where were you, Bradley? Daydreaming?"

"Nah. Just thinking. There's Angel. Come on, let's go."

When they were dropped off at their suites, Angel told

Henrietta she'd left a pitcher of the rum drink she enjoyed. Then she drove off saying, "Call us for anything."

Bradley decided it was time to bite the bullet. "Your place or mine?"

"For our discussion?"

"Yes. Where do you prefer we do it?"

"Yours. I'll bring the rum drink Angel left. See you in five." She let herself into her suite.

Five minutes until he had to face the music. He entered his suite and headed for the patio. In the refrigerator, he found sandwiches Thomas had left for him along with Red Stripe beer. *We are, or we aren't.*

A knock sounded on his door. It was time to shit or get off of the pot. He took in a huge breath before opening the door.

Chapter 55

Carrying her pitcher of rum drink, Henrietta walked into Bradley's suite and moved directly to the poolside patio. She noticed he had not changed out of his bathing trunks. His tanned chest was magnificent. She was glad she'd gotten out of her bikini and into denim shorts and a t-shirt she'd spent a lot of money on at Neiman Marcus. She watched his eyes move from the top of her head to her feet before lowering his gaze to the floor.

She sat opposite the bottle of beer and the large sandwich sitting on the patio table. Her stomach growled, but there was only one sandwich. He got a glass and a plate from the kitchen and slid them in front of her. He placed half of his sandwich on her plate, picked up the other half, and bit into it. She thought he looked nervous. She had no clue what he wanted to discuss. *Yes, you do. Admit it.*

She took a sip of her drink. "You'd wanted us to talk, Bradley." She licked her lips. "So start talking."

"We should get a couple of things straight." His gaze zeroed in on her cool sky-blue one, and he didn't miss that she'd lifted her chin. Since he could read her like a book, she was certain he knew she was ready for combat.

"We have approximately two more weeks down here. I didn't much like being alone in the honeymoon capital of the world until we got together. It made me feel like the proverbial bastard at a family reunion. Yes, it's beautiful and all that, but everything is better when it's shared."

"I find it hard to believe that no females hit on you. I'm sure you could have found company."

He plowed his fingers through his hair. "I could have, but I wasn't interested. I was too busy planning what I would do once you arrived."

"Go on," she urged.

"I guess I thought being here together would be a little like our time together in Houston. It appears now that I was wrong to assume that."

He took a big bite out of his sandwich along with a swallow of beer, stood, and began pacing around the pool. Rather abruptly, he turned and pinned her with his silvery-grey bullets. "I need to know what you want, Henrietta. If it's a platonic relationship, although that's not what I want, I'll do it." He took a long pull on his beer. "But I refuse to allow you to turn me on and off like a light switch. One night you're hot to trot and all over me, and the next night you're colder than hot ice." He sat at his place. "So tell me. What is that you want from me?"

Her heart banged against her ribs, and her hands began to sweat. She reached for the pearls that weren't there and drew her fingers across her lips and chin. *Might as well spit it out, honey. You don't really want to send him away.*

"I do owe you an explanation, Bradley. I had been planning to have this discussion with you, so here goes. I have a huge problem. I don't trust men at all. And even worse, I don't trust myself to know when someone really cares. That's one of the reasons I was so promiscuous. It's easy just to have sex with a man. I expected nothing, and that's exactly what I got. And although I didn't have an orgasm with them, I felt as victorious as if I'd won a battle."

She gulped her drink. "Then you entered my life with a bang. You were different from any man I knew. You made love to me and introduced me to blissful orgasms. And I was happy with that. So happy, that we'd found each other."

Again, she reached for the pearls that were not there. "The night you yelled at me that you were not my Uncle Carl opened my eyes. I realized I didn't trust that you would not hurt me, so I pulled back. And I don't think you trust me, either."

He lowered his head, and she took a bite of the sandwich on her plate. When he looked up, his silvery-grey eyes looked sad. He shrugged and said, "You're right. I was so badly hurt and disappointed at what Saundra and my best friend did that I've been protecting my heart from another hurt. But I have to admit that I ache for you physically, Henrietta. I never ached for Saundra like that. I love being with you, and I want you in my arms and in my bed." He drew in a deep breath and blew it out. "So what do you want us to do?"

"I want you, too, Bradley. But I'm not at all ready for a commitment." She took another gulp from her glass searching for the relaxation that usually accompanied the rum drink. "I'm willing for us to experience all the activities that are available during the next two weeks together." She toyed with her neck with her index finger and thumb. "I care for you, Bradley. I sometimes even think I love you, but again, I'm not sure. So I propose we have fun and sex until we leave, the emphasis being on fun. We may even sleep together on occasion, but not every night. What do you think?"

He sucked in a big breath and blew it out. He wanted more than sex with Henrietta and didn't know if he wanted her on her terms or not at all. *But you have two weeks to get her to change her mind and trust you. Take the deal even though it's not what you want.*

"Agreed," he finally replied. "I think I expected you to tell me to get lost." Then he shot her a sexy smile. "I'm relieved you didn't. Now where shall we have dinner and what will we do tomorrow?"

"Regarding dinner, I think we should choose a place we've not gone to together. How about Barefoot by the Sea?"

"Okay. Now, what about tomorrow?"

"Your choice."

"How about us zip lining?"

She cringed, and her eyes widened. He would pick something that involved heights. "I don't know. I'm not comfortable with heights."

"Didn't you enjoy parasailing?"

"Yes. But I don't know anything about zip lining."

"You knew nothing about parasailing, but you enjoyed it. Trust me, Henrietta. I would never put you in danger. You'll wear a hard hat, sit your butt in a zip harness, and hold on to the glider that slides down a cable."

"I can't see how sliding down what resembles a clothes line in Cut Off is enticing."

"It's a thick cable, and you get to enjoy the incredible scenery you couldn't possibly see from the ground." When she didn't answer, he added, "Do I have to do the chicken act again?"

She frowned. "Please don't. I don't want to, but I'll do it. I hope I don't shit in my pants in fright."

"Maybe you should bring an extra pair." He laughed. It made a loud, bubbly sound. "What time do you want to leave for dinner?"

She glanced at her watch. "Around six-thirty, if that's good with you."

"And make sure you wear underwear tonight!"

It was her turn to laugh. "Just make sure you do, too. Just saying…"

When his knock sounded on her wall at six-thirty, she didn't hear it. She was already outside her door.

Chapter 56

Bradley thought Henrietta looked beautiful in her black pants and short top with cotton lace sleeves. She wore her pearls tonight. He'd noticed the way she always toyed with them when she was nervous or uncomfortable. She was doing that now. He'd chosen to wear his white pants and his white-on-white print shirt. *We're dressed like day and night. Did that mean something?*

The shrimp bisque appetizer and the sea trout with herb and butter sauce were delicious. The Chardonnay was icy cold and good. They chatted and laughed throughout the meal. He thought her blue eyes looked pensive. He wondered why. After all, they'd ironed out everything earlier. *But then again, who the fuck knew if that was so?*

After dinner, he asked, "Would you like to go to one of the clubs?"

"No." She fondled her pearls. "Why don't we head on back to our suites? I'll call Angel and have her mix a large pitcher of Margaritas. I found a Scrabble game today in my suite. Perhaps we could play a game or two."

Although Scrabble was not the game he wished to play, he'd stick to his earlier agreement. "Okay," he said, "we can do that."

He called Thomas to come for them while she called Angel about mixing the Margaritas.

When Thomas arrived, Bradley helped her into the cart and sat next to her. He could see that the corner of the butler's mouth was up, an indication that he was smiling.

Bradley watched her enter her suite before entering his. He shed his pants and shirt and put on kaiki shorts and a white muscle shirt. He slid his feet into flip-flops and knocked on the wall.

Henrietta let him in. She was barefoot and wore denim shorts and a white tank top. Her hair was down. God. He so wanted to kiss her full lips but refrained from making any move. He thought she looked nervous as she chattered too brightly, "Angel made two pitchers of Margaritas. I think she wants us to get drunk."

He shook his head, "That's not going to happen. I need to keep my head straight." *Both of them.*

She set the Scrabble game on the ottoman and placed one of the pitchers into a cooler before taking a seat on the floor. Because he knew she liked her Margaritas on the rocks, he handed her a glass filled with ice and poured her a drink before pouring his. He sat across from her.

At first, spelling the words came easily, but the time between the words got longer as coming up with words became more difficult. They were pretty evenly matched. He noticed she'd consumed two drinks to his one. He watched her posture soften and relax.

After her third drink and during the fourth game, she announced, "I'm tired of this!"

He shrugged and began picking up the letters and the board. "I guess it's time to call it a night."

She rose from her seat on the floor. "I want you to kiss me,

Bradley."

"What about our earlier agreement?" he questioned as his dick began to rise.

"I thought we agreed to fun and sex. Was I mistaken?"

"I'm not sure I can do this," he whispered in a trembling voice.

She moved close to him and put her arms around his neck. "I think you can," she murmured and took possession of his mouth. He tried not to get lost in the kiss, but when her tongue teased his lips open, he gave up the fight. She felt so good in his arms. He wanted this woman in his life and in his bed. But admitting that would almost certainly mean she'd send him away. He would settle for what he could get while he hoped to change her mind.

The kiss lasted a long time. His erection was painful, and she rubbed her pelvis against it. The bonfire grew into a major forest fire. Before he could ask what she wanted, she backed away from him. *Why am I not surprised? She gets me all hot and bothered, and now she'll send me home.*

Her gaze locked onto his. She didn't blink. Neither did he. "I want you to make love to me, Bradley."

He raised both hands in front of his chest. "Are you sure about this, Henrietta?"

"I've never been more sure of anything." She said and moved into his arms.

He crushed her into his body and devoured her with his mouth and tongue. He tore his lips away, picked her up, and carried her to her bed. He removed her clothes slowly and made love to her body with his hands. He loved the way she moaned and groaned with pleasure.

"I want you naked," she said as she began pulling at his shirt. Her hands traveled across his chest.

He grabbed the back neckline of his shirt and pulled it over his head while she unbuttoned his shorts. It took little time for his shorts, shirt, and underwear to land on the floor.

Henrietta stroked his erection until he feared he would come on her belly. He caught her hand in his. "Stop it!" he hissed. "I want this to last, and if you continue your ministrations, it won't."

She moved her hands to his chest and rubbed his nipples with the tips of her fingers. They hardened, and his dick throbbed.

He laved her left nipple with his tongue, and she moaned. He moved to the right one and did the same.

"Oooh, Bradley, my inner core cries for you. Please..." She breathed.

"Please what? Tell me what you want Henrietta."

"I want to come with you deep inside me. Don't make me beg."

He pushed his shaft balls deep into her hot vault."

"Aah..." She crooned. "Yes, that's what I've wanted."

He established a rhythm she quickly followed. In and out... back and forth... His heart banged against his ribs as he tried to hold back his release. Her eyes were getting glassy, and he knew she was close to shattering. He took hold of her legs and set her knees over his shoulders before moving faster, harder, and deeper. Her body tremors told him her orgasm would be explosive.

"Now, baby. Let go," he urged as he pumped into her hard one more time. His release coincided with hers, and she screamed his name. "Way to go, baby," he murmured as her vaginal contractions sucked his dick. He didn't pull out of her, and she kept her legs on his shoulders.

After a couple of minutes, he took her legs from his shoulders and pulled out of her. He kissed her lips softly and sweetly. Now side-by-side on her bed, they lay there until their breathing quieted and slowed.

He turned on his side and pulled her on top of him, kissing her and caressing her body with his hands. "Absolutely the best, Henrietta. I love making love to you."

She kissed him. "Same here. You are incredible, Bradley." She slid off him but remained close. "Time to sleep," she whispered.

When he started to rise out of bed, she stopped him. "Stay here. I want to sleep in your arms tonight."

"Are you sure?" he questioned.

"Yes. Positive."

His heart skipped within his chest. This is what he wanted… to have her in his arms forever. Yes. He loved her more than life itself, but he didn't dare say the words for fear it would cause her to run. He could only hope she wouldn't be ready to send him away tomorrow.

Janet Foret Lococo

Chapter 57

She woke him up the next morning stroking his penis. Of course, it rose to the occasion. After another round of incredibly good sex, they showered together before he returned to his suite to change clothes.

* * *

Thomas drove them to the entrance for their eight-hour adventure. They'd gathered supplies recommended. Her camera hung around her neck. Beach shoes, sunscreen, bug repellant, and a change of clothes were safely bagged in plastic. Henrietta was sure her nervousness was apparent to everyone in the group.

She was pleased to learn that their journey would begin with a horseback ride through the Caribbean Sea that would take them to Reading Heights for a breathtaking view and a stop at one of Jamaica's oldest churches. Although this was her first horseback ride, she wasn't fearful.

After that, it was time to head to a jungle outpost for a tasty, authentic Jamaican lunch. *So far, so good.*

After horseback riding, they hopped together onto a tube

and drifted down the river to the base of a stunning waterfall where she took many photographs. So far, she'd thoroughly enjoyed the adventure. After enjoying the jaw-dropping beauty of the springs, the guide told them it was time to fly high above the land on a zip line and rappelling venture. He bragged about the famous Inter-Parish Express, a twelve-hundred-foot-plus long traverse that would take them gliding at thirty-five miles per hour.

She hoped not to panic. A frisson of fear traveled up her spine. She threw a frenzied gaze into Bradley's silvery-grey eyes. He pulled her close and whispered, "Relax. You'll be safe, double-clipped to a steel cable that's over a half-inch thick," he explained. "You'll love it once you get over your fear."

Henrietta was not at all confident. "I hope I don't shit in my pants or throw up. I don't know which would be worse."

Nervous tremors slid up and down her spine when the guide added that they'd sail over the Great River and glide through a tunnel of trees. Last would be a ride on a rope swing. If she made it through the zip lining without dying from cardiac arrest, she figured the rope swing would be a cinch.

The guides got them harnessed onto the zip line. Bradley was directly in front of her, and a guide was behind her. The guide told her to keep an open mind, counted to five, and they were off. At first, she didn't look down, only straight ahead, her stomach in her throat. But when the guide told her she was missing an awesome view, she got up the gumption to open her eyes.

Oh, my God. Stupendous. Staggering. She swallowed her fear and snapped photo after photo. She even enjoyed the part where they flew over the water and the exhilarating thrill of flying through the tunnel of trees.

Then it was on to the rope swing. The guide said they could be dropped off at Margaritaville afterward.

"What do you want to do, Henrietta? It's your decision."

"I'm glad you insisted we do this. I thought you were throwing away a lot of money for nothing especially exciting. But it was one of the most intoxicating adventures I've ever experienced. It will be super crowded at Margaritaville, so I'd like to return to our suite, clean up, and order dinner.

"So be it," he replied. "I'm proud of you, Henrietta. I know it was difficult for you, but you were great!"

"Call Thomas."

When Thomas arrived with the golf cart, Bradley helped seat her and hopped in next to her. "Are you hungry?"

"Yes. Apparently, excitement burns up a lot of the calories we had for breakfast and lunch. What about you?"

"My stomach feels like my throat's been cut. I want a huge, tender steak with all the trimmings."

"I'd love a great steak, too." She turned her gaze forward. "Thomas, where do you suggest we have dinner?"

"Sundowner serves a great tenderloin steak cooked to your specifications. You may want to order two Mr. Bradley since the filets are only eight ounces." He chuckled. "The sides are good, too, and the coconut truffle cake is to die for. Resort evening attire. No jacket required. If you'd like, I'll see that you get a table with a beach view."

Bradley nudged Henrietta. "What do you say?"

"Sounds good to me. You or Angel can pick us up at seven fifteen."

Bradley saw her to the door of her suite. "I'll shower and take a nap. I'll set the alarm on my iPhone to make sure I wake up in time to dress."

"I'll knock on the wall when Thomas or Angel get here."

* * *

Incredible steaks–juicy and tender with peppercorn sauce– followed the blue marlin appetizer. Thomas had been right. The dessert was unbelievable, and she was stuffed. "Maybe we should walk some of this off on the beach," she suggested.

He agreed. They removed their shoes before hitting the

sand. A balmy breeze blew off the water. It would be so nice to live in a beautiful place close to water. *Bayou Lafourche banks are on the water...* She frowned. No way she'd ever want to live there again. That was probably where Gloria would end up. Back on Bayou Lafourche. She pinched her lips together. *That's Gloria. Not me!*

"Why the frown and tight lips?" Bradley asked. His brows almost met over his nose.

"It was just a thought," she answered.

"Not a good one, I take it."

"No. It wasn't."

"Want to tell me about it?"

"It doesn't concern you, Bradley." She was grateful when he didn't pursue the subject.

Hand in hand, they walked passed the Sundowner pool, the Paradise Resort, the main pool, and whirlpool area. After walking that far, they decided to continue on between the sports complex building and Cucina Romano to their suites.

"Want to come in for a nightcap?" he asked.

"Not tonight. I'm completely bushed."

"I could give you a backrub," he added lifting his brows. "It would feel real good."

"Thanks, but no."

He brushed a kiss as light as butterfly wings across her lips and another at the corner of her mouth. "Goodnight," he whispered into her ear, turned, and walked away.

Chapter 58

Henrietta leaned against the closed door of her suite. She was indeed worn out, but surprised Bradley had not pushed for more. So why was she disappointed? She raised her gaze heavenward. *That's what you told him you wanted, and for a change, he didn't press you. Make up your mind, woman! Don't send mixed messages.*

She slid out of her black palazzo pants and pulled the short, white ruffled top over her head. After turning on country music on her iPhone and tucking it under her pillow, she stretched out on her bed and recalled the day she'd spent with Bradley. At first fearful of zip lining, she'd enjoyed views impossible to see otherwise. She would not have experienced that if Bradley had not insisted. *He's so hot... so handsome... so considerate... so determined to have me.* But was that what she wanted?

She was still uncertain and wondered what it would take to make her realize, without a doubt, what it was she truly wanted. She could do a lot worse than end up with Bradley. But would it be better than what she enjoyed right now. There was something to be said for doing only what you wanted to do, going only where you wanted to go, and having what you wanted to have without depending on a man. That was the real reason she'd gotten an education. She had not wanted to be left holding the bag like her mother–in her case with four children–when her father died unexpectedly, too young, and without adequate life insurance.

Henrietta grabbed her head with two hands. *I want him in my bed, but do I want a committed relationship? Forsaking all others... wait. That was part of the marriage vows.* And she did not under any circumstances want to be married.

Gloria and Jesse came to mind. It is obvious they are really good together. A pang of jealousy struck her heart as she recalled the way they looked at each other with genuine love shining in their eyes. Gloria certainly appeared to be very happy, and Jesse adored her. Their daughter Jessica was precious. Gloria had the best life imaginable. Henrietta shivered when she thought of not having someone to share her life with until she closed her eyes in death. *It must be terrible to die alone.*

"Shit. Shit. Shit." She muttered as she wondered if Bradley was asleep. She ached to feel his arms around her. He was an unbelievably great lover who taught her that making love could be a blissful experience. *Is he thinking about me? Is his body aching with desire for me?* She could have had the answer to those questions had she invited him in and asked him to spend the night. *Face it. That's really what you wanted.* But she hadn't done that. Instead, she was lonely and desperate.

She wanted to knock on the wall and ask him over. What would his reaction be? She finally drifted off to sleep only to dream of Bradley.

* * *

In the suite next door, Bradley was sipping his second drink and thinking about Henrietta. For the life of him, it was impossible to fathom what made the woman tick. He knew that being raped had a lot to do with her fear of a relationship. He'd

316

always thought that women feared sexual liaisons following rape, but instead Henrietta had been promiscuous. Something didn't jive, but he couldn't put his finger on it. She should have been able to ascertain that he was not like her Uncle Carl by now.

Perhaps he should let her go instead of trying to figure her out. He couldn't–and wouldn't–put up with an on again, off again relationship. In his mind and heart, you either loved someone, or you didn't. It was that simple. He'd be damned before he'd be nothing more than Henrietta's sex toy. He was not for sale at Mr. Binky's Boutique.

Bradley didn't pour himself another drink. After three, he was beginning to feel relaxed. He stripped and slid between the smooth cotton sheets hoping for sleep free of dreams of Henrietta. Instead of getting what he'd hoped for, his sleep was filled with dreams of her... on the beach... deep sea diving... riding horseback in the waters of the Caribbean Sea... in his arms... in his bed.

* * *

For the next thirteen days, Henrietta and Bradley experienced everything Jamaica had to offer. They'd continued diving three times a week, had gone tubing and kayaking, gone out on Hobie Cats, enjoyed a ride on a glass-bottomed boat, and even played tennis and beach volleyball, along with enjoying local tours of Negril.

They had dinner together every night, went to bars and clubs, enjoyed almost daily sex, and had spent several nights sharing a bed.

* * *

Friday, June 22nd marked her last day in Jamaica. Henrietta rose early for her daily walk. To her surprise, Bradley awaited her on the beach. They walked hand in hand toward the west portion of the seven-mile beach. They hardly spoke. She was busy cataloging all her experiences in her mind, and she supposed he was doing the same.

317

Henrietta had done more than she'd imagined during her three-week stay. Unfortunately, she had not reached a decision about Bradley. She still didn't trust that a committed relationship with him would not result in a broken heart for her, and she was beginning to doubt that she would ever experience the redemption she so desired. She trusted herself even less. His facial expression was serious, not fun-loving and happy like he'd been all the other days they'd spent together. She sensed he would plead his case tonight and feared the outcome.

* * *

Bradley's thoughts warred inside his head. They'd had a really good time together. Yes, he did love Henrietta but did she feel the same way about him? He wanted a life with her but was unsure of what she would say to that. She was so damn hardheaded and impossible to figure out. Well, it would all come down to tonight. He'd lay his cards on the table... tell her of his love... and ask her to marry him. He could only hope she'd say yes.

He'd signed them up for water skiing in the morning and a final dive in the afternoon. Dinner would be Bradley's personal D-Day. As on June 6, 1944, when Allied troops stormed the beaches of Normandy, France, to fight Nazi Germany, he would storm the beaches of Henrietta's heart. And like General Dwight D. Eisenhower had said, "We will accept nothing less than full victory," neither would he. His mind was made up. It would be all or nothing.

Chapter 59

After a full day of activity, Angel drove them back to
their suites. Henrietta asked, "Where do you want to
go to dinner?"

"It's a surprise," Bradley replied. "Wear something sultry."
He licked his lips. " One of your white bikinis with one of your
sexy see-through cover ups will do nicely. Beach thongs on
your feet."

Henrietta frowned. "I can't imagine where you're taking
me dressed like that, and I don't like surprises."

"Tough," he answered. "Angel will take you to the meeting
place at seven o'clock. I'll be there waiting for your arrival.
And don't even think about pumping her for information.
She's promised me she wouldn't breathe a word to you." He
shot her what he hoped was a killer smile.

After helping Henrietta out of the golf cart, he hopped out
and sauntered into his suite. Once inside, he let out a hearty
laugh before his nerves took over. Please let her say yes. I'm
not at all sure that I can live without her.

* * *

Angel drove her to a spot on the beach Henrietta had not noticed before. In the shallow water, sat a cabana with the drapes drawn. She wondered where that had come from. "So where do I go, Angel?"

Angel pointed to the cabana. "In there."

Henrietta's eyes rounded. "Are you serious? Mr. Bradley is in there?"

"Yes, he waits for you." Angel touched a button on her phone, and the drapes facing the beach opened to reveal Bradley, in his golden brown glory, wearing white shorts, and shirtless.

Henrietta gasped and immediately moved toward the cabana and into his arms. Candles provided the only light. He closed the drapes facing the beach and opened the ones facing the water. She could hear the surf clearly through the slatted floor. A low table held place settings and large pillows on the floor would provide seating. "When did you do this?"

He grinned. "Yesterday. I wanted our last dinner here to be very romantic and delicious. So I arranged for our Kimonos chef to feed us a little of everything. Have a seat facing the water and I'll pour some champagne for our enjoyment."

They feasted on appetizers of Opilio crab sticks, salmon bites with cream cheese and cucumber, and the full tasting menu while sipping on Veuve Cliquot Ponsardin.

Henrietta noted the chef had left another bottle of the fine wine with its subtle notes of peach and anise when he departed. Bradley had probably paid through the nose for the cabana, food, wine, and the chef.

When he suggested they move to the sofa, she did and touched her neck for the pearls that weren't there. She sensed something of catastrophic proportions would shortly occur, and prayed she was wrong.

"I enjoyed dinner, Bradley. I know it took a lot of planning on your part, and I appreciate the effort and the expense."

"I wanted tonight to be extra special," he murmured close

to her ear. "Don't you agree that this time together has been wonderful?"

"I do." She swallowed the nervous lump in her throat. "I sense your apprehension. What's up, Bradley?"

He took her hands in his. "I wasn't sure when I decided to come find you in Jamaica, but I am sure now. I love you, Henrietta, with a forever kind of love. I never thought I'd ever be able to love again after my past experiences. You stole my heart, I think from the moment you knocked me on my ass outside church after midnight Mass. I want to share everything with you, but mostly my heart and soul."

Henrietta's heart thudded in her ears and pounded in her chest. Her breaths were short and close together. *Shit. I knew it would come to this. What to do?* She was not at all ready for this.

She took a deep breath and blew it out. "I like you, Bradley. A lot. I think I probably love you."

"But..." he whispered with his gaze pinned to hers. He sighed. "There's always a but."

"I want to be sure about this, Bradley. I want you all of the time I'm not with you. I need you like the air I breathe." She closed her eyes for a moment and licked her lips. "I'm not ready to make a commitment, though. I still have not achieved trusting myself in spite of daily affirmations. I hope you can understand." She watched his face redden and the veins in his neck become distended. She was certain he was angry and terribly disappointed.

He rose to his feet and began pacing in the cabana. "I understand that you will never trust yourself to love anyone. I had planned to propose marriage tonight, but I refuse to give you the opportunity to reject me again." He plowed his fingers through his hair. "I've had all I can take. It's all or nothing with me, Henrietta. I hope you understand the importance of your decision." He noted her watery eyes but was determined not to let that change his decision. "So what'll it be? All or nothing?"

She thought he stood as straight and stiff as a decorative nutcracker. Rigid. Unbending. "I'm afraid I'm not ready for all." She sniffed.

"Then it's nothing. We're done." He slid one palm against the other. "Don't bother trying to contact me. I'll be busy driving you out of mind and heart." He stepped off the cabana into the water and walked away without looking back.

Henrietta's heart broke. She sobbed into the sofa. *I'll never feel his kiss again... or experience joy in his arms... or enjoy his wonderful lovemaking.* She'd brought it all on herself. *I'm an absolute asshole.* When she ran out of tears, she called Angel to come for her.

In her suite, she poured herself a Margarita from the pitcher in the refrigerator. She reached for her handbag and drew five one-hundred-dollar bills from her wallet. "You've been wonderful, Angel. I want you to have this," she said handing her the bills.

"I have packed your bags, Miss Henrietta." She eyed the money in her hand. "This is too generous," she said as she tried handing three of the bills back.

"No, Angel. I insist you take it all. You're worth more than that."

Angel pocketed the money. "Thank you, Miss Henrietta. I can see you are very sad and have been crying. Did you and Mr. Bradley have a disagreement?" She lowered her gaze to the floor. "I should not have asked. I'm sorry. It's not any of my business."

"Mr. Bradley and I are done. Pick me up in the morning at eight and arrange for a cab to take me to the airport."

"I'll fix your breakfast at seven."

"No breakfast. I couldn't possibly eat a thing. Thank you, Angel. Goodnight."

After Angel had left, she showered and washed her hair. Sorrow and regret almost suffocated her. It was as though she were stuck beneath a huge boulder. Sleep would not come–

only memories of her time with Bradley. And desire. She ached to be in his arms... in his bed... his lips on hers... his tongue in her mouth and on her nipples... his shaft inside her. All her pain could have been avoided if she had never run into him at Christmas. Now she had another reason to hate her hometown.

It was almost time to get up when she finally fell asleep. When she looked in the mirror while brushing her teeth, her eyes were swollen and red from crying and lack of sleep. Makeup didn't help much. *Oh, well.*

* * *

Bradley was unable to sleep at all wondering how he'd go on with his life. He called the airline to change his flight to a later one to avoid running into Henrietta at the airport and on the plane. *Face it. You are royally fucked. You should have known better than to come here looking for her. It's sad that you love her and that she doesn't trust herself to love you back. So wake up and smell the roses. Forget about her.*

Chapter 60

Home again in Houston, Henrietta called Monique as soon as she entered her condo. Ten minutes later, Mo knocked on the door. The happy smile on her face changed to concern as soon as she caught sight of Henrietta.

"What's wrong?" She asked as she hugged her partner.

"Everything!"

"Oh, Retta, I'll pour us some wine and listen if you want to tell me about it."

Between sobbing episodes, Henrietta related the entire story of her time in Jamaica. She left nothing out. Monique tried to cheer her up to no avail.

"I'm sorry I told him where you were. I thought I was doing the right thing. I thought you loved him, Retta. How could I have been so mistaken?"

"You're going to think I'm crazy, and I sometimes think I am. I'm sure that I love him. I prayed for redemption from a complete lack of trust in him and in me that kept me from risking it all with Bradley. You know how I recite affirmations?"

Monique nodded. "Yes. I take it they didn't work this

time." She glanced at her watch. "I'm calling Gloria to come over. Jesse's here and can take care of Jessica." She dialed Gloria's phone, told her to come to Henrietta's condo, and hung up. "She'll be here shortly. So wait to say any more until she gets here."

No more than fifteen minutes later, Gloria arrived. Monique let her in. She took one look at Henrietta and stopped in her tracks. "What happened?"

Monique told her what had been revealed so far.

"So you were reciting affirmations to help you trust Bradley not to hurt you, and to trust yourself to make the right decision regarding risking a relationship. You called it a redemption?"

"Yes. I called it a redemption because I wanted to be saved from my lack of trust with men that has plagued me since Uncle Carl raped me when I was seven years old. The affirmations helped some, but I couldn't trust him not to hurt me in the future. He wanted all or nothing and wouldn't settle for anything less. And like an ignoramus, I couldn't risk a broken heart. So what am I stuck with? A fucking broken heart." She broke into sobs again.

"I can't believe this," Gloria barked. "You had all the answers for my problems with Jesse, but you couldn't get up the guts to admit that you love and want this man. Un-fucking-believable." When Henrietta sniffed, she added, "And don't you start crying again. It didn't help me, and it won't help you. I know I sound like a bitch, but someone has to wake you up."

"It's too late for me to wake up, Gloria. He's gone and even warned me not to contact him. I know I was stupid and that I'll pay the price. I will never subject myself to this again."

Gloria played with a lock of her hair. "That was surely one hell of a coincidence for him to be in Jamaica while you were there."

Henrietta's gaze turned to Monique, who cleared her throat.

"It wasn't a coincidence, Gloria. I told him where she was going and where she'd be staying. He was grateful."

Henrietta piped in, "Don't raise hell at her." She toyed with her pearls as usual when she was upset. "She knew I loved him long before I did. All of my trouble is my fault–nobody else's. Bradley was just too good to be true." She wiped her nose with the back of her hand. "I'll wallow in sorrow for a while, but I'll bounce back. You can both go home. I'll be okay. I'll be at work on Monday, ready to slave over cases to keep my mind occupied."

She longed for the rum drinks that relaxed her while in Negril. After three glasses of wine, she stopped the pacing she'd started as soon as her partners left. A hot shower would probably help her relax. Afterward, she slipped into her nightshirt and stretched out on her bed. The wine worked, and she soon was asleep.

Her dreams were filled with scenes of her and Bradley having fun in Jamaica. She ached to feel his arms around her. He appeared before her completely naked, his body bronzed by the sun. He spread out his arms, and she walked into them. He kissed her with a passion that set them both on fire. When she rubbed herself against his turgid shaft, he smiled and asked, "What do you want, Henrietta?"

"You," she murmured.

"You know that it's all or nothing. So what do you say?"

"I want it all. I love you, Bradley. Now make sweet love to me."

She awakened when his throbbing dick filled her, aching with want and desperate for his touch.

* * *

With a glass of wine in hand, Bradley paced the floor of his apartment like a caged animal. After losing his heart to Henrietta, she'd just pitched it away like yesterday's garbage. He hated the thought of facing her mother at work on a daily basis. After all, she'd created Henrietta with the help of her husband, but it had been her motherfucking brother who caused the mental and emotional damage to an adorable seven-year-old girl.

TRUST. This powerful five-letter word–actually the lack of it–had wrecked his chance with the love of his life. Henrietta had allowed her past experience with Carl all those years ago to come between them. That no-count bastard was responsible for ruining her life. Following that episode, she'd subconsciously built walls around her heart to avoid future hurt and disappointment. And it was those same walls that were keeping him out of her life. Unfortunately, she was the only person capable of tearing them down and risking it all.

Bradley was tired of crying. His eyes burned and felt scratchy. He wanted to drink himself into oblivion but knew that would result in only a few hours of peace. The pain would then return with a vengeance–like a man drowning in the sea, unable to save himself.

He regretted returning Monique's call and going to Jamaica. He'd been doing a little better before running to Henrietta. He recalled a friend saying, "Hope is a wonderful thing." And he had agreed. It was hope that sent him to Jamaica to woo Henrietta. Now, all hope was dashed. Forever.

He wanted to die. His life had no meaning without her in it. And because he couldn't take his own life, he was doomed to loneliness until the day the good Lord called him to his final home. So be it…

Bradley finished his wine and stopped pacing.

It would be easier said than done, but he would give it his ultimate effort.

He buried himself in work on Monday. His colleagues seemed happy to have him back and commented on his glorious tan. He smiled and said, "I had a grand time." Until the last day.

His nights were worse than his days. His sleep was filled with dreams of them together in Jamaica. Every morning, he forced breakfast down and did the same for lunch. So far, he'd held on to the pounds he'd found in Jamaica.

Chapter 61

Time moved on, day-by-day. Before Henrietta knew it, July 4th reared its head. Her partners were celebrating the anniversary of American independence at home while she chose to remain in Houston. Alone. Miserable. She had no plans to return to Cut Off in the near future.

All she had were memories of her time with Bradley. She still ached for him every night as soon as her workday ended. Her nights were filled with dreams of him making love to her. She regretted her unwillingness to risk everything when he'd issued his ultimatum.

Her life was one big question mark. What was he up to? Had he gotten over her? Had he found someone else to warm his bed and his life? Although she wanted to erase Bradley Graham from her memory, she had no clue regarding how to go about it. Of one thing she was certain. She could not continue on this lonely path. With absolutely no social life, all she did was work and remain in her condo. Each day was a repetition of the day before. Complete boredom.

Although everlasting sadness was all she could look

forward to, she woke every morning and reported to their law office like one of those laboratory mice in a maze.

* * *

Bradley was miserable. While everyone chose to celebrate July 4th at their homes, he'd made use of the company beach house in Grand Isle in an effort to escape his memories of Jamaica with Henrietta. It was to no avail. She was embedded in his brain like a font or an image in a computer file.

He'd thought he would be feeling better by this time, but it had not come to pass. He still ached for her, and she continued to fill his dreams. What the fuck was he to do?

During the weekend following July 4th, he received a text message. The sender was blocked from view. The message was only one word: "All."

Could it be? He opened and clenched his fists over and over, and his heart pounded within his chest. Over and over again, he read the single word. Was this really happening? *It could be a joke.* He rolled his lips between his teeth. *No. She wouldn't do that, and nobody else knew about the all or nothing bit.* No one other than Henrietta would send him such a message. His fingers trembled as he pressed the letters on his phone to respond. "As in all or nothing?"

Almost instantly, he received a reply. "Yes. If you're interested, call me."

His heart raced, his breaths were shallow and rapid, and his hands shook. Was she saying she'd risk it all? Did she trust that he'd not hurt her in the future? Could he be that lucky?

Bradley's fingers shook as he dialed her number. She answered on the second ring.

"Hello."

"All?" He queried as he raked his fingers through his hair.

"Yes," she responded.

"Are you absolutely certain?"

"Yes. I've been miserable without you. I've cried so much that you probably wouldn't recognize me. I don't like to risk anything, but I'll risk my heart because I realized I will not be whole without you." She breathed in and blew it out. "You made me do things in Jamaica I didn't want to do–things I was afraid to do. I did them because I knew you would keep me safe. And you did. I didn't realize that I had already experienced that redemption I so dearly wanted. I love you, Bradley, with my whole heart and soul. Do you trust me enough to love me until the end of time?"

He jumped up like a cheerleader and shouted, "Yes. Yes. Yes!" He feared someone might come to check on him if they'd heard his shout. "I'm coming. I'll get the company jet to fly me up there. I should be at your place before dark. I love you, Henrietta, and I need you like the air I breathe."

"I'll meet you on the tarmac where private planes land. Hurry, Bradley. I need you, too."

After informing his CEO, he immediately made arrangements to fly to Houston.

* * *

Henrietta was waiting nearby when Bradley exited the plane. She ran into his arms, and he captured her mouth in a passionate kiss that had her heart racing and shivers running up and down her spine. At long last. When he tore his mouth from hers, she said, "I was so stupid. Please forgive me for hurting you. I love you, Bradley. I'm more than willing to risk everything for your love. You have indeed been my redemption. So what do you say?"

"I've dreamed of this day, but to be perfectly honest, I had given up hope it would ever happen. I love you more than I love myself. Marry me, Henrietta."

"Yes. Yes. Yes," she replied.

Janet Foret Lococo

Epilogue

From a crack in the door leading to the sacristy, Bradley could see the church was filled to capacity on the evening of August 24, 2011, one day after Henrietta's thirty-ninth birthday. She was hidden from view, and he couldn't wait to watch her move toward him. Five-light candelabras on high stands decorated the main aisle, the flames of their fat candles fluttering. Between them, arrangements of pink roses and peonies stood on similar stands. Large baskets of flowers matching the aisle arrangements filled the sacristy. The long, white runner was in place. All was in readiness. His palms were sweaty.

Henrietta had pushed him away so many times that he couldn't help fearing the possibility of her leaving him standing at the altar. *She'd better not.* She was his life… his world.

The priest came out and took his place in the center of the sacristy. Jesse, along with two of Henrietta's brothers and Bradley, took their places to the right of the middle aisle. The organ began to play *Canon in D*, and Gloria began to walk toward Jesse. Monique followed and met with Jeremy. The matron of honor was none other than Henrietta's mother, Mary Ann, who took the arm of her son, Johnny Boy.

Bradley spotted Henrietta at the back of the church on the arm of J.J. and breathed a sigh of relief before swallowing the immense lump in his throat. His heart thumped inside his chest. His gaze remained on her face. She would soon be his.

The organ rang out *The Bridal March.* She was a vision in her creamy-white wedding gown that molded to her slender body. A wreath of the same flowers decorating the church sat on her head, kind of like the flower children of the 1960s. She wore no veil, but a narrow train was attached at her waist.

Shaking in his boots, he watched J.J. kiss Henrietta, take her hand and place it in his. She smiled, and his heart skipped a beat or two. *It's really happening. Today, she officially becomes mine.* "I love you," he whispered before they moved to their places facing the priest.

"Ditto," she whispered.

After the priest had finished the usual lessons about marriage in general, Bradley began his vows.

"I believe I fell in love with you the very moment your eyes met mine." He pinned her with his gaze. *"I, Bradley Graham, take you, Henrietta Blanchard, to be my lawful wife. On this day, I give you my heart, along with my promise that I will walk with you, hand in hand, wherever our journey leads; living, learning, loving, and risking it all, together. I will love you in good times and in bad, in sickness and in health, for richer or poorer, until I breathe my last. I will love you and honor you all the days of my life."*

* * *

Now it was her turn. Henrietta allowed the light of love to shine from her eyes to his.

"I, Henrietta Blanchard, take you, Bradley Graham, to be my lawful husband. On this day, I give you my heart, and completely trust you with it. Free of fear for the future, I promise to walk with you, hand in hand, wherever our journey

leads, even if that journey is on a Harley." She paused to smile. *"I will cherish you in good times and in bad, in sickness and in health, for richer or poorer, until we are parted by death. I will love you and honor you all the days of my life."*

They exchanged rings over the traditional words and finally heard the priest say, "You may kiss your bride, Bradley."

The kiss was light and sweet with a promise of more to come later.

Much later, after a traditional Cajun reception, Bradley and Henrietta left for their honeymoon at her brothers' beach house in Grand Isle on his Harley.

"It's fitting that we honeymoon there," Henrietta murmured into the helmet's microphone. That's where this all started."

The sound of his laughter rang into her ear from the speaker in her helmet. "Nah. It all started when you knocked me on my ass right outside of church on Christmas Eve after midnight Mass."

About the Author

Janet Foret Lococo, retired registered nurse, wife, mother, and grandmother—discovered the joy of reading in the first grade at Baudoin-Foret School in Raceland, Louisiana, at the age of seven.

Her love of happily–ever–after endings began at an early age when she listened to fairy tales on the radio show *Let's Pretend* every Saturday morning. She reads just about anything, but her favorite reading genre is steamy romance followed by mystery mixed with romance. A voracious reader, she reads two to three books weekly.

She discovered the joy of writing after retiring from nursing at the age of sixty–five. Since her retirement fifteen years ago, she has self-published three humorous autobiographies and four steamy romance novels. This marks her eighth work, and she is already working on the last manuscript of the trilogy—The Partners Series - Book 3.

Reader's Comments on Previous Books

"Lost Innocence is a page turner and well-written. The characters are memorable and well-defined. This is a fast-paced read and steamier than a Louisiana summer. However, it also deals with the serious subject matter of a childhood rape which the heroine doesn't recall. This doesn't take away from the romance between the adult heroine and the sexy Cameron LeRoux. Highly recommend this book."   LV

"Lost Innocence is a dramatic and poignant saga of a young woman coming of age in Southeast Louisiana during the 1950's. The main characters are strong, interesting, and exciting. They're easy to relate to. The author is very skillful at bringing the characters' emotions from the page and right into your heart. You'll cry, laugh, sigh and look forward to what will be coming next. Even the secondary characters are interesting and exciting. I found it hard to tear myself from the book. It is a page turner for sure and is full of suspense, twists, turns, and surprises. Even the small towns in Southeast Louisiana are characters in themselves, again, the result of a creative writer who has a way with words and emotions. Her words seem to find their way straight into your heart. The writer is so blessed with the gift of eloquence that I feel like I've seen a movie rather than read a book. Everything she has written in *Lost Innocence* is so glowingly vivid. I can still see the bigger than life visions she has indelibly placed on my mind. Reading this book is the best thing I have ever done and I strongly recommend it to anyone.   NAG

"Once I started reading *Lost Innocence,* I couldn't put it down. Loved the characters, the steamy sex scenes, the storyline etc. Can't wait to read the sequel.   DT

Guilty Pleasure. "After reading *Lost Innocence,* I just had to read the sequel. I was curious to see how Jacquelyn's life played out. Her love story was so beautiful and Jacquelyn's mother reminded me of some of the older people I know! I wasn't disappointed, great book!"   PNY

"*Guilty Pleasure* reminded me so much of what I went through after my husband died. I laughed... I cried... I stayed up all night to finish reading it. Both books were given to me as a Christmas gift. I LOVED them."
                                                                    DEL

"*Guilty Pleasure* is a wonderful love story."   SBS

"*The Prince Wore Cowboy Boots* is Janet Lococo's best book yet! Sexy... sensual...descriptive...a real turn on." ABC

"This exciting and sexy story will keep you engaged until the surprise ending. A Louisiana girl, Catarina, travels to Colorado to work in a hospital, but before she arrives, she meets a handsome hunk wearing turquoise cowboy boots. Josiah, a champion bronco rodeo rider, struggles to convince her he's a good guy." AAK

"*The Prince Wore Cowboy Boots* was a fun, sexy, romantic story. I love how they met and fell in love. A nurse and a cowboy, two people from two different worlds. He provided his love for her. I am ready for another adventure. SBS

"Funny, poignant, heartwarming, and entertaining, these are just a few words to describe Janet Foret Lococo's latest release, *The Prince Wore Cowboy Boots*. You'll find yourself cheering for the heroine, Catarina Rossi; and swooning over the steamy hero, Josiah Taylor. Janet Foret Lococo is a writer NOT to be overlooked. CP

"*Jesse's Girl*, like all the others was awesome. Sure hope you're working on the next one because I'm ready to read it!!! Hurry up with the next one!" WWP

"Yes, and I'm just about done, too, so I agree with Wendy, hurry up with the next one, "Jesse's Girl" is awesome!!!!" KE

"Just finished reading *Jesse's Girl* by Janet Lococo . Another great work. Enjoyed it greatly. Didn't want to put it down." CD

"Love, hot sex, plus a great story. Janet Lococo has everything you are looking for. *Jessie's Girl* is one book you'll want to start early in the day so you can read it in one sitting." CP

Other Books by Janet F. Lococo

Humorous Autobiographies

Novels:

  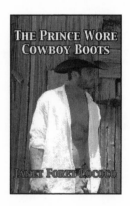

Print editions are available at:
www.createspace.com
www.janetflococo.net

eBooks are also available at:
Amazon.com, Barnes & Noble,
Apple iBooks, Kobo, Scribd, Page
Foundry, Oyster, and Tolibo